# Out of Time

## The Dream Traveler Book One

Ernesto H Lee

ISBN – 13: 978-1723341632

2nd Edition – 5th March 2019

Cover art by Spiffing Covers

# Dedication

Most of all this book is dedicated to Maria – my partner in dreams, my partner in crime and my partner in love. You inspire me, you excite me, you complete me xxx

But it is also dedicated to the dreamers– don't be afraid to cast off the burden of lifes limitations and society's definition of traditional normality.

Living somebody else's dream is a life not yet fulfilled - step away and live your own dream with the one life you have.

Ernesto H Lee
25th July, 2018

# Preface

The one major drawback with what I do is that it is not an exact science, and until I close my eyes I really have no idea as to exactly where, or indeed when, I will end up. There are no classes or textbooks that can adequately teach or explain this, and I wasn't taken under the wing of some Jedi master or guru keen to pass on his art to a young protégé.

My craft, if I can call it a craft, has been honed through self-discovery, trial and error, and often painful experience.

So, am I a time traveler? In a way, I am. But I don't have a time machine and I can't visit the future, so don't waste your time asking me about next week's winning lottery numbers.

It's true I can visit at will any location and any point in time from the past, including the recent past, from the comfort of my own home, albeit plus or minus two or three days and fifty miles, but am I a time traveler? No, I don't think so.

I prefer to think of myself as a dream traveler. This description makes far more sense to me, when you consider that the gateway to my travel is through my dreams. It is also a romanticized description that I particularly like. It was originally penned by a little-known author, Mary Arnold Forster, who in 1921 published a book called Studies in Dreams.

Mary's book describes her own theories and experiences with 'Lucid Dreaming', 'Dream Travel', and 'Dream Control' and, if we are to believe her, she was far more accurate in influencing her dream locations and scenarios then I have ever been.

Considering that her book was published nearly one hundred years ago, her experiences are remarkably similar to my own. As part of my informal dream education, Mary's book has been a source of both knowledge and inspiration to me.

Despite this, and despite the fact that I now have ten years of dream-travel under my belt, I still struggle with precision.

As I said before, it is not an exact science and it is not as simple as using a GPS app on a smartphone.

This then might explain why I am now standing six miles and two days away from where I was intending to be when I closed my eyes.

Sean McMillan

7th February, 2018

## The Past – Thursday, 13th October, 1994

According to the Staines and Egham News, today is Thursday, 13th October, 1994 and the front page has a story about the landing of the space shuttle Endeavour. Other than that, there is nothing much of interest in the paper, and even if there were the voice behind me brings me swiftly back to earth.

"Oy, this is not a bloody library, mate. Are you gonna buy that paper or what?"

I was born in Kingston-Upon-Thames, so not far from here, but the accent sounds much broader than I remember, and the fashion sense makes me smile. In fairness, I was only six years old in 1994, so what do I really know about nineties fashion?

I am mesmerized, though, by the super-gelled hair, spray tan, and gold earrings, which remind me of watching Boyzone on Top of the Pops as a kid. I smile again and wonder to myself why Stephen Gately is working in a newsagents in Staines, but my inane grin is clearly making the Boyzone lookalike uncomfortable and he leans over the counter towards me.

"Are you a bit simple, mate, or are you bloody queer? I asked you if you're gonna buy that paper. If not, put it down and piss off if you're not gonna buy anything."

"Sorry, yes, I will take the paper and a packet of Juicy Fruit gum please – how much is that?"

"Twenty-seven pence for the paper and twenty-five for the gum."

I hand him the money and ask if he knows how to get to the train station.

"You're not from round here, are you, mate? I knew as soon as you walked in with your fancy clothes and your weird haircut."

As he hands over my change, he points towards the door. "Take a right as you go out, then the station is a couple of hundred meters up on the left. Be careful, though – this is a bit of a rough area for a stranger to be walking about in."

I look at him bemused and he gestures towards my clothes. "Mate, you're either a bender, or you're some kind of stuck-up ponce. No one bloody dresses like that round here."

Another challenge with being a dream traveler is having the ability to blend in fully with my surroundings every time I travel. The ideal scenario of course is to be dressed appropriately, to behave properly, to speak the language if needed, and generally to look and act as if I belong, but it is not always possible.

With enough time and planning, I can do the research and bring money and other items that are correct to the period, but the clothes and hairstyles for every possible time period are a real problem, not least because I have a high-profile day job.

Imagine trying to explain turning up for work with a Billy Ray Cyrus mullet or a Beatles-style mop top in 2018. I'm not sure if even I could explain that too easily.

Fortunately, even though I was only a kid, 1994 is not that far away from the present day and, apart from the styles, everything else should be familiar enough for me not to stand out too much.

"No, I'm not a bender, but thanks for asking and thanks for the directions, Stephen."

My sarcasm and Boyzone joke goes right over his head, but as I turn and walk towards the door, he cannot resist trying to get the last word in.

"So, if you're not a bender, what's with those freaky clothes then?"

"It's called fashion. I'm a trendsetter – it's called being ahead of the times. You should try it someday!"

Perhaps twenty-four years ahead of the times is a bit much, but it silences Stephen and I head out of the shop, leaving him standing there scratching his heavily gelled head.

Clearly, either he doesn't know his left from his right, or the fumes from the gel have him confused, or perhaps he was dazzled by my incredible fashion sense. Whatever the reason, the station is actually on the right-hand side of the road.

Because it is just before 6 pm, it is busy with students and commuters heading home.

When I get to the top of the ticket-counter queue, the middle-aged woman behind the glass looks at me as if I am from another planet. Then she gives me a fake smile and hands me my ticket to Feltham. "Platform number two, love. It's due at 6.19."

Behind me, a group of teenagers in school uniform are sniggering, probably at my clothes and hair, but I ignore them and head outside. I cross over the bridge to platform two to wait for the train.

The platform is busy enough, and all the benches are fully occupied, but if the train is on time I won't have too long to wait. One of the things I enjoy most about travelling within my own lifetime is remembering all the things from my own past.

Behind me, a group of students are crowded round one of their mates, who is proudly showing off Donkey Kong on his Nintendo Gameboy and to the side of me a young girl asks her boyfriend if he wants to come over and watch Forest Gump on Friday evening.

"Dad got a pirate video copy from one of his mates at work. It's got that guy in it from Big – Tom somebody. You know, the one where the kid makes the wish and gets big overnight?"

The boyfriend nods and suggests that he bring a couple of bottles of Lambrusco and a few beers so that they can relax better.

Dirty git, I know exactly what the Lambrusco is for and so does she. It's to make her legs relax so that her knickers can slide off better!

The boyfriend catches me staring at them, but before he can say anything, the train pulls into the station right on time and they both move forward with everyone else to the edge of the platform.

It's rush hour, so the train is busy and I have to walk through three carriages before I find an empty seat. Unfortunately, the seat is not entirely empty.

"Don't even think about sitting down, dickhead. That seat is for my boots – keep on moving."

I thought that skinheads faded away sometime in the 1980s, but obviously nobody told this pair of clowns. There is no denying, though, they certainly look the part. Black Fred Perry polo shirts, braces, tight, bleached Levi jeans, Doc Marten boots – and, of course, the obligatory shaven heads, aggressive demeanor, and mangy looking pit-bull dog.

"So, what's this then? Are you and your sisters going to a fancy dress party, or is there a freak show in town?"

Instantly the pair of them are on their feet and squaring up to me.

"What did you say, pal?"

"Calm yourself down, ladies, I was talking to the dog. Now sit down like good little girls before you get spanked."

The pair of them are now positively frothing at the mouth and the carriage is completely silent as the rest of the passengers wait expectantly to see me get my head kicked in. The only difference between now and 2018 is the lack of smartphones to capture the action.

"You had better piss off right now, mate, or my dog is gonna rip your bleeding throat out."

"Okay, lads, maybe we got off on the wrong foot. I just want to sit down and read my paper. Is that okay?"

"Who the hell is this joker? I'm warning you, piss off right now or that paper is going right up your arse."

"Hang on, what about this – why don't you read my paper? You can read, can't you, lads?"

My obvious lack of fear seems to throw them off-balance and they look lost for words for a few seconds.

One of them finally splutters, "Enough of your bloody paper. What the fuck are you talking about?"

"My paper – look, have a read," I explain, helpfully holding it out to them. Neither of them notice how tightly I have rolled it, and as I drop it back down to my side, they also don't notice the way that I am holding it.

"So, what's it to be, lads, can we be friends?"

They both launch at me, but I am way ahead of them. In quick succession, the compacted end of the rolled-up newspaper smashes into their faces and they both drop to the floor with blood pumping from their shattered noses.

As they fall, I reach across, pick up the pit bull by the collar and hurl it through the open window, much to the astonishment of the ticket inspector who has now appeared behind me.

He doesn't speak but I answer him anyway, "What? It didn't have a ticket!"

He looks like he is about to ask me for my ticket, but when he sees the state of the two dipshits on the floor, he thinks better of it and moves away down the carriage.

For the next few minutes, the skinheads sit opposite me, obviously uncomfortable and in pain, but still looking defiant and putting on a brave face for the rest of the passengers. Then, much to their relief, we pull in to Feltham station and they are up on their feet before the train has even stopped.

I am just behind them as they open the door and I can't resist a final dig as they step down onto the platform, "Don't forget your newspaper, ladies."

They ignore me and keep on walking, but as soon as they are at a safe distance, the bravado returns and they both turn back towards me.

"You're bloody dead, you prick! You had better watch your back," one of them yells.

"This is not over," the other one joins in, "you're a dead man walking!"

Outside the entrance to the station, they get into a battered-looking Ford Sierra driven by another Neanderthal and continue to threaten and abuse me until they are out of sight.

I guess my smiling and waving didn't help much in diffusing the situation, but I never have been much of a diplomat, so screw them.

I am just pondering my next move when a hand taps me on the shoulder.

"Excuse me, I saw what you did on the train, but you really should be careful. Those guys are nutters and have a bad reputation."

Being somewhat preoccupied on the train, I hadn't noticed her before. Under normal circumstances, I most definitely would have. She is absolutely gorgeous with long black hair and, if I had to guess, I would say that she is in her mid-twenties with Indian or Nepalese heritage.

"Thanks for the advice, but scumbags like that don't worry me. I can handle myself."

"I think it's obvious from the display on the train that you can handle yourself, but those two scumbags hang around with a much bigger group of scumbags. They won't let things go and they won't be happy until justice has been served."

"Again, thanks for the advice. I didn't catch your name?"

"It's Maria, and no need for thanks – just watch your back is all I'm saying. Anyway, I need to get going or I will miss my bus. Take care of yourself, Superman."

"It's Sean, but Superman also works for me. How about a quick drink before you go home? No strings attached, just a thank you for the advice."

"I can't. Sorry, but I really need to get going – another time maybe."

"What's wrong – husband waiting at home with your dinner on the table, kids to put to bed, or maybe you're late for bible class? It's bible class, isn't it? You have that angelic look about you."

This makes her smile and I can tell already that I nearly have her.

"Cocky bastard, aren't you? For your information, there is no husband or kids and I can't remember the last time I even picked up a bible, but then you knew all of this already, didn't you?"

If she really wanted to leave, she would have left already, so I press my advantage, "Is that a yes then – one drink with Superman?"

"Okay yes, one drink, then I really need to get going. The King George is just around the corner and it's right next to my bus stop. Do you know it?"

I know it very well, although in 1994 I have never been there. It is, however, exactly where I need to be and having someone else with me makes it a damn sight easier to blend in. The fact that she is a stunner is a bonus.

"No, I'm not from around here, but I'm sure it's nice. Let's go."

This makes her laugh. "You're really not from around here, are you? If you were, you would know that the King George is a shithole, just like the rest of the pubs in this town. Just as well I have Superman with me. Come on, let's go."

Inside the pub the air is thick with cigarette smoke and the bar counter is crowded, but Maria is obviously well known.

"Bacardi and Coke, love?" the barman calls over to her.

"Thanks, Barry", and without asking me, "and a pint of Stella for my friend here – is Stella okay for you? You look like a Stella kind of bloke."

"Stella is fine, thank you. And what kind of bloke am I?"

"Well, apart from being Superman, maybe a bit of a wide boy. You don't look or act like any of the blokes around here. Where did you say you were from?"

"I didn't say. Actually, I'm from Romford in Essex. I'm just in town to look up an old friend. What about you? Are you from Feltham?"

"Yes, been here since I was four. My parents moved here from India – we have been in Feltham ever since."

We continue to flirt and make small talk and after four Bacardi and Cokes, Maria has forgotten all about her bus, most of the early evening commuters have moved on, and the pub is starting to fill with the evening regulars.

I might be just using her as cover tonight, but she is the kind of girl I would normally go for: cute, smart, funny, and a good conversationalist. But I still have a job to do, so while we chat I continue to watch the door.

"You said earlier that you were here to look up an old friend – don't you need to go soon?"

"That's okay, he can wait, and he isn't nearly as attractive as you anyway. There's a free table over there by the pool table – shall we grab it before anyone else does?"

I had been waiting for this table to become free since we arrived. It has a good view of the door, is right next to the pool table – and, if my information is correct, my targets should be arriving soon.

"Bit of a charmer, aren't you? It makes quite a change from the usual creeps around here. Get me another drink and I may consider staying a bit longer."

Maria sits down at the table and I excuse myself to get the drinks, detouring first to the bathroom, where the condom machines on the wall and the usual smell of stale piss make me feel I could be standing in any pub bathroom in 1994 or 2018. This is one thing that, unfortunately, hasn't changed much over time.

As I turn to leave, the poster on the back of the door catches my attention. It is an advert for a Pub League Pool Tournament. The King George is due to play against the Three Crowns this coming Saturday at 7.30 pm. I knew this already, but it is still weird to know that I am so close to witnessing something that I have spent months working on.

Tonight is my opportunity to get some insight into what to expect on Saturday and ideally to find a way of gaining an advantage, or something I can use in 2018 to finally close this case.

As I head back with the drinks, another girl has joined Maria and they are having an animated conversation about a hot new boyband from Ireland.

I hold myself back from telling them that Stephen Gately is working in a newsagents in Staines; the humor would be lost on them.

"Oh, hi, Sean, this is my friend Gina. Gina, this is Sean. He beats up skinheads and lures young women into pubs, don't you, Sean?"

I don't know why, but the way she said it actually makes me blush. I always try not to mess with the emotions of anyone I meet when I travel, but when they are as hot as she is, it is hard not to.

"So, you're the guy from the train," Gina said. "You are quite the hot topic – word travels fast around here. I am sure Maria has told you already, but those two guys you flattened are out for your blood. You need to watch yourself, Sean."

I thank her for her concern and offer to get her a drink, but she is already on her feet.

"Thanks, but I need to be getting home. Anyway, I don't want to interrupt you two love birds. Make sure you look after her, Sean."

We chat for another twenty minutes and I answer enough questions to keep her interested, whilst trying not to give too much away. She is particularly interested in what I do and where I learnt to fight.

"You handled yourself well on the train. Most guys would have walked past or backed down right away, but you seemed very sure of yourself. And what was that thing you did with the newspaper? That was very impressive."

"It was nothing really," I replied, trying to sound modest. "I was a special constable for a couple of years, so I know a few self-defense techniques." Not a total lie, and believable enough as an explanation. "The rolled-up newspaper was something I was taught. It's about using everyday items as weapons."

"Oh really? And throwing the dog out of the window – was that also a self-defense technique? Or you just don't like dogs?"

This comment makes me smile. "No, nothing like that. I love dogs. That was about shock factor and making a point. I think it worked. Pit bulls are tough and we weren't going that fast anyway. It would have been fine."

Before we can say anything else, the front door is pushed open and three hard-looking guys in their early and mid-twenties head past us towards the pool table.

Two young guys are already halfway through a game, but the biggest guy in the group leans over the table and picks up the black ball.

"You two, piss off, we need to get some practice in."

They don't argue. They hand over their pool cues and retreat towards the bar while the big guy sets up the balls for another game.

"Right, Terry, get the drinks in and try and get it right this time, ya twat: snakebite and a chaser."

I gesture towards the pool table, "You know those guys?"

Maria nods and says, "Yep, unfortunately, I do. The loud guy is Paul Donovan and his mate is Mark Fletcher. They were in the year above me at school – local troublemakers, but more noise than action – and the guy at the bar is Mark's younger brother Terry. Bit of a simpleton, but he idolizes Paul and Mark."

I watch as they finish setting up the balls and then Paul makes a show of breaking to Mark.

"Watch this, Mark, those assholes from the Three Crowns don't stand a bloody chance."

I am expecting to see something special, but he turns out to be a shitty player. After failing to pot anything, he sulkily moves to the side to let Mark take his shot, muttering, "Bloody cue must be bent."

He is still complaining as he downs half of his snakebite and tips in the whisky shot.

"Terry, pass me another cue."

Terry is five years younger than his brother Mark and from what I know already, and what I can see now, Paul treats him like absolute shit.

This is no surprise to me, though. By all accounts, Paul has always been a bully. But I can't understand why Mark allows it.

"Oy, cloth ears, I said get me another cue."

"Sorry, Paul, here you go," Terry said as he handed him the cue, adding, "I think the one you had is okay, though. It doesn't look bent to me."

You could hear the slap from across the other side of the bar and for just a second the whole place is silent, as Terry struggles to hold back tears.

"Are you trying to make me look like a bloody idiot in front of everyone? What the hell do you know about pool anyway, you bleedin spastic? Now, make yourself useful and get another round in."

Terry was visibly shaken, and it was all I could do to hold myself back from saying or doing something – to the point that Maria put her hand over mine and told me not to get involved.

As it was, she said it a little too loud and Paul turned towards us. "Do yourself a favor, mate, and listen to your slag. Drink your drink and keep your nose out of what doesn't concern you. Time you were leaving and offering that table to us anyway."

Maria tells Paul that we are not ready to leave yet, but I tell her that we should probably get going anyway and Mark walks over and clucks like a chicken as we finish our drinks.

Much as I would love to stay to slap the shit out of them, this is not part of the plan, so we get up and head towards the door as Paul continues to abuse Terry.

"Stop your bloody crying, it was only a slap. Go and get those drinks before I really get angry. Sort that prick out, Mark. Can't believe you two are from the same mother."

It's nearly 9 pm, and the streets are quiet, other than for some kids hanging around outside of the chip shop and a couple of private taxis loitering for business.

Maria is unhappy about what happened in the pub and apologizes to me, but I reassure her that it doesn't matter.

"Don't worry about them. It's time I was getting you home anyway. Those guys are real assholes, but plenty of time to put them straight on a few things later."

"Yes, I'm really sorry about them, Sean. Paul has always been a bit of an idiot. He loves to throw his weight around. The other two are okay when they aren't with him. Unfortunately, most of the time they are with him. As you could see, Paul is a crap pool player, but the landlord is too scared of him to say anything."

Crap is an understatement, but the Saturday pool tournament is the reason I am here, and I know already that Paul, Mark, and Terry are the team from the King George. The game on Saturday is going to be memorable for all the wrong reasons and the quality of the players is not one of them.

"It's getting late, Maria. Let's get a taxi and let me take you home."

"That's very kind, Sean, but there really is no need. My bus stop is just here, and they come every twenty minutes."

Until a few hours ago, I had never heard of Maria, but because of a chance meeting outside the train station, she has suddenly become an extremely important piece of the jigsaw that I am putting together and there is no way I am going to let her get rid of me just yet.

"I really would feel better if I could take you home, Maria. This town seems to have more than its fair share of nutters and I could never forgive myself if anything happened to you, particularly after I made you come for drinks with me."

"I'm not sure, Sean. I'm still trying to work you out, and I haven't decided yet whether you are actually as charming as you make out, or whether it's all just a front to get in my knickers."

For a second, we both go quiet and then we laugh.

"I guess there is only one way to find out. Your taxi awaits, princess – what's the address?"

The ride in the taxi takes less than five minutes. We pull up outside a row of semi-detached houses and there is an awkward silence as we both wait for the other person to speak or do something.

Normally, I would have no qualms about inviting myself in, but I seem to be a bag of nerves around this girl.

Fortunately, she spares me from making a tit of myself with some cheesy chat-up line by asking me if I want to come in.

"Thank God for that," the taxi driver interjects, " I thought you pair were taking up residency. Six quid for the ride, mate."

I hand the cab driver a ten-pound note and without waiting for the change, I get out of the cab and follow Maria to the front door.

"Listen, I live with my mum. She's probably in bed, but she's a light sleeper, so keep your noise down, or we might miss finding out what your real intentions are. Does that work for you, Superman?"

I smile and nod, then follow her upstairs to her bedroom. The décor is typically nineties and the phone in the hallway, plugged into the wall, is a particular highlight that makes me smile. The décor, though, is not what I have on my mind.

Just because technically I am working, it doesn't mean I can't enjoy some of the perks of the job. As long as the job gets done and nothing gets changed, there is no reason at all why we can't have some fun. Maria is most definitely one of the perks.

Inside her room, she gestures to her bed. "Okay, sit there and don't touch anything. I won't be long, just going to the bathroom to freshen up. Try not to beat anyone up while I'm gone."

Based on what Maria had said earlier about Paul and Mark being in the year above her at school, this would make her twenty-five or twenty-six, as I first thought. Her room, though, has a much younger feel about it and it is quite unusual for an Indian girl still to be living at home, or not to be married by now.

I notice also that she has not mentioned her father, just her mother.

Next to her bed there is a table with a lamp and two photographs in gold frames. The first, I assume, is a picture of her mum and dad. Both are very good looking – it is easy to see where she gets her own good looks from.

I pick up the second one for a better look. It is the same man, but he appears to be a bit younger than he is in the other picture. In this one, he is looking very smart in a pilot's uniform and hanging over the frame is a silver St. Christopher pendant.

The patron saint of travelers makes perfect sense to be worn by a pilot, and I suspect that Maria's father has probably passed away.

"That's my dad, or he was my dad. He was killed a year and a half ago, a hit-and-run. They still haven't found the driver."

I was so engrossed in the picture that I hadn't noticed her coming back into the room. "I am so sorry, Maria, I didn't mean to pry. He was a good-looking guy. Have the police got any leads at all?"

It is probably not the right time to ask such a question and I can tell she doesn't really want to talk about it, but I guess it kind of goes with the territory for me.

"Nothing much, it was a stolen car. There were a few witnesses, but people don't tend to say much around here. They are too scared of what might happen. No doubt in a few months, the police will close the case and my dad will be just another statistic."

Sadly, she is probably right, and I don't ask her anything else, but I make a few mental notes. Then I pull her towards me and kiss her on the lips.

"So, have you made your mind up about me yet?"

"I made my mind up about you after the second Bacardi and Coke. You're most definitely a charmer and you're also most definitely trying to get into my knickers. The only difference between you and the other guys is that you're happy to buy me a drink first and I have a feeling that it's not going to be a race to see who comes first."

For the second time tonight, I am lost for words, so she takes the lead and pulls me down onto the bed. "You can take that last part as a compliment, Mr. Charmer. I don't do this very often, so let's do it now before I come to my senses and change my mind."

The sex is mind-blowing and by the time we climax, we are both sweating heavily, and I gladly accept Maria's offer to get me a glass of cold water.

I am starting to think that she might have been exaggerating, though, when she said that her mom was a light sleeper. I know for a fact that I am a noisy bastard when I come, and Maria was not exactly quiet herself, but there is nothing heard from her mother's bedroom.

As she walks back into the bedroom with the water, her figure is silhouetted in the window and I can't help staring at her pert breasts and shapely ass.

"Hey, Casanova, avert your eyes, drink your water and get your clothes on. It's already past two in the morning and my mum is an early riser. Believe me, those skinheads have nothing on my mother. If you want to keep your balls intact, you had better get moving."

It wasn't part of my plan to stay over anyway, but I need to be able to see her again. "Can I see you again, Maria? This Saturday, let's meet in the King George around 7.30 pm and then we can go on somewhere for dinner."

"Wow, the King George, you are such a romantic. But okay – if it means you'll put your pants on and let me sleep, then yes.

Make sure you book somewhere nice for dinner, though. Now go on, get dressed."

By the time she closes the door behind me, it is nearly 2.45 am and the early morning chill has well and truly kicked in. Despite only having a light jacket on, it doesn't bother me. I know it won't be long before my way home appears.

I start walking without any idea where I am going, but it doesn't matter. As I walk out of Maria's street and onto the main road, my two skinhead friends are waiting for me. I wasn't entirely sure it would be them, but it makes sense, as there is nobody else that I have pissed off enough during this trip.

"Hey, dickhead, I bet you didn't expect to see us again so soon," one of them taunts.

On the contrary, I suspected that I would, but no point trying to explain that to this pair of morons. I know that there is no point running either. This needs to happen and the best thing I can do is to do as much damage as I can before I leave.

"Hey, ladies, love the matching plasters. What's this all about? Did you not get the message earlier? Do I need to take you over my knee again and give you another good spanking?"

They both smile and move towards me.

"We told you before, smart mouth, you're a dead man walking."

I don't see them, but I know the rest of their mates are behind me. When the first baseball bat swings towards me, I dodge it easily, but the second one crashes down on my shoulder and drops me to my knees.

From then on, they all pile in on me and we trade punches and headbutts for a few seconds, but there are far too many of them, even for me.

As I go down on the floor for the final time, the Doc Marten boots slam into my ribs and my head. The last thing I remember is the glint of a blade from a Stanley knife as it slashes across my face.

“Not so fucking tough now, are you? Enjoy reading about this in your newspaper, dickhead!

## Present Day – Thursday, 8th February, 2018

I am never late. If anything, I am one of those people that is always irritatingly early, so when I wake up and realize that I have slept through all three of my alarms, it takes me a few seconds to register it and get my bearings.

"Shit, shit, shit, why today of all days?"

I am already skating on thin ice with Detective Chief Inspector Morgan and if I miss his briefing this morning, I am going to go down even further in his opinion.

DCI Kevin Morgan is a by-the-book career police officer with more than twenty years of impeccable service under his belt, and he does not tolerate any kind of tardiness or lack of effort in his team.

Last night took me a step closer to bringing forward some new information for him, but I don't have enough yet and his patience is already wearing thin with me.

I personally requested to head up this case and he has already given me three extensions to explore new leads. If I don't come up with something conclusive soon, he is going to hand over the lead to someone else, which means I can pretty much say goodbye to the Cold Case Squad.

The daily briefing is at 9 am and it is already 8.35. Even if I drive like a lunatic, I am still going to be at least 10 minutes late – and I still need to shave and shower.

As I shower, my mind wanders to the night before, to Maria, to Paul Donovan, and to the skinheads kicking the living shit out of me. The skins are unconnected to my case and I laugh thinking about what they must have thought when I disappeared in front of their eyes. Nobody will believe them, though, or they might put it down to the extra-strength lager they drink, or a dodgy batch of drugs.

Paul Donovan is my focus, and Maria just might be the advantage that I need for a real breakthrough. I feel like a shit for using her, but she said it herself, "People don't tend to say much around here. They are too scared of what might happen."

There has been a conspiracy of silence for too long in this case, but if I can get just one person to speak up, then it may open up the door for others; and surely, they can't all still be afraid after twenty-four years.

I put on my suit and my smartest tie, then I pick up my car keys and my phone. I see that there is a text message from my partner, Detective Constable Catherine Swain, asking where I am.

I message her back to say that I am on my way and that I may be late. Instantly I get a reply: You need to get a move on. Morgan is in a foul mood today. I will try to cover for you but get moving!

Just what I need, another dressing down in front of the team. If I thought I could get away with it, I would try to go back to sleep right now, but that would really do it for me with the boss. Besides, I am not tired enough to stay away long enough.

No, I need to brazen it out today and buy myself a few more days. Maria is the key and I need to focus my attention on her.

I head to the door and am just about to open it when I suddenly remember I have forgotten something. It is the mugshot of Paul Donovan at the side of my bed, taken after his arrest on 18$^{th}$ October, 1994.

To dream-travel with any degree of accuracy, I need a clear stimulus or physical connection to the past or to a case, so yesterday morning I had taken the original mugshot from his file.

I pick it up and look at it for a few seconds. Then I fold it up, slip it inside my jacket pocket and say to myself, "You think you've gotten away with it, Paul. Well, think again, asshole, I am coming for you."

Normally, the drive from my apartment to Blackwell Police Station takes around twenty minutes; today I managed it in fourteen by breaking the limits all the way. I figure at this point that a speeding ticket is preferable to a dressing down from Kevin Morgan.

Unfortunately, by the time I walk into the briefing room, it is nearly 9.20 am and there is a distinct possibility of both. The room is full, and the only spare seat is right at the front of the room, so I can't even slip in quietly.

DCI Morgan is getting an update on a missing person's case from 1991, from Detective Sergeant Sarah Gray. Just for a moment, I think that he might ignore my late arrival, but no such luck.

Sarah finishes the point she is on and Morgan asks her to wait for a moment.

"Very good of you to join us, DC McMillan. Did you have something else important on this morning, or perhaps your colleague's case updates are not interesting enough for you?"

My colleagues around me, apart from a few, make no attempt to hide their sniggers. That's the way it is in the force, always looking for someone else to fall from grace so that they can climb the greasy ladder themselves.

It's not that I am a star performer, far from it. Up till now I have been an average police officer and an average detective constable; it's more just about someone else screwing up and taking the attention off everyone else. I have been guilty of it myself from time to time.

"My sincere apologies, sir. I was working late last night on the Glennister case and I forgot to set my alarm. It won't happen again."

From behind me, someone coughs the word "bullshit" into their hand, which sets off the sniggers again, but Morgan cuts them short.

"It appears that your colleagues are as unimpressed as I am, DC McMillan. I sincerely hope for your sake that your late working last night has produced something worthwhile. I look forward to hearing all about it when we get to your case update. Carry on, DS Gray."

My case update is third on the agenda, so I probably have no more than ten minutes before I need to offer something up to keep my case on track. So, while Sarah Grey continues her update, I flick through my pocket book and add in everything from last night.

Terry Fletcher is definitely the weak link among the three of them, but would he inform on Paul, which would mean implicating himself and his brother also?

No, I still think Maria is the key. Twenty-four years ago, on the night of the pool tournament, she wasn't even in the King George. I need to place her there and I need to make sure she witnesses everything.

If I can get what I need from her, I can put pressure on Terry, and then, with luck, the whole pack of lies should come tumbling down.

My mind is wandering when my phone vibrates in my pocket. There is another message from Catherine: I hope for your sake that you have something. Walker has been pushing Sarah to lobby Morgan to hand over your case to him.

DC Mark Walker is the newest member of the Cold Case Squad. He joined a few months after I did and has made it known that he wants to make detective sergeant as soon as possible.

For now, he hasn't been given any cases of his own to lead, so my failure would open the door for him. I would probably be doing the same if I were him, but it's still shit when we are supposed to be on the same team.

I reply to Catherine: Just keep watching my back. I need three or four days, tops. I am close to breaking this.

Sarah Gray finishes her update and after a few questions from the team, DCI Morgan checks the agenda. "Okay, DC McMillan, how about we let you jump the queue? Tell me that you have made some progress."

I can just imagine how many of the team are waiting for me to stumble through my update, and if Catherine is correct, Mark Walker must be rubbing his hands in anticipation of taking my case.

There is no way I am going to let that happen, though. My appointment to this squad was my way up. I have been a copper for eight years now and most of the guys that went through Hendon with me are already sergeants.

Matt Davies is a bloody inspector and leading a team in the Serious Crimes Squad; so no, this squad and this case is my chance to move beyond being a bloody constable.

The first time I dream-travelled was more than ten years ago. It should have meant that I could travel freely through time, and as a copper this was like winning the lottery, but I never had enough control.

It is only in the last eighteen months that I have been able to travel with any degree of precision, and to have the confidence to apply to join the Cold Case Squad.

After four years as a beat copper and three as a regular detective constable, I finally made it onto this squad. I know that I am onto something and there is no way I am going to make myself look like a dick.

"Actually, sir, yes, I think that I have made good progress. Our three main suspects for the murder of Anthony Glennister were all interviewed again by DC Catherine Swain and myself. All three of them stuck to the story in their original statements and still maintain that an unidentified black male got into a fight with Anthony Glennister and stabbed him to death.

"The other witnesses on the night were the pub landlord, Michael Bell, but he passed away in 2014, the two other members of the Three Crowns pool team and eleven drinkers that were in the bar at the time of the incident. Up to now, we have managed to trace and interview nine of these thirteen witnesses, but they are all sticking firmly to their original statements; not one of them has contradicted the statements given by Paul Donovan and Mark and Terry Fletcher."

Morgan holds up his hand to stop me. "DC McMillan, you said that you had made some progress, how about you save us the recap on what we already know and get to the point please?"

"Yes, sir. It is clear that even after twenty-four years the witnesses are scared witless of Donovan and the Fletcher brothers. The identical statements from all the witnesses is a classic indication of collusion. They are just too similar to have been thought out independently. I think that the level of fear and intimidation is so high that we are wasting our time trying to get anyone to speak. I have, though, identified a new witness. This person was originally placed in the bathroom during the incident, but I have new evidence to suggest that this is incorrect and that the person did in fact witness the entire incident."

Again, the coughing "bullshit" from the back of the room and a few sniggers from my colleagues.

"And are you able to enlighten us on where you got this new evidence from, DC McMillan?"

"At the moment, sir, I would prefer to keep that information confidential. My expectation is that within seventy-two hours I will be in a position to bring this witness in for questioning and then to re-interview Donovan and the Fletcher brothers."

"DC McMillan, this squad was formed to re-examine previously dormant cases for the purpose of reopening them if the Crown Prosecution Service feels that we have found sufficient new evidence to warrant it. You have seventy-two hours to bring me that evidence. After that I am reassigning you and possibly closing the case."

By 10.15 am the morning briefing has finished, and we all disperse back to our offices, and I know that Catherine will be eager to speak to me. As expected, a few minutes later she comes over with two cups of black coffee.

"You probably need this – heavy night, was it? You said you were working late last night on the case. How is it that I don't know about it and why don't I know about this new witness? Correct me if I am wrong, but aren't we meant to be partners on this case?"

Catherine has been collaborating with me in interviewing the witnesses and reviewing the case files, but how do you tell your partner that you are gathering evidence in your sleep?

"Thanks for the coffee. I really was working last night, Catherine. It was something that came up suddenly and I didn't want to disturb you. To be honest, I wasn't sure if it would actually lead to anything."

"Okay, so who is this new witness? We have been through all of the witness statements in minute detail and I don't recall any witness hiding out in the bathroom."

Lying to Catherine is the last thing I need to be doing. She is my main ally, but right now my new witness doesn't even exist as far as this case is concerned.

"I know it's not the way we should be working together, but for now I can't even tell you, Catherine. I just need you to trust me and I promise that as soon as I can, I will tell you everything."

"You do know that the whole office is waiting for you to fall flat on your face on this one? You pushed hard for Morgan to give you your own case – a cocky young DC looking to make a name for himself. Don't make me regret trusting you, Sean. Enjoy your coffee."

For the rest of the day, I do my best to keep busy and to keep Catherine as involved as possible in looking for new possibilities to explore in the Glennister case files.

Anthony Glennister was the captain of the pool team from the Three Crowns playing against the King George on the night of Saturday, 15th October, 1994. Unsurprisingly, given what I now know about the pool skills of Paul Donovan, the Three Crowns won convincingly on the night. According to the witness statements, there was some bad-tempered banter being thrown around by both teams after the game finished.

Supposedly, a glass was thrown across the room by Anthony Glennister, hitting an unidentified black male in the face. All the witness statements then describe a fight between Glennister and the black male, resulting in the stabbing to death of Glennister.

It's all bullshit, though, and even the investigating officers in 1994 knew that. Nobody was able to identify the attacker, no trace of him was ever found. There was no trace of blood or other DNA from this male and no blood on any of the glasses found in the subsequent search of the crime scene.

Anthony Glennister himself was an accountant. He was a light drinker, a committed family man, and had no prior record for violence of any description. He didn't have so much as a parking ticket.

On the other hand, when Donovan and the Fletcher brothers were taken in for questioning, they all had bruises and abrasions on their face and knuckles, which they were not able to account for.

An innocent man has been murdered, and it has gone unpunished for twenty-four years. I know that Donovan and his cronies are involved in the death of Glennister and are intimidating the witnesses into silence; I just need to find the key to breaking that silence.

Maria is part of that key. But involving her means she will also be dragged into the cycle of intimidation. I need something else if I have a hope in hell of getting her cooperation.

By 5 pm, I am ready to give up, but then I go back to the notes in my pocket book and I find what I need.

"Catherine, I need you to pull a file for me. I don't have much to go on, but this is the location, approximate date range, and the circumstances."

"Okay, but what has this got to do with the Glennister case, or is this something else that you can't share with me right now?"

"Sorry, Catherine, I really can't. It's extremely important, though. I think that the two cases could be connected."

Thirty minutes later Catherine is back with a thin Manilla folder; the date on the front is 11th April, 1993.

"Is this what you're looking for, Sean?"

Inside is a picture with a familiar face. For a second, I feel guilty.

"Yes, it is, thanks, Catherine, I really appreciate your help. Let's finish up for the day."

"Sean, I don't know what you are up to, but I sincerely hope that you are not playing me for a fool. If your hunch doesn't work out, then you are on your own. I do trust you, but I don't appreciate being left out in the cold."

She is right, and I would feel exactly the same. I feel like a complete shit, but now is not the time to come clean with her. The best I can manage is a nod and I tell her to have a good evening.

She picks up her handbag to leave. "You too, Sean."

And then just as she is about to open the office door she turns back towards me with a knowing look to say, "And don't forget to set your alarm, Sean, just in case you decide to work late again."

When I get home, I drop the folder onto the coffee table and change into my running gear. I need to be as tired as possible when I hit my bed, just in case I need to travel for longer than I am hoping to.

It is already getting dark and is raining lightly, but I go for a six-mile run, mainly along the banks of the River Thames. This is a familiar route for me and I use the time to think about what I need to do over the next few days and in what order.

Donovan and his cronies are slippery fuckers with equally slippery legal counsel; you don't avoid justice for this long without knowing how to work the system, or how to cover your tracks.

Tonight, I need to go back to 1993. Then, hopefully, if I get what I need, my next move will be to look up Maria. I haven't checked yet if she is still living in this area, but if all goes well I can hand this case over to Catherine to keep her occupied.

It also means that I can put off coming face to face with Maria again for a little longer. After twenty-four years she probably won't recognize me, but it could still be awkward for both of us if she does think that I look familiar.

On the other hand, if I don't get anything that can help tonight, I will have wasted another twenty-four hours and will simply need to appeal to Maria's sense of right and wrong.

There is so much riding on what happens over the next few days and it worries me to think of the consequences of failure. Three thugs will continue to walk free, Maria will have been dragged into a life of fear and intimidation, and I will end up, at best, back on the beat.

It doesn't even bear thinking about and for the last part of the run I put the case out of my mind, speed up my pace, and finish with a sprint.

Ever the copper, as I get to the front of my tower block, I notice Catherine's car parked just opposite the entrance. I assume that she must be on her way up to my place, but I don't pass her in the lift and she is not outside my apartment.

I pick up my phone to call her, but at the last second, I cut off, partly because I think I may have been mistaken about the car, but mainly because I don't want to have another awkward conversation tonight.

If it was her and it is something important she will call me, but for now, I need to shower and to get to work.

By 8.30 pm with a Chinese takeaway and a large glass of Bushmills Irish Whiskey, I am ready to start. I settle down on my sofa with the contents of the folder laid out on the table in front of me.

Two witness statements, two photographs of a burnt-out Ford Escort, a report from the Scene of Crime Officer, three photographs of the victim showing the extent of his injuries and another picture provided by his family, then the autopsy report, and finally the coroner's report recording a verdict of unlawful death.

All in all, a pitiful collection of documents and a sad indictment on the ability of the police to bring justice to the victim's family.

The key to successful dream-travel Is remembering as much detail as I can, so for the next two hours I read through the contents of the folder in fine detail another four times, until I know everything possible about the case and the victim.

I know his age, his date of birth, his occupation, the details of his family, the date, location, circumstances and approximate time of his death and, with my eyes closed, I can picture him exactly.

Satisfied that I am ready to go, I pour myself another small glass of whisky and knock it back in one; then I pick up the victim's photograph and drop it on the bed, before moving to the window to close my bedroom curtains.

My apartment is on the third floor and my bedroom overlooks the street. I notice the car from earlier is still parked in front of my building, although it has moved to a different parking spot, so I assume it probably isn't Catherine's after all. Most likely, it is just a new resident or someone visiting one of my neighbors. I don't give it another thought as I pull the curtains closed, set my alarm, and lie down on my bed.

The date and the photograph are my keys tonight and with my eyes closed I picture the victim and repeat the date in my head, 11$^{th}$ April , 1993, 11$^{th}$ April , 1993, 11$^{th}$ April , 19 ...

Then it comes, always the same, a sudden rush of warmth and a blinding light, powerful shaking throughout my body, then silence and a few seconds of confusion before I fully get my bearings.

## The Past – Sunday, 11th April, 1993

The sun is on my face and it feels like mid-afternoon. The off-licence opposite me is still operating in 2018. I remember it from my days as a beat copper, as this area was part of my patch when I was based at Stanwell Road Station.

As I recall, it went through a full renovation five or six years back, but it doesn't look a great deal different now, apart from the products and the prices.

So far, so good, the right location is always a good start, and for reasons unknown to me, my watch always adjusts itself to the correct time, even allowing for daylight saving.

It's just after 3.30 pm, so I have around three hours to kill until show time. First, I need to confirm the date – obviously, no point hanging around if I have the wrong day completely.

There are plenty of people in the street, but it's always my last resort to ask somebody the day and date. That's the kind of shit you see in a movie when somebody has lost their memory or been abducted by aliens.

No point drawing unnecessary attention to myself and not needed anyway when there is a newsagents right next to the off-licence.

Without even checking the date, I know already that at least I have the right day. The shelves are packed with the Sunday editions of the newspapers and I have a little chuckle to myself when I see the Sunday Sport.

For those that have never heard of the Sunday Sport, it is a tabloid newspaper that has been in circulation since 1986 and is well known for its outrageous stories, nudity, and eye-catching headlines. Some of the more memorable ones are: 'World War 2 Bomber Found On The Moon,' 'He Shagged Our Sunday Dinner

Chicken, But I Still Love Him,' and 'Sex With Greggs Pasty Boiled My Bellend.'

I digress, though. The date is Sunday, 11th April, 1993. So, thankfully, for now there is no need for me to jump off a bridge or get myself knocked out, which, as you have probably realized already, is how I get myself home.

This must sound a bit extreme, but in fairness I don't always need to go quite that far. I do, however, need some kind of shock or a jolt to wake me up. It's just more fun to work out how many different ways I can kill myself or get myself beaten up.

As of now, I still haven't worked out why I need to do this, and during my first few trips I did everything possible to keep myself out of danger. But once I realized that the pain was just temporary, it got much easier to step in front of a train or to drop a hair dryer into my bath.

Anyway, good news, I am in the right location on the right day. Now I need to pick something else up in readiness for tonight.

I scan the shelves but can't see what I am looking for. Then the elderly woman behind the counter looks over to me.

"Is there something I can help you with, love?"

"Yes, thank you. I need a disposable camera, one with a flash. Do you have any?"

The look she gives me suggests that she has no idea what I am talking about.

"Sorry, young man, we don't sell cameras. Try the electrical shop two doors down. I'm sure they have them."

She probably has some somewhere in the shop, but I don't waste time trying to explain to her what a disposable camera is and instead I thank her and head to the electrical store.

The cameras are positioned right at the front of the store, and I find what I am looking for immediately. But then I spot something even better, a Kodak Polaroid camera kit, with batteries, flash, and a free ten pack of film.

The Polaroid spits out pictures instantly, with no time wasted on sending away the film to be processed, so I pay for the camera and then I find a café to grab a bite to eat and a cup of tea to kill some time.

While I wait, I set up the camera and take a couple of pictures to make sure it works. The overall picture quality is poor in comparison to the images that you get from modern digital cameras or from smartphones, but it is good enough for what I need.

After a third cup of tea, the time is getting on for 6 pm. I need to find myself a vantage point to take my pictures from and I can tell that the café owner is getting annoyed with me hogging the table, so I make my way outside.

It is still daylight. If I am correct, it will probably be at least 7.30 pm before it starts getting dark, which makes me even more confused as to why the witnesses in this case were unable to provide any clear description of the suspect.

The two witness statements have the incident taking place at approximately 6.20 pm, just around twenty minutes from now and it is still perfectly light.

Something doesn't add up and I am starting to suspect that the Glennister case is not the only one that might have a whiff of witness intimidation about it.

Just opposite the off-licence and around ten yards further down the road is a public telephone box, which will give me a perfect view of the road in both directions and of the off-licence itself.

At 6.10 pm, I position myself inside and pretend to make a call. I am worried at first that I might be disturbed by somebody actually wanting to make a call, but there is no need to worry about that. Like every other phone box in this area, it has been vandalized and the handset is smashed to pieces, so for the next few minutes I amuse myself reading the graffiti and hookers' calling cards pasted on the windows.

Sure enough, at 6.14 pm a Red Ford Mondeo pulls up opposite the off-licence and a middle-aged guy gets out, crosses the road, and goes inside. He is unmistakable, and, as always, I feel guilty that I know what is going to happen but am not going to do anything to stop it.

That's not part of the game, of course. I don't do this to play God. I do this to put bad guys away and to get justice for the victims and their families; at least that's how I justify it to myself.

I check the camera over and then focus my attention on the door to the off-licence. I know from the statement of the manager that the victim was inside for a couple of minutes and he paid cash for two bottles of red wine and a bag of Kettle chips.

At 6.17 pm, my heart is racing as I see him come outside. He is a proud looking man and he walks with a dignified air, totally unaware that he has seconds to live. He crosses the road and is literally just a few feet away from his car when he drops his car keys and stoops to pick them up. The car heading towards him is speeding on the wrong side of the road and I think to myself that, mercifully, he probably didn't even see it coming.

At the last second, the driver must have seen him, though, and the tires screech and belch out smoke as he slams on the brakes. But at that speed it makes no difference. The front of the speeding car slams into the man with a sickening crunch and he is crushed against the side of his own car.

Even though I know what is about to happen, it is still a shock to see it up close; and for a second, I freeze. But then my instincts and training kick in. I know I have a job to do and I only have seconds in which to do it.

I run from the telephone box and position myself within a few feet of the cars. I can see the driver clearly and I take three pictures as fast as the camera will allow me.

He has a trickle of blood running down his forehead but otherwise appears unscathed. From the crunch of the gearbox, it sounds like he is trying to get into reverse gear. The bastard is so absorbed in trying to get away that he doesn't see me snapping away and he only registers the other two people when they try to pull open the passenger side door.

One is the manager from the off-licence and the other is a young woman. I remember from her statement that she is a single mother with two young children.

Instead of being thankful, their efforts at helping him are met with aggression, and they both pause.

"Get the fuck away from me! Don't bloody touch that door if you know what's good for you!"

They step away from the car and it seems to me that they have both recognized him. He also seems to realize this. He gets out of the car, walks round to their side, and grabs them both by the throat.

"You both know who I am, which means you both know what I can do. Don't forget, I know where you both live. Don't even bloody think of speaking to the pigs."

Then directly to the young woman, "If you even think about giving my name or description to the police, your kids are gonna end up in the river and you two are both dead, you got that?"

They both nod in unison and the driver pushes them backwards into the road before getting back into his car without even bothering to look at the guy he has just killed.

It wasn't part of my plan, but just before he drives away, I step forward, just close enough to be seen by him but not by the two witnesses. I want this bastard to see me taking this picture.

"Hey, asshole, smile for the camera."

As he turns his head and sees me standing there, the look on his face is priceless. He knows that he is caught, but there is nothing he can do about it, and for now he just needs to get away before the police or the ambulance arrives, so he guns the engine and speeds off.

That last picture isn't really necessary. The three photos I have already are more than enough to identify him and his ugly face is already firmly ingrained in my mind. The real point of that last picture is about letting him sweat for the next twenty-five years, knowing that somewhere out there is someone with the evidence to put him away for killing an innocent man.

I'm sure he must have spent the last twenty-five years wondering why that person hasn't already come forward. Well, I have news for you, buddy, the wait is nearly over.

I have what I came for and I move away down the street before anyone else comes along and spots me. A few minutes later I hear sirens. An ambulance passes me heading towards the scene, closely followed by two police cars. I stuff the four Polaroids into my pocket, dump the camera in a dustbin and make my way into a public park to look for a way home.

At first the park appears deserted and I mutter under my breath, "Typical, never any thugs, muggers or winos when you need them." But then I spot a possible opportunity lying on the grass.

Thank God for drug addicts. These two are both completely comatose, but helpfully have left the rest of their stash and drugs paraphernalia lying around for any other passing addicts to take a hit.

I'm not an expert on drugs, but for my purpose I don't need to be, so I sit down next to the two druggies, unroll a cellophane wrap and swallow the remainder of the heroin inside.

I remember seeing Uma Thurman snorting heroin in Pulp Fiction and it messed her up pretty much instantly, so I figure swallowing it should do pretty much the same thing to me.

I am not wrong. Within seconds I feel my heart pumping and I fall backwards onto the grass. I cough up blood and vomit and it is a struggle not to try to clear it from my mouth and nose as I black out and slowly choke to death.

## Present Day – Friday, $9^{th}$ February, 2018

I wake up at around 6.40 am, nearly an hour before my alarm is due to go off. As always after a trip, I lie in bed with my eyes closed for a few minutes memorizing all of the key details.

To say that this trip was a success would be an understatement. I had managed to get everything I needed and more; and exposing myself to take that last picture had been well worth it just to see the look on that assholes face.

I can now hand over the file to Catherine and get her to pull the witnesses back in for interview, while I work on the next part of my plan.

Unable to get back to sleep, I get up and put the kettle on. Then I have a small panic as I remember the Polaroids and irrationally think that I may have lost them, or they may not have made it back. When I pull them out of my pocket, I am massively relieved and breathe a sigh of relief.

Considering how quickly they had been taken, they are actually quite good pictures. Two of them have clearly captured Donovan and his vehicle registration and the other two are focused firmly on his face. What I hadn't noticed before, though, is that in one of the pictures, I have also inadvertently captured the two witnesses approaching the car. The view of them is through the passenger side window and is partially obscured, so would not stand up in court, but it might just be enough to get them to change their statements and agree to identifying the driver.

Yep, it was a good trip and it has kept me on track to put the next phase of my plan into operation. Closing the Glennister case will be a massive feather in my cap, but if I can top it off with also closing this second case, then my career should definitely get a massive boost.

I just need to keep Catherine busy today and keep her on side. It's Friday, so most of the team will be off for the weekend, but my seventy-two hours are ticking away, and I can't afford to waste any of them.

By 7.45 am I am in the office. My case is not on the agenda for today's team briefing, but I wouldn't be at all surprised if Morgan throws me a curveball at the last moment.

It isn't needed, as I know both cases inside out by now. But for the next forty-five minutes, I go through all of my notes and the two case files again to ensure that I haven't missed anything, just in case he does surprise me.

I am so engrossed in reading that I don't notice Catherine standing next to me until she speaks, "You look busy there, is there anything I can help you with?"

Rather awkwardly and embarrassed about being caught out, I push all of the documents back into the files and smile at her. "Hey Catherine, how long have you been standing there?"

"Long enough to see those pictures. What the hell is going on, Sean? I read that file before I gave it to you, an unsolved hit-and-run case from '93. When I gave you that file there were no pictures in it."

"Can we not do this now, Catherine? Straight after the team brief let's grab a coffee and I will fill you in on some new developments and explain the link between the two cases."

She is not impressed, and she doesn't hold back in letting me know.

"Thanks, Sean, that is very gracious of you. I take it you are aware that you are not the only detective in this department? I saw those pictures clearly enough and, even with my limited experience, I can work out the link. If you want me to continue backing you, you need to throw me a bone; I'm not just here to make up the numbers, Sean."

If I felt like a shit yesterday, I feel like an even bigger one today. I am not just playing with people's lives in the past; I am also playing with lives in the present and possibly the future. The decisions I make over the next forty-eight hours will decide how those futures, including my own pan out, but I still can't share everything with Catherine yet.

"Sorry, Catherine, I didn't mean to insult you or to sound condescending. Come on, let's get a decent seat in the briefing room, somewhere at the back. Breakfast on me straight after, I promise."

This last comment elicits half a smile from her.

Despite my earlier concern, the briefing passes off without my having to give any kind of update and by 10.30 am, we are out of the station and in a café with a full English breakfast and mugs of steaming hot tea in front of us.

"I hope that by buying me breakfast, Sean, you're not trying to buy me off. It takes more than a fry-up and a cup of tea for that. Where did you get the pictures and how did you even know to connect the two cases?"

The question about the pictures I am ready for, but the second part throws me off-balance a bit, but I hope it doesn't show and I try to brazen it out.

"As part of the investigation into the Glennister case, I received an anonymous tip-off about another unsolved but connected crime, the hit-and-run. Yesterday I received some additional information concerning the whereabouts of the photographs you saw, and last night I met with the informant."

I am about to say more but Catherine cuts me off.

"You met this informant last night? Exactly what time did you meet this person and where was the meeting?"

It clicks with me that it was her car outside my place last night, and my face gives away that realization to her.

"Oh, the penny drops, Sean. You saw my car twice last night, when you got back from your run and then when you looked out of your bedroom window. So, when exactly did you meet with this informant? I was outside your place until 2 am."

I know that I am caught out and not wishing to answer the question I try to divert the discussion, attack being the best form of defense.

"Why the hell are you spying on me, Catherine? I have asked you to trust me, but clearly you don't. Did Morgan put you up to this?"

"Don't change the subject, Sean, and don't be so stupid. I was outside your apartment because I am concerned about you. Your behavior over the last few days has not exactly been normal, and now you're spinning me a line about an informant. You want me to trust and work with you, but you're not making it easy for me."

I need to find a way out and to end this, but it can only be another lie. It has to be; the truth would end everything now, including my career in the force.

"At 3.20 am, I received another call from the informant, who promised to provide pictures of the hit-and-run suspect on condition of full anonymity.

"At 4.10 am this morning, I met with the informant at a location around ten-minutes' drive from my apartment block and I was given the four Polaroid photographs that you saw on my desk this morning. That's it Catherine, no big conspiracy, no mystery, just a stroke of luck, a stroke of luck that I badly needed. Sometimes that's the way things work out."

I can tell that she is not convinced, and she continues to pump me for more information.

"Why now? Why after twenty-five years does this concerned citizen come forward? Our re-opening of the Glennister case has not been made public. Apart from the pictures, where is the link between the two cases? I don't see any commonality that would connect both cases, other than someone talking, which as we both know is highly unlikely after this length of time."

I don't immediately answer her and after a few seconds Catherine breaks the silence again.

"Look, Sean," her tone is gentler, "I said I trust you and I do. However you made the link and got the photographs is irrelevant at the moment. If you don't want to tell me for now, that is fine.

"The important thing is that we have them now. Just tell me what you need me to do. If we break these cases, it's going to be good for me as well. On the other hand, if we go down, we go down together."

I certainly hope going down together is not what happens, but the mood lightens, and I call to the waitress to refill our mugs.

"Thanks, Catherine. I might seem like an ungrateful twat, but I really do appreciate your support. Now shut up and eat your sausages, then let's get down to work."

Thirty minutes later, we are back in the office and Catherine gets to work tracking down the two witnesses to the hit-and-run. It turns out that the manager of the off-licence is now retired and living in Canada – so we can forget about him.

The young single mother, Carol Baker, is still living locally, although now she is married and living in Walton-on-Thames.

After another fifteen minutes, Catherine tracks down her number and calls her. They speak for nearly twenty minutes and I overhear enough to know that the call has knocked Carol for six.

Catherine confirms as much when she ends the call.

"She is absolutely terrified. You heard me trying to reassure her, but she is scared to death. I almost had to threaten to have her arrested before she would agree to come and speak to me. I hope your hunch is right, Sean."

"So do I, Catherine. If this doesn't play out in the way we need, it weakens my next move with the second case. The photographs alone may not be enough. We need eyewitness testimony to be sure."

At just before 2 pm, the phone on Catherine's desk rings and she takes the call.

"She is here, Sean, and her husband is with her and she Is insisting on having him with her in the meeting. What do you think? It's an informal meeting at this stage."

"Let's go and meet them and assess the mood first."

It is a shock meeting Carol again. It is less than a day since I last saw her, but her face is carrying every one of the last twenty-five years and she looks at least ten years older than she actually is.

"Thank you so much for coming in, Carol, particularly at such short notice. My name is Detective Constable McMillan and my colleague is Detective Constable Swain – you spoke on the phone. And this gentleman must be your husband?"

"Yes, I am, Detective Constable," the man answered, "I am also my wife's lawyer, David Cole. Carol has explained to me what this is about and while she is not currently being accused of anything, I would prefer if we could keep this meeting formal with my attendance."

This works better for me, as it should speed things up. The next step would have been a formal interview anyway – a win-win, as far as I am concerned – so I agree and we make our way to an interview room.

Following on from our morning discussion, Catherine leads the interview and opens up with the required formalities.

"This interview is being recorded. For the benefit of the tape, the time now is 2.19 pm and the date is Friday, 9th February, 2018. Present in the room are Detective Constable Sean McMillan, Detective Constable Catherine Swain, Mrs. Carol Baker and ..."

Carol interrupts her, "It's Carol Cole now, not Carol Baker."

"For the benefit of the tape, also present in the room is Mrs. Carol Cole, formerly known as Carol Baker, and her legal representative, Mr. David Cole. For clarity, I further note that Mr. David Cole is also the husband of Carol Cole. Is that okay, Carol?"

Carol looks to her husband who nods, and she also nods her confirmation, then confirms verbally, "Yes, it is, thank you."

She looks terrified and with good reason. She must have been living with fear and guilt for the last twenty-five years and to get a call unexpectedly, as she did this morning, would have knocked anyone sideways.

It's a shitty part of the job, but we need to do it and Catherine does her best to reassure her.

"Okay, Carol, before we start, I would like to tell you that you are not under investigation yourself. The purpose of this interview is to ask you some questions about a statement you made on 11th April, 1993 in connection to an incident that you were witness to. Do you remember making that statement, Carol?"

She looks again to her husband.

"Just tell the truth, Carol," he responds. "If there is anything I am not happy for you to answer, I will tell you."

"Yes, I did make a statement, but it was so long ago, why are you dragging it up now? I told the police everything I saw at the time."

"Thank you, Carol. We just need to ask a few more questions. Now, before we proceed, please can you confirm that you are Carol Cole, formerly known as Carol Baker and your date of birth is 15th March, 1971?"

She answers the question, but her voice is shaky, and it is obvious that this is going to be a difficult interview. So, before Catherine starts the questioning, I set the expectations.

"Shortly my colleague is going to ask you a series of questions, Carol, and you must answer them truthfully. We have seen the statement you gave, but a series of recent events has caused the case to be reopened and has cast doubt on the version of events that you and the other witness gave on that night."

This hits a nerve with both Carol and her husband and he leaps to her defense.

"With respect, you are completely out of order implying that my client is a liar. If you have some new piece of evidence that disproves my client's version of events, then you need to disclose it now; otherwise we will withdraw our cooperation. May I remind you, my client came here willingly at the request of Detective Constable Swain."

The last thing I need now is for them to walk out, so I apologize and continue, "Your client's willingness is greatly appreciated, Mr. Cole, but twenty-five years ago, a man in the prime of his life was killed in a hit-and-run incident and we strongly believe that your wife is able to identify the person responsible.

"I fully appreciate that this is difficult for her and I also understand that there may have been some extenuating circumstances. I can assure you that if your wife cooperates there will be no repercussions on her. May we continue?"

David Cole leans towards his wife and they have a brief discussion, then they agree to continue.

"I am happy for my client to continue for now, DC McMillan, but I would prefer it if you could get straight to the point and spare my client any unnecessary distress. You mentioned recent events that cast doubt on my client's statement; we would appreciate if you could elaborate on that."

Our game plan had been to take Carol through her original statement first, then to ask her directly if she had told the truth about her ability to identify the driver of the car involved in the hit-and-run. Depending on her answers, we were then going to show her the photographs and look for her reaction.

We had of course considered starting by showing the photographs, but, based on her reaction to the earlier phone call, we had decided to try a softer approach before shocking her completely.

After this last statement from David, I now wonder just how much Carol has told him. I suspect that she has probably come clean and he has advised her to cooperate. Whatever the reason, we can now get straight to the point, so I thank him and indicate for Catherine to continue.

"Carol, in the witness statement you gave on 11th April, 1993, you stated that you were unable to clearly see the driver of the Blue Ford Escort involved in the collision with the victim due to the fact that you were more than thirty yards away. Do you stand by that statement?"

"It was so long ago, I can't be sure, but if that's what I said back then, then yes."

I was wrong – he either hasn't told her to cooperate or she is genuinely confused, so I gesture to the envelope and tell Catherine to continue.

"Carol, DC McMillan is going to show you four Polaroid photographs that were taken on the evening of 11th April, 1993, the same evening as this incident. I want you to look carefully at the photographs and, in your own time, tell me if you recognize anyone in these photographs. Do you understand?"

She nods, and Catherine asks her to speak up for the tape.

"Do you understand what I just said Carol?"

"Yes, I understand."

As I open the envelope and lay out the photographs in front of her, any remaining color drains from her face and she looks like she is about to faint; then she leans forward onto the table and bursts into tears.

Her husband reaches over to comfort her and then turns back towards us.

"DC McMillan, we all know that my wife was intimidated into giving false testimony when she gave her witness statement. You said it yourself when you eluded to extenuating circumstances. On my advice, she is now fully prepared to cooperate but only with the guarantee of her safety and that of her children."

By now Carol has composed herself enough to carry on.

"Is that correct, Carol? Are you okay with my colleague asking you a few more questions?"

"Yes, I am, I want to help. I wanted to help back then, but you have to understand that he threatened to kill me and my kids. The police couldn't protect me. I had no choice."

Catherine takes over again.

"Carol, we know this. Help us now and we will do everything in our power to have him put away for a very long time. These photographs and your testimony are all that we need to bring him in again for questioning.

"Do you recognize the man sitting in the driver's seat in these photographs, Carol, and do you know who he is?"

Our assurances and the words from her husband seem to give her new energy and she responds without hesitation, "Yes I do, I know him very well."

"And is this the man that was driving the Blue Ford Escort that you witnessed crashing on the evening of 11$^{th}$ April, 1993?"

"Yes, yes, it is."

I ask Carol if she is 100 percent sure. "This is extremely important, Carol. If there is even the slightest doubt in your mind, you must say so now."

"It's him – he was a bastard then and he is a bastard now."

I pick up on this comment and ask her what she means. "Has there been recent contact with him, Carol?"

"Why do you think Roger Davies retired to Canada? It wasn't through choice. He was fed up with the regular visits and threats to keep quiet. I would have gone myself if it weren't for my kids. They are grown up now, but the threat is still real. He comes around a couple of times a year, always when David is at work. He doesn't say much; he doesn't need to, just showing up is enough. I have lived with this for a quarter of a century and I want my life back."

From his reaction, this revelation is obviously news to her husband, and listening to her speak I can feel my blood boiling.

One of the first principles of police work is to never get personally involved in a case but being so close to it and knowing just how bad this scumbag is, it is hard not to get involved.

"DC McMillan, as my client's legal representative I have advised her to retract her original statement and to provide a new and accurate account of what happened on the night. Additionally, as both her legal representative and her husband, I want an assurance of her protection and full account taken of the circumstances in which the original statement was given."

This was never an issue for me anyway, so I give full reassurance.

"We are aware that your client was physically threatened at the time of the incident, and with the additional information provided today, you have my full assurance that no charges will be brought against your client. Twenty-five years of intimidation is punishment enough.

"Our priority now is to bring the perpetrator of this crime to justice for the victim's family and to allow Carol to restart her life without the threat of violence from this lowlife hanging over her."

They both look visibly relieved and I tell Catherine to continue.

"Carol, based on the latest information provided, and if you are in agreement, we are going to ask two of our colleagues to come in to take a full new statement from you. Do you agree to this?"

After briefly conferring with her husband Carol agrees to making a new statement and Catherine thanks her and ends the interview. "For the benefit of the tape, the time now is 2.47 pm. This interview with Carol Cole is now terminated."

Catherine turns off the tape and I explain what is going to happen next.

"Okay, Carol, we are going to leave you here for a few minutes, then very shortly two uniformed police officers are going to come and take your new statement. Can we get either of you anything to drink while you wait?" They both decline.

As we go to leave, Carol grabs my hand and begs, "Put this bastard away before he ruins any more lives, promise me that!"

I am embarrassed at the new pain I have put her through, but I console myself in the knowledge that we have made progress today, and, ultimately, I am helping her.

"You have my word, Carol – anything we can do, we will."

I am shocked to see that DCI Morgan is waiting outside the interview room, and I wonder how long he has been observing the interview.

"I'm confused, DC McMillan, and I don't like being confused. It's not how I got to be a DCI. How about you help me clear up my confusion and explain what a hit-and-run in '93 has to do with a murder in '94?"

I am about to explain when he cuts me short. "Not here, my office in ten minutes and bring both case files with you. DC Swain, you can carry on. Don't keep me waiting, McMillan."

Morgan walks away and Catherine says, "You have to give him something, Sean. He is not an idiot and as soon as he sees those pictures he is going to make the connection anyway. Don't even think about trying to hide them from him. For all we know he might have been observing the entire interview."

It had actually crossed my mind to try to bluff it out, but Catherine is right, and coming clean with the new information could work in my favor anyway.

"Thanks, Cath, don't worry. With the pictures and the new statement from Carol, we now have a completely new angle to work on, and I might even be able to get a bit more time from the boss. With any luck, we won't need it, but it would still be nice to have a buffer."

Catherine asks if there is anything she can do for me and I reply, "For now, just keep an eye on Carol while she gives her new statement, and message me if there are any problems."

Morgan is on the phone, but he is not alone in his office. DS Sarah Gray is also there and gestures me to sit down, "Have a seat, DC McMillan. The boss has asked me to sit in and give a second opinion on your progress."

I wasn't expecting to have an audience, but it doesn't bother me. Sarah Gray is a good copper and it's a chance to impress her also. Without a doubt, Morgan would ask for her opinion anyway if I was up for promotion, or if he was looking to assign a case.

For a few minutes we sit in silence as the boss finishes his call. Then he starts, "Okay, DC McMillan, it's Friday afternoon and if I am not in the Officers Club with a gin and tonic in my hand by 5 pm, I will be extremely annoyed. Make it quick, get to the point and don't bullshit me. Clear? Great, go for it, you have ten minutes."

I can feel Sarah's eyes boring into me, but I am confident in what I have, and I feel better now than I have in a long time.

"Thank you, sir. Since my last update on the Glennister case, we have made a significant breakthrough involving another case with a clear link between the two. The second case was an unsolved hit-and-run from April 1993. The case was shelved after initial investigations due to a lack of witnesses able to identify the driver, or the availability of any credible traffic camera footage.

"The two witnesses who were interviewed at the time both gave statements to say that they were too far away to be able to provide any clear details.

"Crucially, two days ago, I received a call from an anonymous informant to say that they had information regarding this hit-and-run case, and then yesterday morning I received another call to say they had photographs of the incident and driver.

"Whilst this was relating to a completely different case, I still went ahead and met with the informant early yesterday morning to take handover of the photographs. Obviously, until that point, I had no idea of the significance of these photographs in regard to the Glennister case, but this connection now gives us a significant advantage."

Morgan points to the hit-and-run file and I lay out the photographs on his table. The connection is obvious, and he asks DS Gray for her opinion, "What do you think, Sarah? This all seems a little too convenient to me. A clear connection – but a random call out of the blue, and to DC McMillan in particular?"

"Yes, sir, I agree," DS Gray replies, "Why would this anonymous informant pick up the phone now after twenty-five years, and are we really expected to believe that somebody stood there taking pictures with a Polaroid camera and none of the witnesses saw it?"

They are both right, and if I were on the other side of the table, I would be thinking exactly the same. But the alternative is telling the truth, which would signal an immediate end to my career and a trip to the psyche ward.

"I don't know why I got the call, sir," I said. "And I agree that it's a completely unlikely coincidence, but you have said it before yourself – sometimes policing is down to luck. Whatever the reason, none of us can deny that the connection is there, and we now have a better-than-average chance of closing both cases."

Morgan is looking down making notes but still asking questions, "Tell me about the interview of Carol Baker."

"Yes, sir," I said, glad to get away from the topic of how I got the photographs. "As you can see, one of the photographs includes Carol Baker and Roger Davies, the off-licence manager. It's not particularly clear, but you can see that they are both right next to the car. Based on this photograph, we brought Carol in for interview and during the course of the interview she admitted to knowing the driver and agreed to give a new witness statement.

"DC Swain is arranging with our uniformed colleagues to take the statement now and she will be monitoring the video feed to make sure there are no issues.

"You should know also that the original statement was given under duress and there has been regular pressure applied by the suspect over the last twenty-five years."

While I have been talking, Sarah has been looking through the Glennister file and now has a puzzled look on her face.

"I'm still not quite there, Sean," she interjects. "If the photographs are genuine and Carol Baker is willing to back up her new statement in court, then the hit-and-run case looks clear-cut. I don't, though, fully see how you are going to close the Glennister case. The photographs provide a clear link, there is no doubting that, but you still don't have a witness willing to speak up."

I am about to lie again and lying to a couple of senior detectives is not the easiest thing in the world. I just hope it doesn't show in my face.

"If you remember from my last update, I mentioned another witness from the Glennister case. I have reason to believe that this witness also has a direct connection to the hit-and-run case. I strongly believe that if I can firm up that connection, then the witness will be willing to give a statement implicating Donovan and his cronies in the murder of Anthony Glennister."

Morgan pushes his notepad to one side, drops his pen onto it, then sits upright in his chair. "Oh yes, that's right, your mystery witness hiding out in the bathroom. And how is that working out for you?"

I would like to say that she is working out amazingly well, but it is not the time or place for bedroom flashbacks and I don't think they are in the mood for my humor anyway.

"It's going very well, sir. I have a few leads to check out this weekend and then I should be able to bring the witness in for questioning. If all goes well, the final step will be to pull Donovan and the Fletcher brothers back in."

"Okay, I've heard enough for now. Sarah, anything else from you?"

Sarah shakes her head and Morgan turns towards his keyboard and starts typing. "Make the most of the weekend, DC McMillan, it looks like you have made substantial progress. Close the door on your way out."

As I stand up and make my way to the door, I can't help feeling pleased with myself. They seem to be going along with my explanation; and getting any kind of compliment from Morgan is rare, even if it is only an acknowledgment of progress. My smugness doesn't last, though. Just as I open the door, he looks up from whatever he is typing and leaves me with a parting shot.

"But don't get complacent. Complacency is the cancer that loses cases. Oh, and if you ever keep us in the dark again about a new case, then you can say goodbye to this squad. I don't take kindly to mavericks and glory hunters – do I make myself clear?"

My face is burning up now, but I probably deserved that, so no point even trying to defend myself. "Yes, sir, understood, thank you."

When I get back to the office, I message Catherine. She replies that she expects Carol's interview to finish within the next thirty minutes and so far, it is going well. Carol has positively identified and named the driver of the car and has provided a lot of detail around the ongoing intimidation.

Based on our earlier interview with Carol, I expected the next interview to go well. But it wouldn't be the first time that a witness lost their nerve at the last minute, so it is a relief to get confirmation that all is well, particularly after my meeting with Morgan and Gray. I would look like a right tit if I had to go back in now to say that Carol had backed out.

I message Catherine to bring a copy of the statement as soon as the interview is finished, then I use the next thirty minutes to review my next moves. One of those moves involves Maria and because I don't want Catherine to know about her just yet I take advantage of Catherine's absence to log onto my computer and do a search of the electoral register.

My plan will go to complete shit if I find out that she has run away to Canada with Roger Davies. But, thankfully, after just a few minutes I find her.

Maria Pinto, 49 years old, living at 247 Collister Drive, Feltham, two persons in the household, no phone number listed.

Unbelievably, she is still living at the same address after all this time. This probably means that she is still not married, and I assume the other person in the household is her mother, who must be in her seventies or eighties by now.

Maria Pinto seems to me to be an unusual name for an Indian girl, but after some googling it turns out to be a throwback to Portuguese colonial influence in India. It is quite common for Indians to have Portuguese-inspired names.

I probably don't need to, but I jot down the details in my notebook anyway. Just as I log off, Catherine comes in clutching a copy of Carol's statement.

"Good to see you in one piece still, Sean. I assume from the way you are sitting that Morgan didn't tear you a new one?"

I'm glad that Catherine has her sense of humor back and I laugh at her comment. "Nope still my original one for now, and hopefully it stays that way. It actually went pretty well, all things considered. How was the interview?"

Catherine hands me the folder. "Here, take a look. Based on what we have in there and the photographic evidence, no jury in their right mind could let this guy walk. Whatever happens with the Glennister case, good work on this one, Sean."

I must have a smug look on my face because Catherine quickly brings me back down to earth by adding, "That doesn't mean you're not a lying bastard, Sean, and it doesn't mean you can continue to keep me out of the loop. When all this is finished, I want to know what you have been up to. I just hope to hell that you haven't been bending the law or compromising yourself to get evidence."

"Wow, Catherine, a compliment and a slap down twice in as many hours – thank God the day is nearly over. I am not sure my heart can take much more of this. Have you been taking pointers from DCI Morgan?"

It's all light-hearted banter, but, like Morgan earlier, I know she is right.

"Thanks again for your support, Catherine, and really excellent job with the interview. Why don't you make a move now and try to enjoy the weekend while you can? Keep your phone on, though, I may need to get hold of you at short notice."

"Sure, no problem. What's your plan for tonight, Sean – or shouldn't I ask?"

"Not exactly sure yet, still thinking out my next move, but I will call you if I need anything."

She knows that I am lying of course, but I can see that she is beyond it and simply smiles as she gets up to leave.

"Have a nice evening, Sean. Feel free to call me if you need any new evidence picked up – Polaroid pictures, smoking gun, signed confessions etc."

Normally I would reply to something like that with something equally humorous or sarcastic, but I am keen to get home myself and I still have a few things to finish, so I just smile and turn back to my computer while wishing her a good evening.

Forty-five minutes later I am finished and in my car heading home. The plan for tonight is clear in my mind and I am excited at the prospect of going back to 1994 again.

Unusually for a Friday evening, the traffic is light and by 5.30 pm, I arrive at my apartment block and take the ramp down to the underground parking garage.

As I pull into my parking space, I spot a familiar-looking man in my rear-view mirror loitering in the lift lobby. But by the time I shut off the engine and turn to face the lobby, he is gone.

Don't ask me why but something about him unnerves me. Possibly I am overthinking things and he is just another tenant or visitor.

Then I spot the envelope taped to the wall in front of my car. The childish handwriting on the front says 'Mr. Pig' and I know immediately who it is from.

It wasn't Paul standing in the lobby, though – it was his whipping boy, Terry. Paul wouldn't risk being caught himself, not when he has a ready supply of lackeys to do his bidding.

Carefully I remove the envelope from the wall, and then I sniff it and check around the edges before opening it up.

Inside there is a single sheet of paper and, in the same childish handwriting, the message: We know where you live, Pig. Along with it is a single rasher of bacon.

I must hand it to those boys – they really are masters of intimidation. Unfortunately for them, I am not Carol and, unlike Roger Davies, I have no intention of running off to Canada anytime soon.

Under normal circumstances, I would be pulling them back into the station. But I have other priorities today and I drop the note and the bacon into a bin in the lobby. Those assholes will be getting their comeuppance soon, so why waste my time on something that would be hard to prove anyway?

Between now and Sunday, I need to dream-travel at least twice, possibly even three times depending on how the first two trips go, plus visit Maria in real time. I need to travel with more precision than ever before and not waste a moment.

My time on this case is running out fast. By Monday morning, I need to have made some major breakthroughs; otherwise I might as well hand over the case to Mark Walker myself.

After thirty minutes pumping weights in the building gym, I have a light dinner and then relax and prepare myself by watching about an hour of TV over a couple of beers. Just before nine I feel ready to go.

I change into the same clothes that I had on during the first trip to the King George. Then I lie down on my bed. Donovan's mugshot is in my hand, but the image of him in my head is as clear as if he were standing right in front of me.

Before I have finished saying the date even once, I am there.

## The Past – Friday, $14^{th}$ October, 1994

I am standing outside the entrance to Feltham train station and the time on my watch is ten past four. The station looks quiet, so either I have landed at the weekend or the evening rush has not fully kicked in yet.

My plan tonight is to visit the King George on the day before the murder, so Friday, $14^{th}$ October, and I am relieved to see some kids in school uniform come out of the station, which confirms that it is not the weekend.

When I see a middle-aged businessman coming out of the station, for once I break my own rule and ask him the date, and without even breaking his stride he confirms that it is $14^{th}$ October.

With this settled, I walk around to the pub and a few minutes later I step inside. For late afternoon it is already reasonably busy.

Like my last trip, there is a heavy smell of cigarettes and a thin cloud of smoke in the air. Looking at all the smokers I wonder what they will make of being kicked outside to smoke in a few years' time.

I spot a gap at the bar and push through, nodding to the barman. It's Barry, the same barman from last night, but he doesn't appear to recognize me, and why would he? I was one of probably a couple of hundred punters last night.

"What can I get you, pal?"

I order a Stella. As he pulls it, he smiles and asks, "Weren't you the guy in here last night with Maria? You were sitting near the pool table for a while."

I nod and confirm that I was. I ask him if he is expecting it to get busy tonight and if he is expecting a big crowd for the tournament tomorrow.

"Tonight will be busy enough – the usual Friday crowd, I guess. The tournament normally pulls in a few extra customers, but mainly just a few of the opposing team's supporters. It's not exactly the World Cup, is it?"

I hand him a tenner and take a swig from my pint. As he returns with my change he turns and shouts to another guy serving at the other end of the bar, "Oy, Mike, this is the train guy. I knew it was all bullshit. It would have been all over today's news if it were true."

Mike must be Michael Bell, the pub landlord. He turns to face us and nods his head to acknowledge me.

"Either that or this fella is a quick healer," Mike replies.

Obviously, I know what they are referring to, but I don't let on. I ask Barry what he is talking about.

"Oh, it's nothing, just a couple of gobshite skinheads putting it about that they carved you up last night. I knew it was bullshit. The police would have been all over the place if it were true."

I take another swig from my pint to hide my smile and then suggest that the skinheads are probably just trying to save face.

As Barry moves away to serve another customer, I turn around to face back into the pub. I am hoping that Donovan and his boys come in for some practice tonight, but for now they are nowhere to be seen. I know, though, from my enquiries that on a Friday they generally come in straight after work, and with the tournament tomorrow it should be a certainty.

It's getting on for five o'clock, so hopefully I won't have to wait long; I need to make another trip tonight and the longer I spend here, the less time I will have to travel again. My intention on this trip is just to observe and see if I can pick up any other useful intelligence that I can use on the next trip, or back in 2018.

By five-thirty, I am back at the bar ordering a third pint, when the front door opens and the three of them come in wearing dirty overalls and boots. Like last night, Paul and Mark head straight to the pool table and Terry goes to the bar.

Fortunately, tonight the pool table is unoccupied, so there is no need for Paul to intimidate anyone into leaving. Instead he loudly announces to the pub what they are going to do to the Three Crowns team tomorrow.

"Listen up, wankers, if you want to see a display of world-class pool skills, make sure you come in tomorrow night. Me and my lads are gonna cream those mincers from the Three Faggots tomorrow night, mark my words."

Clearly, most of the pub regulars are well used to him by now and they don't even bother looking up from their drinks. When he doesn't get the response he is looking for, he calls them all miserable twats and turns his back to set up the table.

Terry then joins them with the drinks and I watch as they play the first two frames in relative silence.

Perhaps they really are concentrating, and in fairness, they certainly appear to be playing reasonably well in comparison to the shit show from last night.

At the end of the second frame, Paul tells Terry to take over and play against Mark.

"You're on, knobhead," he says, "get a couple of games in while I take a shit. I've got a bleedin turtle's head touching cloth right now, so I might be a while."

Mark calls him a dirty bastard and as he walks towards the bathroom he laughs and tells Mark that he might let him smell his fingers if he is lucky.

He certainly is a charmer. If I had ever wondered why he has never married, I am not wondering any more.

As he passes the bar, he looks towards me, but keeps walking towards the bathroom. Then he stops and comes back to the bar.

"Do I know you?" he asks me, not in a threatening way but as though genuinely puzzled. "You look familiar. You're not a regular in here, are you?"

Before I can answer, a spark of recognition lights up his face. "That's right, you're the fella that was with Maria last night. You were gonna have a pop, but your girlfriend took you home to save you from getting a slap."

He clearly doesn't feel threatened by me, so there is no point antagonizing him and possibly ending my trip prematurely, so I play the pacifist and keep things calm.

"Look, I don't want any trouble; I just want to have a couple of drinks before I go home."

Before I have even finished speaking, he calls me a pussy, then turns back around and disappears into the bathroom.

Barry, who was close enough to hear Paul talking to me, advises me to ignore him. "Don't worry about that fat fuck. He is all bark and no bite. With any luck he will shit himself down the toilet one of these days."

Up until now, Barry had not struck me as a comedian, but that was actually quite funny, and I had a good laugh picturing Donovan disappearing down the U-bend.

As it happened, he was gone for a long time and as I ordered a fourth pint, I was starting to think that Barry's prediction might have come true, until once again he loudly made another grand entrance.

"Bloody hell, Michael, you need to rename this pub, based on the size of the shit, I have just left in the pan. It should be called Richard the Turd, not the King George. Go and take a look. It's like King Kong's finger, I shit you not; it nearly split me in half."

Michael ignores him and carries on pulling a pint, but a young woman sitting at one of the tables comments to her boyfriend about how disgusting he is.

I could certainly hear her clearly enough and if anyone was in any doubt whether Donovan could, he soon answered that question.

"Who the fuck asked you, ya stuck up slag? You look like you could do with a good prod from King Kong's finger. I bet you don't get much from needle dick here. If you ever want a real man, you know where to find me."

Wisely, they don't react and without another word Donovan slopes back over towards the pool table and tells Terry to hand him a cue.

"That's better, I'm ready to kick ass again now that I have got rid of that big bastard. Rack them up again, Terry."

It's clear to me that Donovan must have some kind of mental condition or bi-polar disorder. It's not normal to go from passive to aggressive to passive so quickly, as if nothing has happened.

I make a mental note to ask Catherine to look into it, but whether he has a condition or not, it makes no difference. It is certainly no excuse for murder.

Paul Donovan is just an out-and-out thug, lacking in remorse, guilt, and – from what I can see tonight – any kind of manners or self-awareness.

I continue to watch them acting like twats for another hour, but I don't pick up anything new that I can use in the investigation. I decide to observe for another hour before I call it a night.

By now I am six pints in and dying for a piss, so as soon as I empty my glass, I head to the bathroom, which surprisingly smells half-decent tonight.

As I stand at the urinal, I think to myself that either they have given the bathrooms a special clean for the weekend or Michael was forced to go mad with the air freshener, after Donovan offloaded King Kong's finger.

Whatever the reason, it smells a damn sight better than it did last night, so perhaps, ironically, Donovan did everyone a favor.

I don't know if it is the fact that I have necked six pints, or whether he is just a sneaky bastard, but I am taken completely by surprise when I zip myself up and turn around.

Donovan's huge hand is round my throat and slamming me against the wall before I even realize he is there, and his strength is obvious.

I can't play my hand too early, though. If I kick the shit out of him now, it might completely change the course of events and this is something I always try to avoid, so I continue to play the pacifist and don't resist.

"What the fuck is your game, pal? It's been bugging me all night about where I know you from. You're the cunt that took the picture of me last year, and don't try denying it."

Shit, this is not the situation I wanted to be in. I had intentionally worn the same clothes because I had wanted Donovan to recognize me from my first visit to the King George, but it is a major schoolboy error allowing Donovan to recognize me from the hit-and-run scene.

This could screw things up massively and I can't believe that I didn't think of this possibility.

I pretend to be scared, stumbling over my words to buy some time, "U'h, I don't, I mean, u'm what are you talking about? I never saw you before last night."

This of course only makes him angrier and he pulls me forward, then slams my head back against the wall, and I feel the warm sensation of blood dripping down the back of my neck.

"You had better start talking, mate, or this is gonna get medieval. What the fuck do you want? Is it money, is that it? You think you can blackmail me, is that it?"

I need to get out of here before it escalates any further or anyone else comes into the bathroom, so I nod my head and tell him that I want money for the photographs.

This causes him to let go of my throat and he takes a step back, but he stays close enough to grab me again if he needs to.

"You've got some bloody nerve coming in here, pal. What makes you think I won't just beat the shit out of you until you tell me where they are?"

"Because I have made photocopies and left them with my lawyer in a sealed envelope that also contains my statement. If anything happens to me, he has been instructed to hand the envelope over to the police."

Donovan clearly wasn't expecting this and for a couple of seconds he says nothing. Then he moves so close that I can smell his stinking breath and he pushes me back up against the wall and holds me there.

"So, what do you think these pictures are worth then, big man?"

I play along and throw out a number that I think might sound reasonable, "Twenty thousand, I want twenty thousand for the pictures."

This obviously doesn't meet with his satisfaction, though, and he grabs me by the throat and starts to squeeze. "Try again, pal. You can do better than that."

I am not acting now. He is incredibly strong and I can feel myself choking. "Ten thousand, ten thousand," I manage to get out.

This number makes him smile and he once again releases his grip on my throat and I fall forward and suck in the fresh air; then he pulls me up and makes a show of straightening up my jacket.

"See, that wasn't so hard, was it? Play nice and we both get what we want. Ten thousand sounds okay, but I also want the copies and the statement. Do we have a deal?"

There is no way that Donovan is ever going to hand over ten-thousand quid to a wimp, but I continue to play along and agree to his terms. It doesn't matter now anyway; I have already worked out how to get home.

"Great, now why don't you tell me where the pictures are? Then I can arrange to get your money."

Only a complete idiot would give him the location before getting the cash. But I need to get going anyway, so I decide to have some fun before I leave.

"The pictures are in Upyer," I tell him.

He looks confused and jabs me in the shoulder with his huge index finger. "Upyer, where the hell is Upyer?"

As soon as I laugh, he realizes I am taking the piss and is already swinging before I even finish answering, "Up yer arse, you fat bastard."

His fist hits me so hard in the face that my head slams against the wall again and the last thing I remember before I pass out is a deafening crack as my skull splits open.

## Present Day – Saturday, 10th February, 2018

Now the good thing about drinking during my dream-travels is that no matter how much I drink and how drunk I might feel, once I wake up, those effects are gone, and I don't get a hangover.

Which is just as well because by the time I wake up it is nearly three in the morning and I am kicking myself for making such an obvious mistake. Donovan recognizing me from the hit-and-run could completely mess everything up and I might now have panicked him into going underground.

Particularly when you consider that I disappeared right in front of his eyes.

This is not what I need and whilst I still have enough to get a conviction for the hit-and-run, the whole course of events leading up to the Glennister case will change beyond recognition.

Now, you are probably thinking that surely this is a good thing. If Donovan doesn't show up at the pool tournament, then the fight and the murder will never happen.

Unfortunately, this is not how it works; the whole point of what I do is to solve crimes, without changing actual events too much.

Changes to the past can set off a chain reaction with a devastating impact on the future. The only thing I can do to set it right is to go back immediately and do what I can to sort out my screw-up.

The only problem now is that I am wideawake and my mind is working overtime, so no matter how hard I concentrate on Donovan's mugshot image, I can't get back there.

Eventually, after trying for another fifteen minutes, I get up, put the TV on, and pour myself a large whisky in the hope that a few drinks will get me sleepy enough to try again.

The irony of all this is that the more I want to sleep, the less tired I feel; so, after flicking through the channels for an hour, I take drastic action and pour myself a full glass of absinthe.

I am going to have a beast of a hangover in the morning, but I don't have any other choice. It will be morning soon and my plan for a trip to the evening of the pool tournament is already at risk tonight. So, after a deep breath, I knock back the drink in one.

The absinthe burns my throat and it is all I can do to hold it down, but after a few minutes it starts to kick in and I can feel my coordination going.

I lie down again on my bed and close my eyes.

## The Past – Friday, 14th October, 1994

This time it works perfectly. I am back outside the train station and I turn around just in time to see the school kids coming out, closely followed by my businessman friend.

I don't bother asking him the date this time; it would be too much of a coincidence if I were here on another day and I just go with my instinct that I have the right day. Also, this time I have no intention of going to the pub. I know already that I am not going to pick up any useful information tonight and I know now that I need to avoid Paul Donovan for as long as possible.

The less he sees of me, the less chance he has of recognizing me later; plus, the other benefit of skipping the pub is that I won't have to listen to the graphic description of his bodily movements again.

Avoiding him tonight should be enough to put things right, but just to be sure I decide to stick around in Feltham a bit longer before I head home.

Twenty minutes later and after a slow walk, I am outside the chip shop opposite the King George. I am intending to grab some fish and chips and watch from here to make sure Donovan arrives and leaves without any incident. I also want to do something to make sure that Maria shows up tomorrow.

In 2018, I could have called her cell phone or sent a message, but in 1994 very few people have a cell phone. So, before I go into the chip shop, I walk a bit further down the street to a florists and pick out the biggest bouquet of roses and lilies in the store.

There is still a possibility that she might not show up, but I am reasonably confident that this grand gesture will push the odds in my favor. I write a suitably romantic message on the card and sign it Superman.

After giving the address details and paying the assistant, it is now getting on for 5 pm, so I head back to the chip shop and take a seat in the window to wait for Donovan and crew to arrive at the King George.

Sure enough, at five-thirty and despite the double yellow lines in front of the pub, a white transit van with the name 'Donovan Building and Plastering Services' pulls up and parks. Donovan and the Fletcher brothers get out and go inside.

So far so good – I just need to bide my time now and wait for him to leave to be sure that everything is back on track. Based on our bathroom confrontation at just past 7 pm, I probably have at least a couple of hours to wait.

The cup of tea that I have been nursing for the last thirty minutes won't buy me enough sitting time, so I order cod, chips, and mushy peas and I pick up a newspaper from another table and start on the crossword to keep myself occupied, which it does for twenty minutes until something else catches my eye.

Three skinheads have just passed the King George and are now crossing the road towards the chip shop, which is not what I need right now.

None of them are the twats from the train, and I don't recognize them, but they are more than likely part of the same mob that worked me over with the baseball bats, so I bury my head in the newspaper and hope that they just grab their food and leave.

There are a few people waiting to be served, but they push their way to the front of the queue. To my relief, one of them orders three portions of fish and chips for takeaway.

My relief is short-lived when the guy behind the counter tells him that it will be ten minutes for the fish and they sit down at the table right next to me and start smoking.

For a few minutes they chat among themselves, but then they get impatient and start to get abusive to the staff and customers.

"Where the hell is our food? Are you still trying to bloody catch the fish or what?"

The guy behind the counter apologizes and tells him it will be just a few more minutes, but then one of them turns his attention in my direction.

"That's alright, I'm sure this guy won't mind sharing his chips, isn't that right, pal?"

Without waiting for a reply, he pushes my newspaper down, reaches over to my plate, and scoops up a handful of my chips. As he stuffs them into his mouth, the look on his face signals a spark of recognition.

"What the hell? Where the fuck did you go to last night? We carved you up good!"

His mates have also recognized me and look like they are ready to fight, but I can see that they are as confused as the chip thief, so I still have a chance to stop things escalating and to save the situation.

"Look, lads, we can do this the easy way, or the hard way and we all know how the hard way ends up. You can either get your food and piss off now with no hard feelings, or you can take your chances against me, this fork, this bottle of vinegar, and this newspaper – what's it to be?"

I can tell that they want to fight, but my disappearance last night and my bravado now has them caught between a rock and a hard place. They can either fight and risk being beaten by one guy in front of witnesses, or they can back down and lose face.

When a hand reaches forward to take more of my chips, it is clear that they have opted for the hard way, which I was expecting anyway.

Before he can grab a chip, my fork has pinned his hand to the table and he is blinded by a big splash of vinegar in the eyes, which means he doesn't see the blow from my fist that knocks him out.

His mates are on their feet, but seeing the fork sticking out of his hand they hesitate and seem unsure what to do.

"I suggest you forget about your takeaway and piss off with your girlfriend here before I really get warmed up."

This is enough for them and when they agree to leave I pull my fork out of the thief's hand and they lift him up between them and leave without waiting for their fish and chips.

Once I am satisfied that they have gone, I apologize to the staff and wipe up the blood from the table and the floor with a napkin. Then I sit back down and continue with the crossword.

A few minutes later, the owner comes over and places a new portion of fish and chips in front of me. "This is with the compliments of your three friends. Enjoy."

I thank her and the next hour and a half passes off without any further incident. As I watch the pub, various people come and go. Finally, at just past seven-thirty, Donovan emerges alone and drives away in the transit van.

The brothers must still be inside, but that's fine. For now, I am happy that Donovan has left and everything appears to be back on track.

I need to get going to see how much of the night I have left, and I don't want to hang around anyway and risk getting into any more trouble. I leave to find a way home.

I have been walking for a few minutes in the direction of the train station when I see the headlights of two cars coming up fast in front of me.

When they skid to a halt next to me and seven guys jump out, I can't believe how bad my luck is. "For God's sake – seriously, girls, are we really going to do this again?"

My friend with the bandaged hand tells me to shut the fuck up, then the rest of the skins grab me, bundle me into the boot of the first car, and drive away. My two friends from the train are among them.

I can hear them laughing and talking, but I can't make out clearly enough what they are saying. No doubt they are discussing what they are going to do to inflict maximum possible pain on me.

So now I have a choice. Let them take me and possibly die a slow and lingering death or find a way to end it now and get home immediately.

It's not such a tough decision and, with time against me, I pass on the lingering death and start to look for a way out.

Within a few minutes, my eyes have adjusted to the dark in the boot of the car. But all I can make out is a wheel brace, a rusty chisel, a half-empty can of deicer, an old car stereo, and a set of jumper cables.

For a second, I consider swallowing the deicer, but it would probably just make me spew up, so I carry on looking and eventually pull back the carpet to see what is underneath.

When I see the mess of cables I figure that they probably run to the lights or to the stereo that is pumping out in the front of the car, and I get an idea.

As quick as I can, I use the chisel to strip back the insulation on a red cable, then straight afterwards I do the same on a black cable and attach the crocodile clips from the jumper cables onto the exposed sections.

You probably know already what's coming next, but as I attach one of the clips to the skin on my stomach I have no idea whether this is going to work or not.

I take a deep breath, then I open my mouth and bite down on the second clip, with the full expectation of electrocuting myself to death.

For a few seconds nothing happens. Then there is a blinding flash and a loud bang, and I can smell burnt flesh in my nostrils as my body convulses.

I don't die, though, and I am fully conscious when the car stops and the boot opens.

"Jesus Christ, would you look at the state of him. The stupid bastard has electrocuted himself. It smells like bloody roast pork in here."

They argue among themselves about what they are going to do to me. For a few minutes it's a toss-up between ditching me by the side of the road and taking me somewhere to be killed.

In the end, bandage boy and my two friends from the train win out and the decision is taken to kill me, so they get back in the cars and drive me away again.

Because of the pain, I drift in and out of consciousness. I don't know how long we drive for, but by the time I am pulled from the car we are in a secluded woodland area and I can see that they have already dug a grave for me.

I think for a second that they might be considering burying me alive, but then I see the knife in the hand of one of the train skinheads.

"Come on, drag him over to the edge, I don't want to carry him and get blood all over me when it's done."

They pull me to the edge of the grave and he pulls back my head and positions the knife across my throat in the same way that ISIS behead their prisoners.

He is shaking like a leaf, though, and I can sense his hesitation. They might be thugs, but I doubt this lot have ever killed anyone before.

I don't have time to mess about, though, and with the last of my energy, I spin my head around as hard as I can so that I am looking up at him and taunt, "What the fuck are you waiting for, faggot?"

This does the trick and the blade slices easily across my throat and severs my jugular vein, causing a spray of bright red blood to cover his face and clothes.

As I fall backwards into the shallow grave, they are already shoveling dirt over me as fast as they can and the last thing I remember Is the taste of blood and dirt on my lips.

## Present Day – Saturday, 11th February, 2018

I have no idea how long my phone has been ringing for, but when I reach over for it, it stops and I can see that I have three missed calls from Catherine and one missed call from my mother.

More importantly, it is nearly eleven in the morning and I have missed my chance to go back to the night of the tournament, until at least tonight.

I should probably call Catherine back, but my head is banging, and my mouth feels like a dog has taken a crap in it, so for now she will have to wait. I really can't handle any kind of conversation with Catherine while I have the hangover from hell, so I pour myself a glass of water and knock it back with a couple of paracetamols, then I lie back down on the bed with the room spinning.

Yesterday evening everything had seemed so simple, one trip to Friday the fourteenth of October to see what other information I could get, then back home to get ready for a trip to Saturday the fifteenth to meet up with Maria and keep her in the King George long enough to witness the murder.

By this morning, I was hoping to be able to pay an informal visit to give her some information about the death of her father and to ask for her cooperation with the Glennister case.

Fat chance of that now – I am only just managing to keep the vomit down and can only hope that my hangover clears before this evening.

My head is thumping like an absolute bitch, so I keep it as still as possible on my pillow. Soon I find myself drifting back off to sleep. But then my phone rings again and brings me back to reality.

It's Catherine and I know if I ignore it she will just keep calling until I answer her, so I pick it up, trying not to sound too much like I am dying.

"Hey, Catherine, what's up?"

"Finally! I was getting worried about you. You mentioned yesterday that you might need me. I was just checking in on that."

I can barely concentrate on anything she is saying, and I would gladly hang up on her right now, but I don't want to arouse any kind of suspicion, so I force myself to talk.

"Yes, sorry for missing your earlier calls, I was in the gym and the shower. Nothing new to report for now. Just keep your phone close to hand and I will call you if I get anything, thanks, Catherine."

I go to end the call, but she starts to ask me whether we should pull Donovan or the Fletcher brothers in for more questioning and I only just manage to tell her there is no need yet and hang up the phone before I violently vomit on my bed and all down myself.

Thankfully, spewing my guts up was actually a good thing and after a long hot shower, two cups of tea, and a couple of slices of burnt toast, I am feeling much better and ready to get back to work.

It is only just after 2 pm on Saturday, so if I get my shit together I can still get all the pieces in place by Monday morning in preparation for making my closing moves.

I call Catherine, who is obviously surprised to hear from me so soon – and who would blame her after the way I ended our last call?

"Hi, Sean, I didn't think I would hear from you again today. What's on your mind?"

"I need you to call Paul Donovan's lawyer. Tell him that we want Paul to come back into the station today. Don't tell him what it's for. Tell him that if Paul refuses we will send uniform to arrest him. Call me straight back after you have spoken to him."

Catherine confirms what I have just told her, then hangs up to make the call, and twenty minutes later she calls me back.

"As you can imagine, they are not happy, Sean. His lawyer is making noises about police harassment, but they will be at the station at 4.15 pm. I'm going to head in now, so I should be there by 3.30. Any chance of getting a quick brief on your plan before we go in?"

I thank her and tell her that I will fully update her once I get there, then I quickly shave with my electric razor before dressing and driving to the station.

Catherine is already at her desk when I arrive, and I spend the next thirty minutes taking her through the game plan. But she is worried about it.

It's really not much of a plan. I am going to ask him exactly the same questions I asked during his previous interview, but I intend to wind him up in the hope that he will lose his temper and let something slip.

Catherine is not impressed. "You know, without presenting any new evidence, his lawyer is going to jump all over this," she points out. "You will be lucky if there isn't a serious complaint of harassment on Morgan's desk by Monday morning. Again, I hope you know what you are doing, Sean."

In all honesty, and now that my hangover has completely gone, I realize that it's probably a mistake to be bringing him in today just to screw him around, but if I cancel the interview now he will think that he has got one over me and I can't have that.

"I just want to keep the pressure on him, Catherine. There's no harm in bringing him in for a few questions. Let me lead on this interview. Don't worry, I won't let it get to the point that they have something to complain about."

By 5.20 pm, Donovan and his lawyer have arrived and are sitting in one of the interview rooms, but I tell Catherine to wait for ten minutes before we go in.

"Let them wait, Catherine. It will do them good to sweat for a bit. This case has gone on for twenty-four years already, another ten minutes won't make a difference."

We both stand and watch them through the observation window and it pisses me off to see Donovan laughing and joking with his lawyer. This is all just a big game to him, and after so long he clearly thinks he is untouchable. The murder of Anthony Glennister is a big joke to him, and his lawyer is no better.

Desmond Carter is in his late sixties and has been the defender of choice for scumbags across the south of England for the last forty years. No matter how abhorrent the crime, there is no case and no suspect that he will not take on if the price is right, and in the case of Donovan and the Fletcher brothers, it is well known in the force that he has been in their pockets since at least the Glennister case and possibly longer.

Additionally, and for many years, rumors have also circulated that he has bent coppers and judges in his circle of cronies. But no substantial evidence has ever surfaced, or even been looked for to my knowledge, which in itself seems to lend credence to him having cops on his payroll.

I think that once I have finished putting Donovan and the Fletchers away, the boss might let me loose on this crooked bastard.

For now, though, Donovan is the prize, and at just after five-thirty I nod to Catherine and we make our way into the interview room, where, not unexpectedly, Carter makes his presence immediately felt.

"How very nice of you to make an appearance, DC McMillan. I would like to start by saying that it is highly irregular to drag my client in at such short notice at the weekend, not to mention the threatening manner in which we were summoned by DC Swain. As you are already well aware, my client is an upstanding citizen and has had an unblemished record for more than twenty years. I would like it noted that, despite my advice, my client will not be filing any claim for police harassment at this time, which I am sure you will agree is clear testament to his character and respect for the police service."

All the while, Donovan has been slouching back in his chair looking smug. The face of course is much older, but I am picturing the younger Donovan choking me in the bathroom of the King George.

How I would love to be able to punch this asshole right in the middle of his fat smug face right now; it would almost be worth getting suspended for. But for now, I satisfy myself with flashing a smile designed to irritate.

Despite my promises to Catherine, I know I am deliberately winding them both up already and Carter puffs himself up again to speak.

"It's nice that you seem to find this amusing, DC McMillan, but let me assure you, harassment is not a laughing matter. I suggest that you start by explaining why my client has been called in for questioning once again when he gave a clear statement twenty-four years ago and again last week, and all other witnesses exonerate him and my other clients fully.

"You really would be better employed focusing your efforts on finding the real killer of this young man, so brutally cut down in the prime of his life."

Before he can continue his rant any longer, I hold up my hand to stop him. “Mr. Carter, we all know what kind of man your client is, and to describe him as an upstanding citizen is an insult to your own intelligence, let alone mine.

“Your client is back here for further questioning because, frankly, I think he was lying in 1994 and I think he is lying now. I trust that answers your question?”

Since we arrived in the room, Donovan has not said a single word and has been happy for his lawyer to speak on his behalf, but now he is noticeably flustered and turns to Carter.

“Are you gonna let him get away with that, calling me a liar? Bloody say something!”

Carter gestures to Donovan to calm down, then turns back towards us. “I strongly suggest that we start this interview and keep to the facts. Wild accusations are not going to be accepted by me or my client.”

For some reason, these two are really getting under my skin, but fortunately, and before I say anything else to make things worse, Catherine speaks.

“Yes, I think we should start the interview, Mr. Carter, if that is okay with you and your client?”

Donovan nods to Carter to indicate his acceptance and Catherine stands up to start the tape. But then Donovan speaks again.

“Hang on, princess – before we start, how about a cup of tea? My tongue’s as bleedin dry as Gandhi’s flip flop.”

Calling Catherine ‘princess’ is a sure-fire way to wind her up, but unlike me she is keeping her cool for both of us today and without flinching she calls reception to arrange his tea.

Now me, on the other hand – I can't resist having another crack at winding Donovan up. "You sure we can't get you something to eat as well, maybe a nice bacon sandwich?"

He knows exactly what I am referring to, but as before he just sits there smiling like a spastic. "That's awfully nice of you, cuntstable – sorry, I mean constable. I think I might pass this time, though, and stick with the tea. Pig products tend to give me the shits."

Catherine throws me a confused but disapproving look and starts the tape. "This interview is being recorded. For the benefit of the tape, the time now is 5.41 pm and the date is Saturday, 10th February, 2018. Present in the room are Detective Constable Sean McMillan, Detective Constable Catherine Swain, Mr. Paul Donovan, and Legal Counsel, Mr. Desmond Carter.

"Mr. Donovan, I would like to inform you that this interview is in connection with the death of Anthony Glennister on the night of 15th October, 1994 and follows on from the witness statement that you made on 15th October, 1994, the interview after your arrest on 18th October, 1994, and your recent interview on 29th January, 2018. At this time, you are not under arrest and are free to leave at any time. Do you understand what I have just said, Paul?"

I would be extremely surprised if he didn't understand. With Donovan's criminal past, he probably knows the legal system better than we do, but he still waits for the confirmation from Carter before answering.

"Perfectly clear, princess. But if it's all the same to you, I'm gonna make a move – now that I know I'm not under arrest."

He makes a joking attempt to stand up but thinks better of it when he sees the annoyed look on Catherine's face.

"Jesus Christ, don't panic, sweetheart, just having a bit of a laugh. You lot need to get yourselves a sense of humor. Always happy to help the bacon out in solving crimes. Let's bloody get on with it then, shall we?"

I think at this point Catherine is more likely to knock this fat fuck out than I am, and as I start the questioning, I have a good feeling that we are getting under his skin almost as much as he is under ours.

"Okay, Paul," Catherine begins, "tell us again about the person you identified as being responsible for the death of Anthony Glennister. You gave a very clear description of the suspect, which was matched perfectly in all of the other witness statements.

"Strangely, nobody had ever seen him before, or were able to name him. I find that very strange, Paul. This was a tight-knit local pub and this stranger just happened to come in, on his own, on the night of the pool tournament. Don't you find that strange, Paul?"

Clearly bored already, he slouches back in his chair again and throws me a dismissive look. "To be perfectly honest, this is all getting a bit boring now. I have already told you and the other coppers back then everything I know. It was a blackie that done him in, stabbed him right in the guts.

"It was his own fault, though; the fucking daft bastard started throwing his weight around after the tournament. You can't be messing with these African boys. They all think they're still killing tigers in the jungle – isn't that right, love?"

This guy is an ignorant bigot, but it is a waste of time pointing out his ignorance to him. He is just trying to provoke a reaction and I am conscious now of keeping an eye on Catherine, who is now in danger of losing her cool.

"The description you gave," Catherine continues, "was of a heavy-set black male, approximately six-feet-four-inches tall, around twenty-five to thirty years old with dreadlocks and a goatee beard. This is not someone that you might easily miss; yet in a later identity parade, you failed to point anyone out even remotely close to this suspect."

Carter leans forward and answers for Donovan, "Detective McMillan, may I ask exactly what the point of this questioning is? This is old ground that we have been over many times before. My client has more than adequately explained his reasons many times over for not being able to provide more details or to identify anyone from the identity parade."

Before I can reply, Donovan sits up in his chair again and pushes Carter to one side, "No, it's okay, Des, I don't mind telling them again, apparently they don't understand English too well."

The last part of the sentence was meant for both of us, but when he said it he was looking straight at Catherine and I can guess already the context of what is coming next.

"Now listen carefully because this is the last time I intend to answer this question. The reason nobody ever properly identified the black bastard is because all those blackies look the same. You know it, I know it, and every other proper Englishman knows it. I'm actually quite impressed how you manage to recognize the African Queen here; maybe it's her stink."

It is all I can do to hold Catherine back and she is nearly halfway across the table and swinging at Donovan before I finally manage to pull her back down in her chair.

"Okay, I suggest that we take a break to calm things down. And, Mr. Carter, I strongly suggest that you advise your client against the use of racially inflammatory language, unless he wants to be facing a charge of racial abuse.

"The time now is 5.59 pm and I am suspending this interview for a fifteen-minute recess. Detective Constable Sean McMillan and Detective Constable Catherine Swain are now leaving the room."

Catherine is absolutely livid, and I have to usher her out of the room to stop her launching at Donovan again or saying anything. Donovan, though, is basking in the glory of this small victory and he makes sure that we hear the comment that he makes to Carter as we are leaving the room.

"Fucking hell, she's a bit precious, isn't she? Must be the time of the month. It's always a problem for the darkies, you know. They can't get the lion skins in London to line their knickers."

This last comment would have been enough for anyone to lose it, and it's all I can do to stop her going for him again and to get her out of the room.

"Leave it, Cath, the bastard is just trying to wind you up. Believe me, when the time is right, you can have the pleasure of slapping the cuffs on him, and if you want to get in a few digs, you won't be getting any complaints from me. Come on, let's go and grab a coffee in the canteen."

By the time we sit down at the table with our coffees and a couple of doughnuts, Catherine has calmed down, and I ask her if she is okay.

"I'm okay, Sean, more bloody annoyed with myself for letting that racist prick get to me. I have been putting up with ignorant assholes like him my whole life.

"It was bad enough growing up and when I was out on the beat, but for that arrogant son of a bitch to look me in the eye and abuse me in the bloody police station – that is a whole new low. Whatever happens, this bastard needs to be put away. And, believe me, if I can get away with it, it will be more than a few digs that he gets. My Taser is going to be fully charged on that day."

I laugh and smile, which lightens the mood instantly.

"Let's just keep the pressure on," I tell her. "I only need a little longer, then we should have enough to charge him. I am absolutely convinced that it was either him or one of the Fletcher brothers who murdered Anthony Glennister. My money is on Donovan, though."

Catherine nods. "Take whatever time you need. Whatever doubts I may have had about whatever you are doing to get evidence are irrelevant now – just get the evidence, Sean, and I will back you all the way."

I never doubted that I had Catherine's full support anyway, but it is still nice to hear it from her and I reach over the table and squeeze her hand.

"Thanks, Cath, that means a lot. Let's finish our coffees and get back to it. Eat your doughnut first, though. You never know when you might need some extra energy to take down a suspect."

Back outside the interview room and through the observation window, we can see that Donovan is reclining in his chair, with his feet up on the table and Desmond Carter is talking to someone on his cell phone.

I ask Catherine if she is ready to continue and she confirms that she is, but then she pulls me back from the door. "Before we go in, how about bringing me in on the whole bacon sandwich thing. Is that a private joke between you and Donovan?"

There is no point or need to lie about this to her, so I explain quickly about the envelope on the wall in my parking space, with the note and the slice of bacon inside.

"It's not even worth getting stressed over, Cath. I have had much worse threats in my career and I am sure I still have many more to come. Let's just focus on the bigger issue and nail this bastard."

We re-enter the interview room, just as Carter finishes his call and hangs up. Catherine points at Donovan's feet and he swings them off the table.

This time, we don't bother with any kind of pleasantries or an introduction and after Catherine starts the tape, I recommence the interview.

"For the purposes of the tape, Detective Constable Sean McMillan and Detective Constable Catherine Swain have re-entered the room to continue the interview with Mr. Paul Donovan and the time now is 6.22 pm on Saturday, 10th February, 2018. Also still present in the room is Mr. Desmond Carter, Legal Counsel to Paul Donovan. Paul, you are still not under arrest and you are free to go at any time, do you understand?"

Paul shrugs his shoulders – the break has clearly done nothing to alter his attitude. When Carter tells him to answer the question, he says, "Yes, I understand. Let's just get on with this bloody circus, can we? I've got better things to be doing than hanging around here all bloody night."

It's obvious he is intending to wind us up again, but we have no intention of rising to anything he might say or do this time and I ignore his shitty attitude.

"Paul, before we took a break, I was asking you about the suspect in the murder of Anthony Glennister, and you made it very clear that it was a black male. In your original statement, you said that you were no more than four or five feet away when the fight started and that you clearly saw the suspect stab Glennister in the chest.

"Did you attempt to stop the fight at any point?"

Before he has a chance to answer, Carter leans over and whispers something to Donovan and he nods, then leans toward me and answers, "No comment."

Obviously, while we had been getting coffee, Carter has advised him to say nothing and I am probably going to get the same response regardless of the question, but this makes no difference to me. I have every intention of carrying on.

"Paul, you do have the right to remain silent, but it really won't help you in the long run. If we don't get the truth from you, we will eventually get the truth from Mark or Terry Fletcher, or perhaps even from one of the other witnesses."

"What about Terry? Maybe an offer of immunity from prosecution might encourage him to turn you and Mark in. Let's face it, a guy like Terry won't last five minutes inside; the other cons will be all over him like flies on shit."

This hits a nerve with Donovan and his face is growing visibly redder as his blood pressure rises.

"No fucking way," he spits, "there is no way that Terry would say anything about me or Mark." He is about to say more, but Carter halts him and he goes silent again.

"But Terry does have something to say – is that what you are saying, Paul?"

"No comment."

"Why didn't you try to stop the fight, Paul? You're a big lad."

"No comment."

"There wasn't any black guy in the pub on that night, was there, Paul?"

"No comment."

"It was you that started the fight. You and your boys had just been humiliated in the pool tournament by Anthony Glennister and the team from the Three Crowns. You were drunk and throwing your weight around – isn't that right, Paul?"

"No comment."

"No trace of the mysterious black suspect was ever found because he doesn't exist. It was you that lost your temper and stabbed Anthony Glennister in the chest, and it is you that has been intimidating all of the witnesses into silence for the last twenty-four years."

"No comment, no comment, no bloody comment. For fuck's sake, Carter, what the hell am I paying you for? How much more of this shit do I need to listen to?"

I had been so focused on Donovan that I hadn't noticed Carter fidgeting with his phone. As he looks at Paul, it is obvious that he has just received a message from someone.

"Don't worry, Paul, this should be over soon enough. DC McMillan has nothing new to put on the table and is simply hoping that by trying to intimidate you, you will admit to a crime so that he can close the book and get himself a promotion."

As he finishes speaking, his phone beeps and vibrates to signal a new message, and as he reads it I already have the sinking feeling that we are about to get some bad news.

"DC McMillan, this interview and the investigation and harassment of my client is over. Check your phone, please."

I had felt my phone vibrating a few minutes earlier for a call, and a few seconds later for a message, but had ignored it while I carried on with the interview.

Without replying to Carter, I reach for my phone in my pocket to check my messages. I don't know what kind of game they are playing or what kind of strings Carter has pulled but, as I show my phone to Catherine, I feel like spewing up again.

The message is from DCI Morgan.

Stop the interview with Paul Donovan immediately, I will be in the station by 7 pm. Meet me in my office and bring Catherine Swain with you.

The look of smug satisfaction on both of their faces is something that I won't easily forget, and as I end the interview, Donovan is on his feet before the tape has even stopped. Before they leave Carter tells us that he expects the matter is now closed.

"I sincerely hope, Detective McMillan, that this is the last we will be seeing of each other and that my client will now be left in peace."

It is all I can do not to punch him in the face. In the end, I ignore the question and tell him to find his own way out. "You both know the way out well enough. Don't let us keep you any longer."

Catherine is as pissed off and as perplexed as I am, "What the hell was all that about, Sean? Who the hell did he call?"

I don't know any more than she does, but in ten minutes the boss should be in his office, so no doubt we will find out soon enough.

When we step out of the lift, I can see that Morgan is already in his office. Judging by his tuxedo, he looks like he is either on his way to an event or he has just left one. Whichever it is, I am sure that he is decidedly unimpressed about being called into work on a Saturday evening, so as I knock on his door and go in, I am fully expecting to get some kind of dressing down from him.

"DC McMillan, DC Swain, take a seat please, this gentleman to my right is Detective Superintendent Clive Douglas. DS Douglas is the head of the Serious Crimes Squad at Scotland Yard, and he would like to speak to you about the Glennister Case, in particular the ongoing questioning of Paul Donovan."

I vaguely remember Clive Douglas from a TV appearance that he made a couple of years back where he was appealing for witnesses to a triple murder, but other than that I have never met or had any dealings with him.

He looks like he is in his mid to late fifties, but even though he is sitting down, his physical presence is powerful. It is no surprise that he is heading such a high-profile squad. Why, though, would he be involving himself with a cold case and a lowlife like Donovan?

"Thank you, Kevin, and thank you both for the fine work that you have been doing on the Glennister case. DCI Morgan was just telling me that you have been making great progress and are close to finding the killer of Anthony Glennister. The work of the Cold Case Squad is truly invaluable, and I have the utmost respect for the work that you do in delivering justice to criminals who think that we have forgotten about them."

It's standard practice when delivering unwelcome news – flannel them with the compliments to soften the impact, then deliver the killer blow as if you are doing them a favor.

"However, in the case of the Anthony Glennister case, you are barking up the wrong tree with Paul Donovan, and I have asked your boss that you cease, with immediate effect, any investigations into him.

"DCI Morgan has assured me of his department's cooperation with this request, but as a professional courtesy I wanted to meet you both and explain my position in person."

The smell of a cover-up is almost choking me, but as a mere detective constable what am I supposed to say when a highly respected detective superintendent and my own boss are telling me to stand down on my prime suspect?

But I am not giving up without a fight. "With respect, sir, as you have just said, we are making extremely strong progress on this case and Paul Donovan is a key player in our investigation. May I ask why we are being asked to back off from him?"

Morgan remains stony-faced, but DS Douglas leans slightly forward in his chair and casts me a look that he probably normally reserves for his suspects.

"I didn't ask you to back off, DC McMillan, I instructed you to cease and desist immediately, and that is exactly what you will do. Paul Donovan is a cooperating witness on several other high-profile investigations and my department has already satisfied itself regarding the statements given for the Glennister case. I strongly suggest that you focus your investigation on finding the suspect already identified by multiple witnesses. Do we understand each other, DC McMillan?"

A cooperating witness, that's nice; we normally refer to them as an informant, a grass, or a snout. Whatever he is, the smell of bullshit is overpowering, and I wonder why Morgan is not making more of an issue of this.

"Yes, sir, I understand fully. Can I take it that there is no objection to us continuing our investigations into the other witnesses?"

"No objection at all, DC McMillan, just stay away from Donovan; focus on your main suspect, and if the Serious Crimes Squad can be of assistance, don't hesitate to call."

Douglas then turns to Morgan and says pleasantly, "Kevin, thank you for seeing me at such short notice. Enjoy the Commissioner's Gala Dinner. I may try to drop in for drinks later."

And with a curt, "DC McMillan, DC Swain, good luck with your investigation, enjoy the rest of the evening," he is gone.

Enjoying my evening is the last thing on my mind after that bombshell, and Morgan is more than aware of it. Before I can vent my frustration, he holds up his hand.

"Listen, Sean, sometimes there are bigger issues at stake than the one or two cases that we may be handling. This has gone all the way up to the Assistant Chief Constable, so for now we need to cooperate and play the game."

I am so angry at the potential derailment of my case that I don't pick up on the subtleties of what he is saying at first.

"This is not right, sir, we have Donovan in the bag already for the hit-and-run, and we are a whisker away from being able to nail him for murder, we just ..."

"DC McMillan, you're a smart lad, I wouldn't have trusted you with this case if I didn't think you were up to it. But forget the emotion for a minute and engage your brain. I don't like this any more than you do, and as the head of this team, I take it as a personal insult when I am instructed to halt a murder investigation without being given all the details. As far as I am concerned, everything continues as it was, apart from direct contact with Donovan or his lawyer. Find another way to get what you need, son. You have my word that if you find anything to firmly implicate Donovan for the murder of Anthony Glennister, I will bring Donovan in myself and deal with the consequences afterwards."

I had expected Morgan to halt the case completely, so I guess this shows that I really don't know him as well as I thought.

A few minutes ago, I was ready to jack it all in, but now my faith in the force has been restored, and I am more determined than ever to bury this asshole.

"Thank you so much, sir, I really thought that we were at the end of the line. You have my word that we can finish this and put Donovan away for a very long time."

Morgan is already on his feet and is no doubt keen to get to his event. "Just remember what I said yesterday about complacency, Sean. Good luck."

I slump back into my chair and it is Catherine that breaks the silence.

"Well, that was interesting," she says. "If Paul Donovan is an informant for Serious Crimes, then I'm Mother Teresa of Calcutta. What the hell is going on, Sean?"

Her sentiments echo my own thoughts exactly and I suspect Morgan is probably thinking the same.

"I really wish I knew, Cath. Something stinks, and I have a feeling that if we don't close this case soon, we might get another visit from our new friend, Clive. I think deep down he took a bit of a shine to me. You can't blame him, though – I am pretty hot."

Catherine laughs and smirks at me. "Somehow, I don't think you're quite his type, but Morgan on the other hand – that is the first time I have ever heard him call you 'Sean'. Close this case and you might just be his new golden boy."

Now it's my turn to laugh. "Yep, I did wonder about that. He called me 'son' as well. Maybe it's just his off-duty manner. Anyway, let's get out of here, tomorrow is another day. Keep your phone switched on, Cath, I think things are about to get interesting."

Tonight, I am going to try for my date with Maria, but I am nervous as hell. If I don't get it right, I could massively mess up again and set myself back another day.

Donovan will be focused on the pool tournament, and provided I keep a fairly low profile, there is only a minimal chance that he will recognize me as his hit-and-run paparazzi. Regardless, I am still worried.

I am also extremely nervous about meeting Maria again. Despite the circumstances, I have that first-date feeling, the only difference is that generally I don't take my dates to a murder scene and risk ruining their lives. Well, I hope I don't anyway.

By 11 pm, I have finished the remains of a bottle of Bushmills and I feel ready to go. Given that I am on a date tonight, I shave, shower and put on a freshly laundered shirt with a blue jacket that I hope is not too poncey for the King George.

Finally, I gel my hair to change my appearance slightly. Then I throw on a splash of my best cologne, before settling down on my bed with the mugshot of Donovan gripped firmly in my hand.

The King George, 15th October , 1994, the King George, 15th October , 1994, the King George, 15th October , 1994, the King Geor ...

## The Past – Saturday, 15th October, 1994

I know straightaway that I am not even close to Feltham or the King George, but it's only just past five in the afternoon, so I should have time to get myself back on track, assuming of course that I have the right day at least. Thankfully, I am on a busy high street and with any luck there should be a cab passing soon.

It could be a lot worse. A few times I have ended up in a forest or the countryside with no idea where I was. In those situations, I tend to give up after an hour or so and go looking for a way to kill myself. As you can imagine, due to the lack of skinheads and junkies in a forest or a field, I have had to get a bit creative. In the past, I have found some quite ingenious ways of topping myself, including lying down in the path of a combine harvester while the farmer gathered in his crops, or filling my pockets full of rocks to drown myself in a lake.

Luckily, there is no need for anything like this, and after waiting for a couple of minutes, I flag down a black cab and ask him to take me to the King George in Feltham.

"No worries, mate. You want me to take you along Stanwell Road – it's a bit longer, but it's a straight run and you will be there in twenty minutes."

I agree to his suggestion and ask, "Is it the fourteenth or the fifteenth today?"

"It's the fifteenth of October, pal. Where are you off to tonight? You look a bit overdressed for the King George."

He is right of course, but Maria will be expecting us to go out for dinner at some place decent, so it's important that I look the part.

"Just meeting a girl there for a drink, then going out for dinner. It's a first date, so I wanted to look smart for her."

The driver turns around to face me, and it's a miracle that he doesn't crash. "I knew it, that explains the gallon of bloody aftershave you're wearing. I thought to myself you're either a poof or you're on the sniff for fanny. Don't get me wrong, I ain't got nothing against poofs, each to his own and that, I'm just more of a fanny man myself."

As he turns back to face the road, I can't help thinking that it has probably been a long time since this guy even got a sniff of a fanny, and thankfully, we make the rest of the journey in silence before eventually pulling up outside the King George at just after five-thirty.

Cabbies are not generally known for their silence or discretion, though, and as I pay and get out of the taxi, he leaves me with a last shot of his worldly wisdom, "Give her one from me, son, and don't forget, don't go for anal right away, save that for the second date."

As he drives away laughing his head off, two thoughts come to mind. Firstly, no, I don't think I will give her one from you, and secondly, how have I ever managed to get through a first date without going for anal!

I was hoping that Donovan would not have arrived yet, but the sight of his van on the double yellow lines again ruins that hope. With two hours before Maria is due to arrive, I can't risk going into the pub yet.

Donovan and his boys are probably on the pool table practicing, but I doubt that the pub is busy enough yet for me to stay out of sight, so I cross the road to the chip shop again.

As I walk in, the manager recognizes me. She gestures to my jacket and says with a smile, "You do know that we don't have a dress code, don't you? This is only a fish and chip shop, not the Ritz. What can I get you, love?"

"If it's okay, can I just get a cup of tea and hang out in here for a while? I was due to meet up with someone, but I got the time wrong, and I have an hour and a half to kill now."

She smiles again and pours me a large mug of tea. "The milk and sugar is at the end of the counter – help yourself."

I take the same table as last night and I can't help smiling when I see the fork marks in the table top. Those assholes will absolutely shit a brick if they bump into me again tonight. They would have already been confused about my apparent good health last night, so seeing me resurrected from the dead would really freak them out. It might be worth bumping into them again just for the giggles.

Unlike last night, my stint in the chip shop passes off peacefully. After watching the comings and goings for over an hour, I head across to the King George at seven-fifteen to get a table and wait for Maria to arrive.

Inside, it is not much busier than it would be normally, and I remember what Barry the barman told me last night about it being a local pool tournament and not the World Cup.

He of course shouldn't remember saying that because, if my second trip was successful, I never even came in last night. If he does remember, I am already screwed and might as well go and find my skinhead friends right now.

As it happens, he barely even gives me a second look as he pulls me a pint of Stella, and I settle down at a table far enough away from the pool table to not be obvious, but still close enough to have an unobstructed view of the action.

Donovan and the Fletcher brothers are hogging the pool table. Even though Glennister and the Three Crowns team are already here, it is apparent that Donovan has no intention of letting them get a feel of the table. They stand patiently to the side, waiting for the tournament to start.

Anthony Glennister looks even more like an accountant then he does in his mugshot. In person he is the stereotypical nerd, with wire-rimmed glasses, pudding-bowl haircut, and god-awful fashion sense.

I can't be sure from this far, but if I were to guess, and knowing that he is nearly teetotal, I doubt very much that his glass of orange juice has any alcohol in it, and quite frankly he doesn't look strong enough to even be holding the glass, let alone throw it across the room at an angry, heavy set, six-feet-four-inch black man.

None of this is a surprise, of course, but I do wonder what he is even doing in a pub in the first place. He looks like he would be more at home in a library or at a spelling contest.

I watch for another ten minutes as Donovan loudly showboats on the table with a few well-prepared trick shots to impress the watching spectators. No doubt this is also a tactic to intimidate or unnerve the Three Crowns team. If so, it isn't working as Glennister and his pals seem oblivious to it.

Just before seven-thirty, I head back to the bar to get another pint and a drink for Maria.

Still concerned about Barry recognizing me, I go to the other end of the bar where the landlord, Michael, is serving and after a polite nod he pulls me another pint, then pours a double Bacardi and Coke for Maria.

At the same time, Barry is serving Terry Fletcher, who orders nine pints of snakebite and nine vodka chasers, and I watch out the corner of my eye as Mark joins him to carry them back to the pool-table area.

Obviously, the boys are stocking up in readiness for the start of the tournament; but somehow, I don't think this is the last trip Terry will be making to the bar tonight.

By 7.40 pm the tournament has started and the first frame between Mark Fletcher and one of the guys from the opposition is underway, with Mark slightly ahead.

There is still no sign of Maria, though, and with the ice melting in her drink I am starting to think that I may have been stood up, which is not something I have prepared for. If she hasn't shown up by the end of the tournament, I will need to make a hasty exit before the murder and come up with another plan to make sure she is here next time.

As I think through the possibilities, the first frame ends, and we are left in no doubt by Donovan who the winner is. "Get in there, you absolute bloody beauty. Good one, Mark, the first of bloody many. Right, that's me up next."

This frame is against Glennister and as he sets up the table, it is obvious from the outset that Donovan has already been knocking the booze back, even before Terry's trip to the bar to stock up.

"Come on, specks, get a bleedin move on, you're like watching snot dripping down a wall."

If Donovan was expecting any kind of reaction from Glennister, he doesn't get it, and he leaves him to finish setting up and knocks back the remainder of another snakebite.

Donovan wins the break and smashes the white ball as hard as he can down the table with an 'if in doubt, give it a clout' tactic, which actually pays off for him with two striped balls potted.

"Did you see that, boys? Bloody skill on legs I am. You might as well sit back down, specky boy."

This guy really is an absolute gobshite and if I didn't have more important things to do, I would quite happily get up now and wrap a pool cue around his fat head.

I am so engrossed in thoughts of caving in Donovan's skull that I don't see her approaching the table.

"Hey, handsome, is this seat taken?"

To say that she is a stunner would be an understatement. Seeing her standing in front of me, I feel like a complete and utter bastard for what I am going to put her through. She is wearing an off-the-shoulder, knee-length dress in emerald blue that shows off her curves beautifully, and I have no doubt that she bought it specially for tonight. Her hair and makeup are perfect, and the killer heels complete the package perfectly.

"Wow, Maria, you look absolutely stunning. Please sit down. I hope you don't mind – I got you a Bacardi and Coke. Is that okay? I can get something else, if you prefer?"

"Bacardi and Coke is fine, Sean, and thanks for the compliment and the flowers. You look pretty good yourself – nice jacket. Have you been waiting long?"

She sits down, and I can't help thinking that keeping an eye on the game is going to be difficult with such a beautiful distraction sitting next to me, but I can't fuck up tonight. The impact on tonight's events and the future would be catastrophic, so I do my best to keep Maria interested and to keep my focus where it needs to be.

She sips from her drink and by the look on her face she has realized it is a double. I am expecting her to ask me if it is, but she just smiles and takes another sip.

"So, Sean, where are we going tonight? I hope you are not going to disappoint me."

Unfortunately, disappointment is exactly what she is going to get, but I need to keep her occupied in the pub until the time of the murder at around 8.50 pm, which is in less than an hour, so it should be manageable.

"We have reservations for nine-fifteen at Francine's, the fancy new Italian place on the high street. A few of my friends have been and they highly recommend it. I hope you like Italian food."

When she smiles, I feel like even more of a shit. But what can I do?

"Oooh very nice, I have been wanting to go there. I love Italian food. Good job so far, Mr. Charmer. I think I might change to red wine now. Let me buy you a drink, though."

Normally, I would be reluctant to let my date pay for a drink, but tonight it suits me, and I let Maria go to the bar, which allows me to focus on Donovan again.

Despite his early lead, he is now trailing with three balls still on the table, compared to one for Glennister, who pots it easily, then follows up quickly and sinks the black ball, much to Donovan's disgust.

After a few insults to nobody in particular, Donovan slinks back to his table and starts on yet another pint, topped off with two vodka chasers, while one of Glennister's teammates sets up the table for the third frame against Terry.

Maria returns with our drinks and we chat for the next twenty minutes about everything and nothing. Occasionally, Maria sees somebody she knows and chats with them, which again allows me to focus on the pool table.

The tournament is the best of nine frames and with six frames already done, the King George team is four frames behind, with only Mark Fletcher winning the two frames he has played so far.

As expected, Donovan is getting louder and more abusive as the night goes on, and as a result of his behavior, many of the early spectators have already left. There are probably no more than twenty people in total left in the pub now.

The police took sixteen witness statements on the night of the murder, so the current crowd is consistent with that, give or take two or three, but now I am worried that with the pub so empty, we might catch Donovan's eye too easily.

A few minutes later, he gets up and stumbles past us towards the bathroom, without even looking down at us, and he is so far gone already that I needn't have worried.

He gets back just in time to see Mark miss his shot and accidentally pot the black ball, giving the Three Crowns another win, which goes down as well as syphilis in a brothel.

"You fucking bellend, Fletcher, what the hell was that? That's the kind of bollocks I expect from Terry, for Christ's sake. I'm gonna play the next two bloody games and save the day, like I always do."

With seven frames done, and the King George five frames down already, they have already lost, but Donovan is either so drunk, or so stupid, that he genuinely thinks they can still win, until one of the guys from the Three Crowns foolishly points out his error.

"Actually, it's over. We have won already. There are only two frames left, so you can't win."

Being told what he can and cannot do is clearly not something that Donovan has ever been used to, and to be told it when he is half-cut is like a red rag to a bull.

"Who the fuck are you, talking to me like that? This game's not over, until I bloody say it is. Get the table set up again, asshole!"

The poor guy is trembling in his shoes and even the Fletcher brothers move in to calm Donovan down, while

Glennister and his two mates get ready to leave. Terry tells him that he will get more drinks, and Mark holds him back from making a grab at any of them.

"Come on, leave it, Paul," Mark says, "It's not worth it. We were just unlucky, that's all."

While this is going on, the rest of the pub is completely silent, and Maria takes my hand and whispers in my ear, "Let's get out of here. We can go now. If our table is not ready yet, we can get a drink at the bar."

I want so much to be able to go and to spend the night with this beautiful girl, but I can't and I tell her we should wait a bit longer and finish our drinks.

"Let's just finish these, beautiful, then we can take a slow walk down, I promise."

When I look back to Donovan, Mark has managed to calm him down and he is setting up the pool table for another game. Then he shouts out to the departing team, "Oy, before you leave, one more game, just to show no hard feelings, what do you say?"

If they had just carried on walking, Anthony Glennister would still be alive today. But to keep the peace, he tells his mates that one more game won't hurt, and they head back to the pool table.

Donovan chalks up his cue and points it towards the three guys from the Three Crowns. "Right then, which of you boys wants a shot at the title?"

In fairness, I doubt any of them do, but after a quick discussion, a guy called Ryan Bayliss steps forward. Donovan pushes him to one side.

"No, not you, you sit your ass down. I think specky here owes me a rematch – he cheated in the last game, didn't you, specks?"

Maria squeezes my hand again and tells me I should do something. "Sean, if he loses, this is not going to end well. Can't you do something before it goes too far?"

I reassure her and promise that I will step in if needed, but I tell her that we shouldn't get involved for now.

"Let's just stay until the end, just to make sure nothing kicks off, then we can go. Hopefully, this won't take too long."

This time Glennister breaks, and on his first shot he puts down both a spotted and a striped ball, so he has the choice of which to take. He opts for stripes and I am almost willing him to mess up, but within a minute he drops another three balls into the pockets before missing his next shot.

Some people have all the brains but no common sense. Unfortunately, Glennister is one of them. That doesn't mean he deserves to die, but for God's sake, let Donovan win and save yourself from the obvious.

Every other person in the room is now probably praying for a miracle to allow Donovan to win and to diffuse the situation, but I know that's not going to happen.

Donovan is so drunk he has no chance against Orange Juice Man, and with a sad air of inevitability he misses his first shot completely. To make it worse, he pots one of Glennister's stripes.

Surprisingly, Terry gets to his feet and tries to pull Donovan away from the table. "Paul, come on mate, it's over. Let's just have another drink and call it a night."

I almost feel sorry for Terry when Donovan slaps him.

"Sit the fuck down, Terry, this game is not over. That's the last bloody time I will say that. What the hell are you waiting for, specks?"

Again, Maria pleads with me to intervene, but again I tell her to wait.

The tension in the air is chilling, with a few more people leaving to avoid the coming trouble, and I know that within minutes I will need to get out of here myself.

Glennister has two final balls to pot, which he drops easily, and leaves himself nicely setup for an easy shot on the black, when Donovan moves in close behind him, still holding his cue.

If this is not enough of a warning, I really don't know what is, but completely oblivious to the threat, Glennister takes a deep breath, then lines up and smoothly plants the black in one of the middle pockets.

Terry and Mark are both on their feet, but before they can stop him, Donovan has already smashed the fat end of his cue into the side of Glennister's head, then he spins back around and swings at the brothers.

While Glennister's mates help him up, I am surprised to see the Fletcher brothers fighting with Donovan in an attempt to stop him from doing any more damage. But even in his current state, they are no match for him.

Donovan lands a brutal uppercut on Mark's chin that sends him crashing across the table, then he flattens Terry with a crippling punch in the side of his ribs, before turning his attention back to Glennister and his mates.

We are already on our feet, and by now I have seen enough. Donovan must have a knife on him and he is about to use it.

Maria is shouting at Donovan to stop, and she looks around to me for help, but instead she sees me heading towards the bar to find the back door.

"Sean, where are you going? He's killing him! Don't leave me, you coward. Come back!"

I don't stop, though, and I don't look back. In a few minutes it will all be over, and the police will be on their way.

The back door is unlocked and leads out into a yard where they keep the empty bottles and beer kegs, and at the back there is a gate, which also thankfully is unlocked. This takes me into a back alley and eventually onto the main street again.

Trying not to look too suspicious, or out of breath, I head into the chip shop for the second time tonight and without ordering anything, I sit down to wait for the police to arrive.

The time now is 8.53 pm, and around two minutes have already passed since I made my exit, so I am surprised that I don't see anyone coming and going from the pub. In fact, by the time I hear sirens, another twelve minutes have passed before Michael Bell, the pub landlord, opens the door and steps out to meet the first police car on the scene.

Twelve minutes is long enough to cook up a story and to sufficiently threaten all the witnesses into cooperating, and it makes sense anyway. The witnesses all gave their initial statements tonight, so this was the only real opportunity for Donovan and the Fletchers to get everyone to toe the line.

I watch for a little longer. Roughly a minute after the arrival of the first police car, two more arrive, accompanied by what looks like an undercover vehicle and finally by two ambulances.

Satisfied that I have seen enough and pleased at how things have gone, I step back out onto the street and watch as the police set up a cordon around the entrance to the pub. The usual crowd of gawkers have already started to gather near the barrier tape. Nothing much has changed procedurally over the years, so I am not surprised when I don't see any of the witnesses coming out of the pub.

They are probably being kept inside, while the police take the first statements and piece together what has happened. So, not wanting to draw any attention to myself, I walk away to find my way home.

I already have a plan tonight and after walking for a few minutes I climb into a taxi and tell him where I want to go.

Without questioning my reasons, he drives me in silence and fifteen minutes later he drops me off at the entrance to Stanwell Road Park.

If my junkie friends are not at home tonight, or are comatose again, then I might need a new plan, but like all creatures of habit, or in their case, creatures with a habit, they are in the same place as they were previously. Only now there are four of them and they are not the two guys that I took the heroin from previously.

I had forgotten that my last trip to Stanwell Road Park was in April 1993, nearly eighteen months before tonight, so more than likely the other two guys have overdosed long ago.

No matter, though, these guys will probably do just as well for what I need. As I approach them, they are eyeing me up with a mixture of fear and suspicion.

"What do you want? Piss off and leave us alone. You're not the police, so fuck off!"

They are wrong, of course, about me not being the police, but that's not why I am here. "Hey, don't be like that, boys. Just wondering if you have a little bit of H that you want to donate to a fellow junkie in need?"

Before they can answer, I move forward and start pulling at their coats, in a show of trying to look for drugs.

"Fuck off, mate, get your own bloody stuff! We don't have anything."

I know they are lying, but I'm not looking for drugs anyway. I am hoping that if I provoke them enough they will kill me in another way, and sure enough after I pull one of the junkie's jackets off, one of his buddies pulls out a knife.

"Give him his jacket back. Don't bloody think I won't do it. I'm warning you, don't push me."

This is exactly what I want, and I turn to face the knifeman, while holding out the jacket to him. "Come on then," I taunt, "take it, come on, what are you waiting for?"

He hesitates, unsure at first, but then with the confidence of having the knife in his hand, he steps closer towards me and reaches for the jacket. At the same time, I let it fall to the ground.

He is so close now that before he has a chance to react, I grab both of his wrists and jerk him towards me, and the pain is instant and excruciating. I had wanted to feel the same pain as Anthony Glennister, to experience what he had felt when Paul Donovan took his life, and I had got my wish.

The junkie is staring down at my stomach with a look of pure terror in his eyes, and I can feel the warmth of my blood pumping out and over my hands. Within seconds, my strength goes, and I release my grip and clutch my hands over the gaping wound in my guts. The junkies are already running, and in a last act of morbid humor, I shout after them as I drop to my knees, "Thanks, lads, let's do this again. It was fun."

## Present Day – Sunday, 11th February, 2018

My alarm is set for 6.30 am. When it goes off, I open my eyes immediately and skip my usual routine of hitting the pause button to get an extra ten minutes of sleep.

Last night went exactly as I hoped it would, and today there is a lot to get through. So, full of confidence of finally nailing Donovan, I get dressed in my running kit and head out for an early morning run to clear my head.

It's Sunday morning, so the roads and the paths along the river are quiet. I am feeling good about the day ahead and run easily, despite that fact that there is a heavy frost.

I am not planning on calling Catherine until around nine, so I run about six miles and use the time to think about what I need to do today.

First on the list is a home visit to Maria. I want to ask her about the death of her father and to show her the picture of Paul Donovan. I am certain that once she finds out that Donovan was the guy driving the car that killed her dad, she will be only too willing to change her statement and agree to testify against him for the killing of Anthony Glennister.

I then want to put the thumbscrews on Terry Fletcher. With a witness statement from Maria, and a promise of immunity for himself and Mark, I am sure that I can get him to roll over.

After what I saw last night, it looks like both Terry and Mark did what they could to stop the fight anyway, so the least they deserve is immunity from prosecution after all this time.

Not even Detective Superintendent Douglas will be able to save Donovan if I have that much evidence. At the very least we will have him for the murder of Glennister, the manslaughter of Ravi Pinto, and for perverting the course of justice through witness intimidation.

Yep, it's going to be a good day, and that slippery bastard is going to go down for a very long time if all goes to plan.

By the time I get back to my apartment it is nearly 7.45, and after a long hot shower, I grab a couple of slices of toast and a strong cup of tea. At 8.50 I call Catherine to give her the day's instructions.

"Hey, Cath, are you dressed? We have work to do. Meet me at the station in thirty minutes. I want to visit Maria Pinto at home this morning. She is the daughter of our hit-and-run victim Ravi Pinto, I want to ..."

Catherine cuts me off before I can finish speaking, "Sean, are you okay? What the hell were you drinking last night? I think you might be mixing things up a bit. Maria Pinto is one of our victims – is this a wind-up?"

I feel like I have just been hit in the stomach by a freight train. I can feel my legs about to buckle under me as the implication of what she has just said hits me. I need to get into the station right now and get the files from my desk drawer, but I feel like I am going to puke, and it is all I can do to keep standing.

"Of course, it's a wind-up, Cath. I was just checking you were awake and alert. Make sure you are ready to go as soon as I call. Thanks, Cath."

As soon as I hang up, I head into the bathroom and splash my face with cold water. This must be a mistake. When I left the pub, the fight was all but over. But then I remember something important – there were two ambulances, not one.

Thank God it's Sunday morning. The roads are quiet and so it only takes me just over fifteen minutes to reach the station. A few minutes later, I am at my desk and staring at the drawer.

I am almost too scared to open it for fear of what I will discover, and for a few seconds I consider going home again. But this is not the kind of person I am, and I reach in and lift out the two case files.

The hit-and-run file is on top, and the cover is exactly as I remember it: same case number, same date, and the same victim name. Inside the contents are also still as I remember them, including the fresh statement from Carol Baker, so my chance meeting with Maria outside the station must have remained unchanged, otherwise I would not have known to make the connection.

My heart skips a beat, though, when I push the file to one side and look at the second one: same case number, same date, but victim names, Anthony Glennister and Maria Pinto.

I have screwed up before, but never on this scale. This is the mother of all screw-ups, and because of me there are now two victims instead of one. I can't understand what happened, though, so I flip open the file to read the statements. Like before, they all tell a near identical story.

Only this time, they all now describe a fight after the pool tournament between Anthony Glennister and an unidentified male. During the fight the suspect pulled a knife to stab Glennister, and during the struggle Maria Pinto tried to intervene to save Glennister. By the time the fight was over, both Anthony Glennister and Maria Pinto had sustained fatal knife wounds and the unknown assailant had fled.

If this is not bad enough already, there is worse to come as I read through the description of the suspect, provided without exception by every one of the witnesses.

'White male, twenty-five to thirty years old, approximately six-feet tall, smooth complexion, gelled light brown hair, smartly dressed in a white shirt, cream-colored trousers and a blue jacket.'

If I am in any doubt at all where this is leading, all doubts disappear when I flip over the photofit picture and stare down at myself.

So not only have I screwed up and got Maria killed, I am now my own prime suspect for a double murder that took place when I was six years old – absolutely bloody wonderful.

If I am to have any hope of salvaging today, I know I need to go back to 15th October, 1994 immediately, but with everything that has happened, I am hyperactive. I know that I won't be able to sleep so soon without something to help me along.

After my last couple of trips, I only have a few beers left in my fridge, and the rest of the bottle of absinthe. But I can't face another hangover like the previous one, so on my way back home, I stop off at a shop for a fresh bottle of whisky.

It's not even ten in the morning yet, and the normal Sunday licensing laws don't normally allow for the sale of alcohol this early; but after flashing my badge, the salesman hands me a liter bottle of Jameson in a plastic bag, and I continue home.

To get ready I need to re-create the exact same look as I had previously – which, unfortunately, is easier said than done. Due to my excitement on waking up earlier, I had ditched my jacket, shirt, and trousers on the floor of my bathroom, so now they are damp and wrinkled to fuck, and I spend the next forty minutes drying them with a hairdryer and ironing them again, while knocking back as much neat Jameson as I can.

Eventually, though, I am satisfied with my efforts. I finish again by gelling my hair and splashing myself with the same generous amount of cologne. Then I settle down in front of the TV with another large glass of Jamey.

It's not long before the effects of the booze start to kick in, and with more than half of the bottle gone, I once more lie down on my bed and go through my now familiar routine to start my travels.

## The Past – Saturday, 15th October, 1994

When I open my eyes a feeling of déjà vu washes over me. I almost cry with relief at how precise I have been this time. Everything is exactly as it was before, and if I needed any more confirmation of that, I get it a few minutes later when I hail the same cab and tell him to take me to the King George.

The trip is exactly the same as it was previously, but as I get out in front of the pub, my sense of humor gets the better of me. Before the cabbie can impart his wisdom, I get my own parting shot in first.

"Do you think it's okay to try for anal on a first date?"

Feigning disgust, he calls me a dirty twat, then pulls up his window and drives away as I piss myself laughing on my way over to the chip shop.

From that point, everything carries on as if I had hit the rewind and replay buttons on a DVD player, and at 8.50 pm Maria turns to me for help, "Sean, please do something. He is going to kill him. Don't just stand there – I saw what you did to those skinheads on the train."

I desperately want to do something, but this needs to play out until the end. Only this time I can't leave until I am sure Maria is safe, so I tell her we can't get involved.

"This is different, Maria. Look, he has a knife, there is nothing we can do."

The look of utter disgust she gives me is almost as painful as being stabbed in the guts, but she follows up with something just as bad.

"You're not the man I thought you were, Sean, you're a coward. If you're not enough of a man to help out, then I will. Get away from me, Sean."

I am ready for what happens next and before she can move towards where they are fighting, I wrap my arms around her in a bear hug and pull her back.

"Let me go, Sean – he's gonna kill him, please Sean, let me go!"

It was never in my plan to witness the murder myself, but to keep Maria safe I have no other option. As we watch Donovan plunging the knife into Glennister's chest, I feel her go limp in my arms, and I help her sit down.

For a few seconds nothing is said, then Donovan turns to face us with the bloodied knife still in his hand. "Mark, go and watch the bloody door, nobody goes in or out. Now listen up, all you bastards had better pay attention."

So, as I suspected, Donovan and the Fletcher brothers spend the next twelve minutes concocting a story and threatening us all into silence, but I think I was the only one that had any clue that Donovan was staring right at me when he was describing the person he wanted us to tell the police about.

Either he is even more stupid than I first thought, or he has recognized me from the hit-and-run scene and wants to use this opportunity to get something over me. Does he seriously expect me to give a description to the police that matches my own? It's just as well that I won't be around much longer.

Exactly at 9.05 pm, we hear the sound of a police siren and Donovan tells Michal Bell to go outside, and then he gives the rest of us a final warning. "If any of you even think about changing the fucking story from what you have been told, just remember, I will be out in ten years or less, and I know where you all live. Even from inside, I can get to you, or my boys can – just keep your mouths shut and this will all be over soon."

As he finishes speaking, he disappears behind the bar, presumably to wash the blood off his hands and stash the knife. As he re-joins us, Michael Bell comes back inside with three police officers following him, and I know that I need to get away now, before they get themselves organized.

Maria is sitting with her head between her knees and is crying into her hands, so I quietly try to edge myself backwards towards the bathroom and the back door. Miraculously, the three cops are so intent on listening to Michael Bell explain what has happened that they don't notice me, and I make it outside into the backyard unnoticed.

I am just about to open the gate to go out into the alley when the gate opens, and I am shocked to see two guys in their mid to late twenties in suits come inside the yard.

"Going somewhere, are we, pal? Stand right there and don't bloody move. DS Douglas, take him inside and get his details."

This just gets better and better. I am staring at Detective Superintendent Clive Douglas, circa 1994, only now it must be Detective Sergeant Douglas. I had no idea until now that he had been part of the response team on the night of the Glennister murder, and I wonder now what other connections he might have.

Now, though, is not the time to wait around to exchange pleasantries or to ask questions, so before they can say anything else, I scramble up a stack of beer kegs in an attempt to get over the wall, and they both come after me.

Unfortunately, the stack of kegs is not as stable as I would have liked, and before I can get high enough up, a truncheon slams into the back of my right leg and two pairs of hands roughly pull me backwards.

Ironically, they have done me a favor. As my head slams into the side of a steel keg, the last thing I remember is the light from a torch and Douglas's familiar voice.

"Where the fuck did he go, Tom? I had hold of his leg. Not a bloody word of this to anyone, okay? We will look like a right pair of tossers if we have let the knifeman get away."

## Present Day – Sunday, 11th February, 2018

It is already dark when I wake up, and yet again my head is banging like a bitch. But I am happy to see that it is only 7.32 pm, because I now need to decide whether to travel again tonight, and to where.

Before I can even begin to decide, though, I need to know if my trip was a success, so I reach over the side of my bed to where I had left the case files on my bedroom floor and am massively relieved to see that the front of the file only shows one victim: Glennister.

The contents inside the file also now include a witness statement from Maria Pinto, following the same outline as all the other statements, including the description of the unknown white male.

Unsurprisingly, none of the statements has mentioned my name, as I remember Donovan telling us to say that the suspect was a complete stranger, which of course makes sense. Any hint of familiarity would prompt more questions from the police.

Another change to the file is the photofit picture, which is now even more like me, because previously he was describing me from memory, and this time he had the benefit of being able to stare me in the face.

I look through the file for something else, and I quickly find it. Handwritten at the bottom of each witness statement is a signature that I had not paid much attention to previously, but based on my chance meeting with Clive Douglas, it is now possibly as important as any other aspect of this case.

The signature is not completely clear, but I am sure that it is Clive Douglas's, and whilst it looks like he didn't take an active part in the witness interviews, he has checked and countersigned them all.

My next step should have been to visit Maria at home as I had originally intended this morning, but with this new twist, I need to understand better if there is any deeper connection between Douglas and Donovan, before moving ahead any further.

If DS Douglas and Paul Donovan are connected in any way, other than a simple informer and handler relationship, then I could be stepping too far into dangerous territory, and there could also be other senior police officers involved.

With this in mind, my next step is clear. I need to go back to 15th October, 1994 yet again and find a way to see what happens after the arrival of Douglas on the scene. But I feel like absolute shit, and I don't think my liver can take another hammering so soon.

Thankfully, my head is still spinning from the effects of the earlier booze, and this time my clothes just need a quick run over with the iron. So, after another quick shower and spruce up, I pick up my camera bag and am ready to go back without needing to drink any more whisky.

## The Past – Saturday, 15th October, 1994

Remarkably, I arrive at exactly the same spot for the third time, and as I climb into the back of the taxi and greet the driver, he is starting to feel like an old friend.

"Hey, good to see you. Let's go to the King George again. Take Stanwell Road – it's a bit longer, but it's a straight run and we can be there in twenty minutes."

Of course, my joke goes straight over his head. As he pulls away, he sarcastically says, "Thanks, pal, I would never have known that. Why would I after only thirty-three years as a bloody cab driver?"

Then under his breath, "Bloody pooftas, think they know everything, and then have the nerve to bloody stink out my cab."

For the rest of the journey, nothing else is said between us, and as he drops me outside the King George, I don't bother with the anal question this time around; he already thinks that I'm gay, and I don't think his fanny-loving heart could take it.

As before, the chip-shop manager smiles, indicating my jacket and making the same comment about not having a dress code. Then as she pours my mug of tea and I ask her if it would be okay to leave my bag behind the counter for a couple of hours.

"Well, we don't normally allow people to leave stuff here, but as long as it's just a couple of hours, I guess it's okay. Enjoy your tea, love. The milk and sugar are at the end of the counter – help yourself."

After leaving the chip shop, and for the third time today, I sit through the pool tournament and witness the murder of Anthony Glennister. Only this time around, as soon as Donovan starts to concoct the story he wants us all to tell, I get a definite feeling from the look on his face that he has recognized me from the hit-and-run.

Last time, I had been half-listening and half-concentrating on comforting Maria, but now with the benefit of hindsight I am certain he has recognized me, and he wants me to know it.

I don't intend to let him have it all his own way, though, so I interrupt him with my own suggestion. "That description sounds like me. There is no way I am going to tell the police that. We should say it was a black guy."

My interruption is clearly not welcome, but Donovan needs everybody to be united, and with the clock ticking, he doesn't have time to argue with me.

"Okay, smart lad, we say it was a black guy. Listen up, everyone, and get this right – it was a heavy-set black guy, he was tall, maybe six feet four inches, around twenty-five to thirty years old, with dreadlocks and a goatee beard. Has everybody bloody got that?"

Even if they hadn't got it, nobody is going to say anything to a man standing in front of them with a knife and blood on his hands. So, with the sound of the police siren in the distance, Donovan gives us his final warning, then disappears behind the bar to wash his hands and hide the knife.

As soon as Michael returns to the bar with the three police officers, I do my disappearing act and quickly find myself in the backyard, where I conceal myself behind a stack of beer kegs, just as the gate swings open.

I can't see them, and even if I didn't know already that it is Douglas and his colleague, Douglas's voice is now instantly recognizable to me.

"Let's not take too long over this, Tom, let's see what plod have got to say, then leave all the donkey work to them. We can check over the statements once they are done, then we can palm it off on one of the new DCs."

Once they are inside, I take my chance and slip into the back alley. Then I cross the road and head to the chip shop as fast as I can, without looking too conspicuous, to retrieve my camera bag.

Right on schedule, I watch as the next two police cars arrive, followed by the ambulance less than a minute later.

By now, the uniformed officers have started to set up their cordon and with all the flashing blue lights and me snapping away with my fancy Nikon long-lensed camera, it was inevitable that I would get some attention.

Fortunately, though, it is just the chip-shop manager.

"I wonder what's going on with all the police? It must be serious if they are putting the tape out, somebody must be hurt. Are you a reporter or something?"

I nod, but don't give her anything else. She has lost interest in me anyway, heading outside to join the rest of the ghouls behind the cordon, while I keep my eyes firmly focused on the entrance.

For more than an hour, apart from the arrival of a forensic team and more police vehicles, there is no other movement in and out of the pub. Then at 10.15 pm, the ambulance crew appear and load Glennister's body into the back of the ambulance.

For the next ten minutes, the witnesses are escorted out in groups of two or three and loaded into police cars, presumably to be taken to various police stations to go over their statements.

The last to come out are Donovan and the Fletcher brothers, and I am surprised when Mark and Terry Fletcher are placed into the back of a marked car, and are driven away accompanied by Douglas's colleague, but Donovan himself is put into the unmarked car, which is driven from the rear of the pub by DS Douglas.

I need to know which station Douglas is taking him to. As they pull away, I jump into the passenger seat of a cab at the taxi rank. Just like in the movies I tell the cabbie to follow that car, and he then rewards me with the obligatory cabbie rant and words of wisdom.

"Sure thing, guvnor, what's with the camera? Are you one of them paparazzi blokes? It looks like some poor bugger has been done in. It's not like the old days. You used to be able to leave your doors open all day around here. I blame the immigrants myself."

After driving for more than twenty minutes on the motorway, it has become clear that Douglas is not taking Donovan anywhere even close to a police station. After another ten minutes we pull into a quiet residential street in Luton, and I tell the cab driver to stop at the end of the street.

The magnitude of what I am seeing is almost overwhelming. As they go inside a large detached house together, it is obvious from Donovan's demeanor that he is not under arrest – in fact, he looks like he doesn't have a care in the world.

Detective Superintendent Douglas is one of the most highly respected detectives in the entire Metropolitan Police and has probably been responsible for putting away more criminals than any other officer of his generation, but corruption is no respecter of rank or experience and from where I am standing right now, it looks like Douglas is as bent as they come.

Mere suspicion alone proves nothing, though, and without real evidence, not only would my suspicions never see the light of day, but even if they did, Douglas would bury me before I even got close to anyone taking me seriously.

I need to get closer and find out what the hell is going on, but the front garden and approach to the windows is way to open and illuminated by security floodlights. Douglas will almost certainly have some kind of camera system as well, so I make my way to the rear of the property to look for a better option.

At the rear of his house, there is a poorly lit alleyway that separates Douglas's row from another row of houses, and his back garden has a six-foot panel fence, with a thick patch of tall pine trees in front that obscures the view into his house.

His gate is locked, but his neighbor's gate is open. I don't see any obvious sign of cameras, so I go inside and climb carefully up onto a compost bin to look into Douglas's garden.

If they are still in the front of the house, I am screwed. But my luck holds; after a short wait, Douglas appears in his kitchen window and a few seconds later, I catch sight of Donovan.

They are talking, but I can't hear what they are saying, although it looks to me like they are not totally in agreement with each other, until finally Donovan nods and Douglas leaves the kitchen.

Soon after, he comes back to the kitchen, and then Donovan goes out of sight for nearly seven minutes, and I am starting to think that he may have already left.

When the back door opens and the rear security light switches on, it takes me by surprise, and I think at first that they might have seen me, but as soon as Douglas lifts the lid on his BBQ, I know immediately what is going on.

Donovan steps out from the kitchen wearing a full set of new but ill-fitting clothes, and his hair is still damp from having taken a shower.

In his hand is a black bin bag that no doubt contains his other clothes, and he is also carrying a rolled-up tea towel that probably contains the knife.

Even from where I am hiding, I can see that the fire has not really got going yet. But as soon as Donovan tips the bag of clothes onto the grill, Douglas empties the best part of a bottle of lighter fuel onto it, and soon he has a nice little inferno going.

"Okay, Paul, get the knife on there as well. The handle will burn away completely and any DNA on the blade will be long gone by the time this has burnt out. It's not like anyone is ever going to find it anyway. Let's give it a few minutes, and then we need to get going and get you into a station before anyone starts to wonder where we are."

Without thinking of the consequences, I point my camera at the BBQ just as Paul unrolls the towel and lets the knife drop into the flames.

My shot captures the BBQ, the knife, Donovan, and Douglas perfectly, but it also illuminates the entire street as the flash goes off. Without a second's hesitation Douglas is running towards the fence, and I fall backwards off the compost bin and into the arms of his equally burly neighbor, who pins me to the floor.

"Clive, I've got the dirty fucker. Hurry up, mate, he's a strong bastard."

Seconds later, Douglas is over his fence, closely followed by Donovan, and I am pulled to my feet by his neighbor, who excitedly explains to Douglas what I was doing.

"This pervy bastard was trying to peep in at you. Janice saw him from our window and we were going to call the police, but we thought you might want to deal with him yourself. Shall I call the police now, Clive?"

Douglas looks me up and down without speaking, then Donovan leans in and whispers something to him. They both move forward and take hold of my arms.

"Thanks, Frank, no need to call anyone for now. I'm heading into the station soon myself anyway. You and the wife get yourself back to bed now. We can look after Mr. Peeping Tom here. Goodnight, Frank."

As they lead me out of the garden and around to the front of Douglas's house, I have a sneaky feeling that I am about to be old-school questioned, and it's not going to be pleasant.

Inside, they lead me through and into a garage on the side of the house, then Donovan binds my hands and feet and enthusiastically gaffer tapes me to a deck chair.

"I guess you know already that I'm a police officer. Of course, you do – that's why you were snooping around with your fancy Japanese camera in the hope of getting something to blackmail me with. Is that why you were in the pub tonight, for a bit of blackmail on Paul? Don't look so innocent. Paul has already told me about your little stunt with his traffic accident last year. Did you think he wouldn't remember you?

"Only you got a bit more than you bargained for tonight, didn't you? A nice little stabbing, and to top it off nicely, you think that you've hooked yourself a bent copper. I bet you thought you were onto a nice little earner, didn't you? Well, sorry to say, your camera should be nicely barbecued by now. So why don't you save yourself a whole lot of pain and tell us where the other pictures are?"

I really couldn't have summed it up better myself, and I know that they are not going to let me leave here alive, so I might as well use the time to find out what I can.

"I don't think anything. I know you're bent and the pictures prove it – just like the pictures of Paul's little accident prove that he ploughed into an innocent man and drove away like a bloody coward, leaving him like a pile of hamburger meat on the side of the road."

Paul's fist slams into the right side of my head so hard that he knocks the chair completely over and I feel my left shoulder dislocate as my body slams into the concrete floor.

"Easy, Paul, we don't want to kill him just yet. We need the pictures from last year. Let's try and be a bit more subtle, can we? Now, pick him up and dust him down."

My head is spinning, and my shoulder is throbbing like a bitch, but I am far from done yet, and I know that if Douglas has his way, this is going to go on for a while before I pass out enough to get home.

"Now, unless you want me to let my friend here loose on you again, how about you be a good lad and tell me where those pictures are? I promise if you tell me now, I will make it quick for you. What do you say, have we got a deal?"

The blood from a cut above my eye is running into my mouth, and I make a show of choking while I try to speak, "U'gh, the pictures are in Upyer."

Douglas looks at Donovan and asks, "What did he say? Something about Upyer – I couldn't hear him properly. Tell him to speak up."

Donovan reaches forward and grabs the lapels of my jacket. "You had better start talking or you're going to regret it. Where the fuck are those pictures?"

"Are you bloody stupid? I already told you. They're in Upyer."

"What the hell are you talking about? Where the hell is Upyer?"

That joke really never gets old, and the look on Donovan's face as I deliver the punchline is priceless, "Up yer fat ass, ya baldy bastard!"

Neither of them see the funny side, though, and Douglas nods to Donovan. "Go on then, but for God's sake, don't kill him yet."

I know already how strong he is, but tonight as he wraps his hands around my throat, the sadistic bastard is actually smiling as he starts to squeeze on my windpipe. After just a few seconds, I can feel my eyeballs starting to bulge out of their sockets.

A little more of this and I will be home, so I force myself to smile as he crushes my trachea. Just as I am on the verge of passing out, Douglas pulls him away.

"This asshole can wait for now. We need to get you to Crompton Road Station. Get yourself into the kitchen and wash your hands again, while I get some more tape on the comedian here."

Five minutes later, I hear the front door close, then the sound of a car driving away, and I blink my eyes to try to clear some of the blood that has congealed in the corner of my left eye.

Before he left, Douglas finished off the roll of gaffer tape on me, including a big piece over my mouth and then he used a few cable ties to secure the chair to a drainage pipe on the wall, so for now I am well and truly stuck.

Crompton Road Station is around twenty-five minutes from here, so I figure that by the time Douglas has handed Donovan over to the duty detective, I probably have no more than seventy-five minutes before he comes back and goes to work on me again.

For the next forty-five minutes, I desperately try to free my hands, but he has me bound up so tight that I make absolutely no progress. With time against me I decide on desperate measures and start to rock myself from side to side in the hope that if I tip the chair, the cable ties will break.

Trying to get momentum is difficult, but each time I manage to tilt just a little bit more until eventually my center of gravity reaches the point that I keep falling – and then I stop, tilted over at forty-five degrees and totally unable to move.

Screw this, I really don't care about him killing me, but I would rather not disappear in front of his eyes. It leaves too much to chance, and always has the possibility of influencing future events, so hopefully he will drop me in a lake with concrete boots on, or something else along those lines. You never know, I might get lucky.

Thirty minutes later, I hear a car pull up and park outside the garage and then I hear somebody pottering around in the kitchen for a few minutes before Douglas comes into the garage wearing shorts and a t-shirt.

"Well, will you look at this guy, he thinks he's a gymnast. Let me straighten you up there and take that tape off your mouth."

He then leans forward and rips off the tape in one fluid motion and asks me if I want a cup of tea.

"It's no problem, the kettle has just boiled anyway. There is no need for us to be uncivilized."

Before I can answer, he disappears into the kitchen and returns with a mug of tea in one hand and the kettle in the other. Then he pulls up a chair and sits down in front of me and puts the kettle on the floor.

"I sincerely hope that you had a chance to think about your situation while I was gone. Why don't you start by telling me who you are, and exactly what you are up to, and don't even think about lying to me. I can smell bullshit at five miles. It's my job. So, who the hell are you?"

Even after the earlier beating and hanging to one side in the chair for forty-five minutes, my attitude is still on form. I lean as far forward in the chair as I am able and say, "I thought you were a detective. Why don't you work it out, Hercule Poirot? I thought you said you were getting me a cup of tea – did you forget about it?"

"Some people just don't know when they have got it good. If you think you are going to walk out of here without telling me what I want to know, then you are wrong. Things are going to get really nasty if you don't start talking. Have it your way for now, though, if that's what you want."

Douglas then stands up and I think he is about to punch me, but instead he leans forward and rifles through my pockets looking for identification. He finds nothing, apart from some loose cash, a pen, and a receipt from the chip shop for a cup of tea.

"What kind of person comes out with no wallet or ID? You're not a reporter or a private detective – no, I think you're just a bloody chancer. What's your name, son? Tell me now or you are going to get that cup of tea, only it won't have any milk or sugar, you get it? So again, what's your name?"

"It's Mark Mai."

"Is that right? What kind of name is Mark Mai? Don't play me for a fool."

I smile again. "It's true, my name is Mark Mai. Mark my bloody words, you're going to prison, you bent bastard."

Unlike Donovan, Douglas is a professional and doesn't lose his cool easily. This guy instils terror through calm and calculated movements.

Despite knowing I really have nothing to worry about, when he puts the tape back across my mouth, lifts up the kettle, and pulls my collar away from my neck, I am genuinely scared.

The pain of the boiling water cascading across my shoulders and down my back is like nothing I have ever experienced before, and I fancy I can feel the blisters growing on my skin as I scream out in muffled agony.

Then as soon as it started, it is done. He rips off the tape again and sits back down in front of me. “How was the tea? Do you want a second cup?”

My skin is on fire and it is all I can do to block out the pain, but I need to keep provoking him. So, through gritted teeth, I force another smile.

“Actually, you should know something, I’m more of a coffee guy – a cappuccino would be nice, and a blueberry muffin wouldn’t be bad. Be a good lad and run down to Starbucks.”

He doesn’t react to this. He just smiles and stares at me for at least thirty seconds before he speaks again, “I don’t think you’re going to tell me anything, are you? Even if I torture you all night you still won’t give me anything. Under any other circumstances I might find it admirable. It doesn’t matter, though. When you die, those pictures will die with you. I don’t think I want to waste any more time with you. It’s getting late anyway, so I think we should go for a drive somewhere to cool off those burns for you. Now, you just hold tight there for a few minutes, I won’t keep you long.”

A few minutes later, I hear his car start, and then the garage door opens from the outside. He comes back in and cuts away the tape that is securing me to the chair, but leaves my hands and feet tightly bound as he lifts me into the boot of his car.

For the next twenty minutes, and judging by the speed, we must be driving on a motorway.

We slow down and after another ten minutes, it feels like we are on a rough country track, or even driving over a field. We drive for another five minutes, until we stop.

When the boot opens, the fresh early morning air is welcome. I am ready to die now.

"Come on, Douglas, get a bloody move on, I need to be at work in the morning."

He pulls me out of the boot and to the edge of the cliff, so that I am looking down on the flooded quarry below.

"You really are something. Even now you still think I'm bluffing and you think you're going home."

Then he pulls me away from the edge and shows me the lump hammer that he has brought with him.

"Your choice – I can smash your skull in before you go over, or do you want to try holding your breath? It makes no difference to me."

Drowning is not something that I particularly enjoy, so I nod my head towards the hammer and I tell him to make sure he doesn't miss.

"Aim right between my eyes, Clive, that should do the trick nicely."

He has obviously never dealt with anyone with as relaxed an attitude to imminent death as me. For a second, he looks confused, but then he shrugs his shoulders and splits open my skull with one powerful blow from the hammer.

I am still alive, though, as he drags me to the edge of the cliff and rolls me off. Then I plummet downwards and drown in the icy water below.

## Present Day – Monday, 12th February, 2018

Well, that has to be one of the more interesting and prolific dream-travel weeks of my life so far, with seven trips notched up since last Wednesday evening.

When you consider that I have been beaten, slashed, strangled, burnt, electrocuted, and thrown into a quarry to drown, I don't think I am looking too bad this morning.

Let's also not forget the copious amounts of alcohol I have put away, and my heroin overdose, which was both a first for me and a personal highlight

No, all things considered, I could be looking and feeling a damn sight worse than I do. Now I need to decide what to tell Catherine about my weekend, and in thirty minutes DS Morgan will be expecting an update at his Monday morning briefing.

With my camera destroyed, any evidence against Detective Superintendent Clive Douglas is long gone, so for now any line of enquiry around him is a complete non-starter.

In the cold light of day, I am not sure a few pictures supposedly taken twenty-four years ago would have been enough anyway, and I realize now that it was a mistake to use a modern camera. Using modern technology, any good forensic officer would easily have seen that the pictures were taken recently or might even surmise that they had been doctored.

Equally, a powerful and slippery bastard like Clive Douglas will have connections everywhere, so I doubt that any other senior officer would take me seriously anyway, without something much more compelling.

It's fine, though. Despite the fact that this dirty bastard tortured and murdered me as easily as if he were taking a walk in the park, I literally have all the time in the world to bring Clive down, and I fully intend to use that time.

At 8.45 am, Catherine walks into the office and catches me deep in thought again. “Good morning, Sean, you look like fucking shit. Judging by the fact that you didn’t call yesterday, it must have been a big night. Given everything that happened on Saturday with our visit from DS Douglas, I thought you might be keen to get moving in other directions.”

One other big drawback of my dream-travel is keeping track of what has happened and what has been said, both in my dreams and in reality.

In my mind, I had called Cath on Sunday morning to say that we were going to visit Maria at home in connection to the hit-and-run.

Cath had asked me if I was winding her up, but as far as Cath is concerned, I never made that call. After re-visiting the murder scene and stopping Maria from intervening in the fight, it changed the course of events for everyone except myself.

“Hey, Cath, yes, sorry for not calling you. I was feeling a bit rough when I woke up, so I took a few aspirin and then pretty much conked out for most of the day, but I did have a good chance to do some thinking about the next steps.

“Obviously we can’t go within a mile of Paul Donovan, but I do want us to pay a visit to Maria Pinto at her home today.”

Catherine looks confused and asks me why we would be visiting Maria. “I assume from the surname that she is related to our hit-and-run victim, Ravi Pinto, but what’s your angle, Sean? Where does Maria Pinto fit into all of this?”

“Maria Pinto is, or should I say was, the daughter of Ravi Pinto. She also happens to be my witness in the bathroom of the King George on the night of Anthony Glennister’s murder.”

While Catherine is still digesting what I have told her, I flip open the Glennister file and hand her Maria’s witness statement.

She spends five minutes silently reading through it, occasionally looking up at me with a disbelieving look on her face.

When she finishes, I can tell that she is about to have another rant at me for not sharing information with her.

"Where did you get this, Sean? That statement is from 1994, and I know for a fact that it was not in the file before. Have you known all along about this? You told Morgan that you had a witness who had originally said they were in the bathroom but could be willing to change their statement. You also lied to me again when I asked you about this after the briefing on Thursday."

In fairness, I hadn't exactly lied to her. I had in fact told Catherine that I couldn't tell her everything yet, but I guess this is just semantics and I really don't want to get her any more pissed off than she already is. But now I need to lie again.

"The statement was in the file, Cath, but I wasn't sure who I could trust, so I removed Maria Pinto's statement from the file as soon as I realized that we might be able to use her against Donovan."

"That's bullshit, Sean. If you removed it, you must have removed it as soon as you were assigned to this case. But that must also mean that you knew about the photographs from the hit-and-run much earlier then you said you did. How else would you have made the connection?"

This is why I like Cath. She has a sharp mind, and if I were able to give her more information we would be a great team. But for now, she knows I am talking out of my ass, and I need to bring her back on side again.

"Listen, you want that arrogant racist bastard put away as much as I do. As soon as I show Maria Pinto the pictures of him at the scene of her father's death, I am certain that she will change her statement and implicate Donovan and the Fletcher brothers. I can't do this on my own, though, Cath. I need you to keep backing me, and when this is all over, I will totally respect your decision if you don't want to carry on working with me. If everything goes pear-shaped, the decision will probably be out of my hands anyway."

She is completely unimpressed but doesn't say anything else for now, and as we make our way to the briefing room and take our seats, I know that I am far from forgiven.

Right now, though, we have a much bigger issue to deal with. That smug bastard Douglas is sitting right next to DCI Morgan and he is staring right at me as I whisper to Catherine, "What the hell is he doing here?"

"No idea, Sean, but I think we are about to find out. Look at the agenda – you're first up, Golden Boy."

Bang on nine o'clock and with the team fully assembled, Morgan stands up and introduces DS Douglas to the team.

"Good morning, ladies and gentlemen, I hope you have all had a productive weekend. Before I start today's briefing I would like to introduce Detective Superintendent Clive Douglas. I'm sure that most of you are familiar with DS Douglas, but for those of you that don't follow the news, DS Douglas is the Head of the Serious Crimes Squad at Scotland Yard. He is joining us today out of professional interest in the work that we do in this squad, but he has also taken a personal interest in the Glennister case."

You can say that again. The dirty bastard has taken a personal interest in making sure that his torture buddy remains free for another twenty-four years, and in making sure that he doesn't get implicated in anything as a result of Donovan getting charged.

"So, with that in mind, DC McMillan, perhaps you would be so good as to start us off today with your update and next steps."

I had already planned to say as little as I could get away with this morning, but now I need to say even less, so that I don't give Douglas any more reason to interfere.

"Thank you, sir. As you know, Paul Donovan was brought in for questioning on Saturday, but we are now satisfied with his statement and will be refocusing our efforts on trying to identify the black male mentioned in the statement of all of the witnesses. If we can make any headway in identifying him, then we will be in a strong position to start tracking him dow ..."

Douglas is itching to ask me a question and he does so, before I even finish speaking.

"DC McMillan, may I ask how you intend to identify him after all this time, when our colleagues twenty-four years ago failed so miserably?"

"Thank you, sir, I plan to interview all of the witnesses again. Even after so long, there is a possibility that one of them might just remember a small detail about our suspect that could give us the break we need."

He knows that I am lying, but he can't say anything. He nods his approval and says, "Good, don't hesitate to ask if Serious Crimes can be of any assistance."

Morgan then speaks again, "Thank you DC McMillan. If there are no more questions let's move onto the next update. Sergeant O'Connor, you're up next."

The speed in which DCI Morgan ended my update is a good sign that he has my back. He obviously doesn't want to give Douglas too much either.

Predictably then, after less than five minutes of O'Connor's update, I see Douglas making his excuses to Morgan and he leaves.

The only reason he was here today was to make sure that I go nowhere near Paul Donovan. I think I am going to be seeing a lot more of Douglas until he is happy that the case is closed to his satisfaction.

For the next forty-five minutes, I am totally preoccupied with my own thoughts and struggle to concentrate fully on the updates my colleagues are giving to Morgan. I count myself lucky that there is not a test at the end.

When the briefing finally finishes at just before ten, I can't get out of there quickly enough. After picking up the Pinto case file, I head down to my car in the underground parking garage, with Cath following behind in heels that are not built for speed.

"Sean, slow down, are we still going to see Maria Pinto? If we are, shouldn't we at least check first that she is home before we waste our time driving to Feltham?"

"Yes, we are. Today's plan still stands, but we will just have to take our chances on her being home. I don't want to spook her by calling ahead."

The drive to Feltham is less than six miles and with the early morning traffic already gone, we pull into Collister Drive by ten-twenty, and the memories of my previous time here come flooding back.

Maria was in her mid-twenties when we made love together, and now just a few days later, I am going to be meeting her as a forty-nine-year-old woman. If that is not a mindfuck, then I don't know what is, but it comes with the territory and I have to put any emotion or disbelief to one side.

As we park outside number 247 and get out of the car, my mind wanders to my skinhead friends and I laugh when I realize that if any of them are still alive they are possibly fathers or even grandfathers now, with decent jobs and knitted jumpers. But then Catherine snaps me back to reality.

“So, are we going in then, or are you going to stand there admiring the flowers all day?”

The front garden is much simpler than I remember. Previously it was laid out with shrubs and flowers, but most of that is now gone and has been replaced with a simple lawn and a few garden ornaments. The wooden front door and windows have also been replaced with modern UPVC; other than that, the house is exactly as I remember it.

My heart is racing and I almost want to turn around and leave. Before I can, Catherine takes the decision out of my hands and rings the doorbell.

We wait for nearly thirty seconds, then Cath rings again and I prepare myself to see Maria again, but as the door opens, it is a young man standing there and I am momentarily lost for words.

“Good morning, sorry to disturb you, my name is Detective Constable Catherine Swain and this is my colleague Detective Constable Sean McMillan. We were hoping to speak to Maria Pinto. Is she at home?”

He doesn’t answer, but he shouts back over his shoulder, “Mum, the police are here. They want to speak to you about something. Have you been shoplifting again?”

When she appears in the doorway, other than the slightest touch of grey and a few fine lines around her eyes, she is still a stunning woman, despite what I have put her through. I can’t help thinking that she has aged well in comparison to Carol Baker, who is just a few years younger.

“Good morning, ignore him, I am not a shoplifter. What is this about please?”

I am happy to let Catherine do the talking for now, glad that Maria is focusing on her and not me.

"Ms. Pinto – is it okay if I call you Ms. or would you prefer just Maria?"

"Maria is fine," Maria answered.

"May we come in to talk with you in relation to a statement you made in 1994?"

She knows immediately what Cath is referring to, and the color noticeably drains from her face. "Please come in. Ben, you get yourself off to uni or you're going to be late for your exam."

"Mum, what's this about? What statement is she talking about?"

"It's okay, Ben. Just something from before you were born. It's probably a routine follow-up. Isn't that right, officers?"

We both nod and reluctantly Ben leaves.

Maria shows us into her living room and takes a seat directly opposite Catherine.

"Has something happened? Nobody has asked me about this in years. I really don't remember very much about that night. I was in shock."

I remember only too well how she was on that night, and she looks like she in in shock now, but hopefully we can bring this to an end for her and for all of the other witnesses.

"Maria, if it's okay, I would like to ask you some questions and DC Swain will be making some notes in her pocket book. Is that okay, Maria?"

"That's okay, DC … uh'm, DC … "

"It's DC McMillan, Maria, thank you. Can you tell me how you know Paul Donovan? Did you know him before the night of the murder?"

As soon as I mention Donovan's name, her reaction is almost exactly the same as Carol Baker's. She is visibly trembling as she answers my question, "We were at the same school together. He was in the year above, though. I knew of him but didn't really know him that well."

"Okay, thank you, Maria. When Paul Donovan made his statement, he said that he tried to stop the attacker, along with Mark and Terry Fletcher, but they were beaten back by him. That guy must have been incredibly strong to fight off three fit young men. Is that what happened, Maria?"

She is already struggling to speak, but we need to push her to the point where we can pull her back and give her a reason to speak out against Donovan.

"Is that what happened, Maria? I know this is bringing back painful memories for you, but we need you to answer. Was Paul Donovan telling the truth in his statement, Maria?"

"Yes, he was telling the truth. The guy that killed Anthony Glennister was a big black guy. They tried to stop him, but when I think about it now, maybe he was on drugs. I think some drugs make you think you are invincible, don't they?"

Catherine stops writing for a second and looks towards Maria. "How often do you see Paul Donovan now, Maria?" she asks.

This question clearly rocks her and she stumbles over her words, "Uh'm, sorry, I don't understand, what do you mean?"

We had discussed this tactic in the car on the way here. I was going to open up the questions, and then Catherine was going to probe for ongoing intimidation from Donovan.

"It's a simple enough question, Maria. How often do you see Paul Donovan – once a week, once a month, are you still friends?"

This last part of the statement really hits home and her voice visibly rises, "Paul Donovan was never my friend. He was just in the same school as I was. Occasionally I might see him in the street or in a shop, but I haven't seen him for a few years."

Catherine quickly glances in my direction and I nod for her to continue. "Are you sure about that, Maria? Some of the other witnesses have told us that they see Paul at least two or three times a year. Apparently, he likes to give reminders about what might happen if you step out of line and change your story."

We are on dangerous ground with this line of questioning. If Maria chooses to make a complaint against us, it will soon become clear that none of the other witnesses have spoken to us about Donovan, apart from Carol Baker for a different case.

"I don't know what anyone else has said. I haven't seen him for a couple of years, and I don't know what else I can tell you."

I take over again from Catherine and turn up the aggression a notch. "You can tell us the truth and stop lying to us. We know that on the night of the murder, Donovan and the Fletcher brothers threatened you all into silence. We also know that he has been paying regular visits to you all ever since to keep you silent. There was no mystery black man, was there, Maria?"

Maria has tears in her eyes and is up on her feet now. "I want you to leave, unless I am under arrest, please leave."

At this point Catherine steps back in to calm things down. "Maria, please sit down. I know this is distressing, but we only have a few more questions. Sean, why don't we move onto the other matter?"

If there is any spark of recognition at the mention of my Christian name, then Maria certainly doesn't give anything away. And before she does get a chance to think about it, I drop the next bombshell.

"Maria, I would like to ask you something about the death of your father. He was …"

"What has my father's death got to do with this? How dare you try to involve my father in this? He was a good man – get out, both of you!"

Maria is on her feet again, and is screaming at us to get out, "Please go, get out, I don't want you here, get out and leave me alone."

We both remain seated, and eventually when she realizes that we are not going to leave, she sits back down and composes herself.

"I am sorry, but I don't even like to be reminded about my father's death. Why are you asking me about him now? Nobody else has cared for twenty-five years. His file is probably gathering dust in a cupboard somewhere."

I place the file on the coffee table and carefully lift out the packet of photographs inside. "Maria, part of the reason we came today is to let you know that your father's case is not forgotten. We do care and we have something that we would like to show you. Do you recognize the person in the driving seat in these photographs?"

The tears are welling up in her eyes again, and it is all I can do to stop myself from pulling her into my arms to hold her close. Because of me, she has been living in fear for the best part of her life, and it would be the least I could do, but I need to keep pushing.

"Maria, please concentrate, do you recognize the person in the driving seat in these photographs?"

"You know I do. It's Paul Donovan. So, does this mean what I think it means? Is Paul the bastard that drove away and left my dad to die on the side of the road?"

I confirm that it is, and Catherine sits down next to Maria to comfort her as she breaks down and sobs uncontrollably into her hands. Catherine hands her a box of tissues and, apart from her crying, there is an uncomfortable silence for a few minutes while we allow her to compose herself.

I feel like a total shit again when I break the silence. "Maria, we also now have a witness who has given us a statement about what happened on that night, and they are also willing to stand up in court to testify against Paul Donovan. We are going to put him away for killing your father, but with your help we can also put him away for the murder of Anthony Glennister."

Maria wipes her eyes with a tissue and takes a deep breath. Then she turns back to face me with a defiant look in her eyes.

"Where have these pictures been for the last twenty-five years? And why has this witness suddenly decided to come forward after all this time? My dad's death was swept under the carpet and nobody has given a fuck about it since. What's changed now?"

This is the first time that I have heard Maria swear, but I can understand her anger.

"All I can tell you about the photographs is that they were handed over anonymously," I explain, hoping I sound convincing. "I can't tell you any more than that about them, but it was these pictures that gave us the break with the witness. The most important thing is that we now have enough to bring charges. Help us put him away for the murder as well. We know that Paul Donovan has been threatening you and making your life a misery for the last twenty-four years, but if you agree to revise your statement and tell us what really happened to Anthony Glennister, I am certain that we can also get some of the other witnesses to cooperate."

I can tell that I am getting to her, but I am not so naïve to think she will simply agree to change her statement because of a ten-minute discussion with two coppers that she has never met before, and certainly not after a lifetime of intimidation.

Catherine takes her hand and squeezes it reassuringly. "Maria," she says, "what DC McMillan is saying is that if you agree to change your statement, there is a real chance that we can convince two or three other witnesses to also change theirs.

"With that, there is a real chance that we can charge Paul Donovan with murder. Combined with the death of your father and perverting the course of justice, we can put him away for at least fifteen to twenty years, if not life, but without you, we have nothing. Please help us, Maria."

I can see that Maria's mind is working overtime, and for a few seconds she doesn't speak. Then she focuses on me again.

"Which case were you working on first – the murder or the death of my father?"

I am not sure where she is going with this but, considering what we are asking her to do, she has every right to ask questions.

"We were assigned the murder case first. Is it important to you which came first? Our priority is to convict Paul Donovan, or if it wasn't Paul, convict whoever did kill Anthony Glennister."

"Yes, it is important to me. I need to know whether you actually give a shit about my dad, or you're just using me to close the murder case.

"It is okay if you are. I can see that the evidence you have to prove that Paul killed my dad makes me the weak link. Just don't sit there and make out that this is all for me when I know it is not."

I am about to answer her when her cell phone rings.

"It's my son. He is probably wondering what is happening. Give me a minute please."

They talk for a few seconds, then she hangs up after reassuring him that everything is fine.

"Sorry about that, he was just checking up on me. Do you see my point about my dad's case? I need to know that his life meant something to somebody, other than my mother and me. You are asking me to speak out and put my life and my son's life at risk. Tell me that you care and that you are not just using me as a pawn in a game."

I would like nothing more than to be able to tell her that she is not a pawn in a game, but she is and she knows it and I choose my words carefully.

"I joined the police because I care, Maria, and I joined this team because of the work it does in reviving old cases that should never have been left to go stale in the first place. Believe me or don't believe me, but we care passionately about getting justice for you, as much as we do about getting justice for Anthony Glennister's family. Paul Donovan is a bullying thug and he left your father dying on the side of the road. We also believe that he killed Anthony Glennister, and for all we know he may have killed others. I personally will not rest until he is behind bars for a very long time. Be the break we need, Maria, come to the station with us and give a new statement."

She is clearly torn between doing what is right, and fearing the consequences of speaking out against Donovan and the Fletcher brothers, and who could blame her?

"You think it's so easy, don't you? You haven't had to live with it all this time like I have. I thought watching Anthony Glennister die was going to be the worst thing I was ever going to experience in my life. I was wrong. Dying a slow death over the last twenty-four years has been far worse. I put up with it, though, because of Ben. He is the sole reason that I go on living each day. I don't care about myself, my real life ended in 1994, but I will not risk any harm coming to my son. I'm sorry that you have had a wasted trip, but the answer is no. Now please leave."

As she stands up, I know that we have lost her for now, and that there is no point in continuing to push her. If we do, we will push her even further away.

"Maria, we can protect you both, and we can give you your life back. I know that it is a lot to take in, but please give some thought to what we are asking. One way or another Paul will be going to jail for killing your father, but with a good lawyer he may get away with five years and be out in three. Don't let Paul Donovan or anyone else ruin the rest of your life, or Ben's."

It's a shit's trick, but as I hand her my business card, I know the reference to Ben will have stirred something in her.

"This is my card – please think seriously about speaking to us again. If you want to talk to me, please call day or night; it's no problem."

She takes my card but doesn't say anything else as she walks us out and closes the front door behind us, but my own feelings of guilt are almost overwhelming. As we get in the car, I am questioning in my own mind if it is all worth it.

"What's up with you, Sean? You're not normally this quiet, and all things considered I think it went reasonably well."

"Sorry, I was just thinking about what we should do next. You're right, it went okay. She is a decent woman, but it was a lot for her to take in. I think that once she has had a chance to digest it all, she will do the right thing. Now how about an early lunch: Maccers or Burger King?"

"Wow, Sean, you really know how to treat a lady, don't you?"

"Yep, I certainly do. If you play your cards right, we might even dine in!"

In the end, we opt for McDonalds, and ten minutes into our meal Catherine nods towards the door. "Don't turn around now, Sean, but I see a familiar face walking towards us, and I don't think he is here for the Big Macs."

"DC Swain, would you give me a few minutes with DC McMillan? Why don't you wait in the car for him? I won't keep him long."

Catherine gets up to leave, and Clive Douglas squeezes his bulky frame into the chair opposite me. Then he helps himself to the remains of her meal.

"I hope you don't mind, I hate to see good food go to waste. Oh, and sorry for breaking up your lunch – you both looked quite cozy together. I hope I wasn't interrupting anything important?"

I Ignore the obvious innuendo and attempt to get under my skin, but as I reply I am also trying to work out how he knew where to find us.

"That's quite alright, sir. I'm a bit surprised to see you, though. Is there something new on my case that I need to know about?"

The ignorant bastard says nothing for nearly a minute, but he keeps looking up at me as he finishes off the last of Catherine's burger and fries, then he loudly slurps the last of her drink, before belching towards me.

Clearly, he has been watching too much Pulp Fiction. If he thinks this tactic will unnerve or intimidate me, he is wrong. All it does is repulse me with his gross eating habits.

"How did you get on with Maria Pinto today? Did she reveal any new nuggets of information?"

Okay, so now I know how he found us. He must have checked the log at the station and followed us to Maria's house. If he is feeling the need to follow us, he is even more worried than I first thought.

"To be honest, it was a bit of a waste of time, sir. She didn't give us anything that we didn't already know. I am thinking of pulling some of the other witnesses in again, but after this morning I am not as hopeful as I was before."

This makes him smile, but that means nothing. After the length of time he has been a detective, he must be a master of wrong footing a suspect, so I don't take this as an indicator of his agreement or acknowledgement.

"I think you could be right, DC McMillan, my advice is to go back to the database. You have a clear description of the suspect, and with the information and technology we have at our disposal these days, it is the best chance you have of getting a match. Take it from me, though, if you don't get a match, close the case and don't waste any more of your time. There is no disgrace in admitting that the case is unsolvable. You will look like a bigger fool if you drag it out and still don't get a result. Careers have been ended for less, DC McMillan. Do you understand what I am saying?"

I understand all right. I understand that he is shitting a brick at the thought of me charging Paul Donovan, and then Donovan singing like the proverbial canary in return for giving information about a bigger fish. Well screw you, Clive, Donovan is going down and if it means you going down too, then all the better.

"Thanks for the advice, sir, but I think we can push for a while longer on this one before we pull the pin. The killer is out there somewhere and I know we can catch him."

Douglas leans towards me and I have a flashback to him leaning over me with the hammer in his hand.

“Be careful what you wish for, DC McMillan, and be sure to pass on my thanks to your girlfriend for the fries.”

I wait until I see him get in his car and leave, then I get up myself and re-join Catherine in my car to update her on my conversation with him.

“Come on then, Sean, put me out of my misery, what did he want?”

“Well, Cath, there is some good news and some bad news. The bad news is that he thinks we are wasting our time and should concede defeat. The good news is that the fat bastard ate the rest of your fries and burger, so fewer calories are going to be landing on your thighs today.”

As you can tell, humor is one of my defense mechanisms when I am under pressure, and it makes me feel instantly better when Catherine laughs at my joke.

“Cheeky bastard, I have lovely thighs. But seriously, what was said? Does he really think we are wasting our time?”

“He followed us to Maria Pinto’s house. I told him that we hadn’t got anything from her, and he didn’t give any indication that he knows about her connection to the hit-and-run. He suggested that we go back to the database and give it up as a dead duck if we don’t get anything. Telling us to leave Donovan alone is one thing. Trying to influence us to close the case completely is another thing entirely.”

Catherine agrees with me and suggests that I report the conversation to DCI Morgan. “Basically, he is warning us off, Sean. Why the hell would a detective superintendent give a shit about our case? Even if his intentions are totally above-board, which I don’t believe for a minute, we should keep Morgan in the loop. If nothing else, he needs to know that Douglas is interfering with one of his cases.”

She is right and I call Morgan immediately. We speak for nearly ten minutes as I relay the conversation with Douglas and update him on our visit to Maria Pinto, then I end the call and turn to face Catherine.

"Okay, so you probably got the gist of what we were discussing, but basically he has told me to ignore any advice from Douglas completely. We still can't go anywhere near Donovan, but we have as long as we need to get enough evidence to be able to pull Donovan in, without Douglas being able to come to his rescue. Obviously, he wants us to let him know immediately if we have any more run-ins with Douglas, but otherwise we have his blessing to carry on as normal."

"That's great news, Sean. So, what do we do now?"

"We do what Douglas told us to do. We go back to the station and we play the bastard at his own game. For the benefit of anyone that is watching us, we are going to make a show of going through the database looking for our mysterious black man – no offence of course, Cath."

"None taken, Sean. You're almost as sneaky as Douglas and I might be close to forgiving you for lying to me. Keep it going and you might be back in my good books by the end of the week. Come on then, let's get back to the station and give them a show."

For the rest of the day we do just that. Catherine enlists the help of a couple of other DCs and searches through hundreds of possible suspects on the police database, and I call around to other departments, including the Serious Crime Squad in Scotland Yard to request access to any other case files with similar suspects.

With any luck, my request will make it onto the desk of DS Douglas, or at the very least he will be informed of it.

I don't think for a minute that this will completely get him off our scent, but it might at least give us some breathing room.

By six o'clock, my head is wrecked, and I am sure Catherine's is as well, so I put on my jacket to leave.

"Come on, let's call it a day, Cath. We can start the show again in the morning. It's been a good day, and thanks again for all your support, it really does mean a lot."

"It's nothing, Sean. I know we have had a few rocky days, but you're a good detective and I really like working with you. With Douglas sticking his nose in, I want more than ever for us to nail Donovan. It also helps that Donovan is a foul-mouthed bigot. Have a good night, Sean, see you tomorrow."

On my drive home, my mind is filled with a million thoughts, and most of them revolve around Maria, and how soon we should follow up with her. We can't even think about talking to any of the other suspects until we have a new statement from her, and the longer it takes, the more likely it is that Douglas will be onto us again. On the other hand, if we blunder in again too soon, we might risk losing her completely, and any chance of closing the case will be gone.

Thank God I don't need to travel again tonight. Hopefully, a decent night's undisturbed sleep without any alcohol will help me think more clearly.

Whilst all of my dream-travelling is done from the comfort of my bed or sofa, it is still mentally and physically exhausting and after so many trips in such a short space of time, I am looking forward to a quick session in the gym to de-stress, followed by an early night.

My local gym is just a five-minute drive from my building, and after giving my apartment a quick clean and changing into my gym gear, I arrive at just after 7.30 pm.

Apart from a couple of meat heads admiring themselves in the mirrors, and a young woman on one of the rowing machines, the gym is empty, so I have a free run on most of the equipment. I opt to start with a short run on the treadmill to get a sweat going.

I push the speed up to six miles an hour, then raise the incline to ten percent, and feel my pulse quicken and the sweat rising on my forehead.

MTV is blasting out One Kiss, by Calvin Harris and Dua Lipa, but my mind is fixed firmly on Paul Donovan, Maria, and Detective Superintendent Clive Douglas.

Last Friday I had been one hundred percent convinced that within a few days I would have enough evidence to nail Paul Donovan for the hit-and-run death of Ravi Pinto and the murder of Anthony Glennister, but with the intervention and subsequent discovery that Clive Douglas is crooked, now I am not so confident of a quick result.

My meeting with him in 1994 has left me in no doubt as to what kind of man he is. I need to tread extremely carefully from now on, if I don't want to end up with my head caved in at the bottom of a flooded quarry – for real.

I drop the incline back down and increase the speed to eight miles an hour for the last mile.

I am already tired, but I push myself hard and by the time I finish and hit the stop button, the sweat is pouring off me and my heart is racing.

After three more minutes of a warm-down on the treadmill, I am so preoccupied with checking my stats on the machine that I don't notice the newcomers in the gym. In fact, I hear them before I see them.

"What the fuck is that smell, Mark? It smells like someone took a dump in their shorts, that's bloody rank!"

"Nah, Paul, I don't think it's shit, it's much worse than that. It smells like bacon, or maybe a sweaty pig. Yep, that's what it is, a sweaty fucking pig."

Donovan and the Fletcher brothers are using one of the multi-gyms, although none of them is wearing gym gear, and Paul and Mark are watching Terry, who is lying back and using the bench press.

I have been specifically warned to stay away from Paul Donovan, but it appears that the warning doesn't apply the other way around. They are obviously here to try to provoke a reaction from me, so for now I ignore them and continue my workout with some dumbbells, but I can see them in the mirror looking over at me and grinning.

When Mark and Terry burst out laughing as Paul starts loudly oinking, I can't ignore it anymore and I drop the dumbbells and walk over to them.

"Judging by the bellies on you boys, this must be the first time you have ever seen the inside of a gym. I guess it's not a coincidence that it's this one. You should all be careful, though; you could do yourself some serious damage at your age."

Terry sits up on the bench, and Paul and Mark self-consciously suck their bellies in and straighten themselves up, but clearly Paul thinks they are untouchable.

"It's Constable McDipshit, isn't it? What a nice surprise seeing you here. I was just telling my friends that there was a nasty smell in the air. I think it's shit, but Mark thinks it's the smell of a sweaty pig. Have you seen any sweaty pigs by any chance?"

Up close and pushing fifty, Donovan is far less intimidating than he was when I met him in 1994. Nonetheless, his sheer size still makes him a tough opponent to floor, and I am looking forward to doing just that sometime soon.

As soon as I get the opportunity I am going to knock the smile right off his face in the most public way possible, but for now I will toe the line and let him keep his teeth.

"Enjoy the moment, Paul, it won't last. Don't make the mistake of thinking that you are above the law. As soon as you slip up, I will be all over you like a cheap suit."

"Oooh, did you hear that, lads? PC Plod thinks he's a bit scary. Go back to your weights, McMillan, and get yourself some muscles. Me and the lads are just here for our work-out, and we don't appreciate you harassing us."

Before I can respond, my phone rings with an unknown number, but I recognize Maria's voice immediately, and she sounds terrified.

"DC McMillan, it's Maria Pinto, I'm sorry to call you, but you said I could call anytime. Someone has just thrown a brick through my window and my car has been vandalized."

"Maria, calm down and tell me exactly what happened. Have you called the police?"

"I haven't called anyone else yet. Is this connected to our talk today? I was in the kitchen and I saw a man run across my garden, then the brick came through. It only just missed me, and I think that he might still be outside."

By rights, I should send a squad car to her house, but I can't risk having other coppers involved until I know what, or who, I am dealing with.

“Okay, don’t call anyone else yet, just make sure that your doors are locked, and I will be there in fifteen minutes. Call me straight back if anything else happens.”

In all the excitement, I forgot about Donovan and crew, but as I grab my gym bag and head to the door, I am reminded by the new oinking sounds from Mark and Terry, and some final words from Paul.

“They say, ‘and pigs might fly.’ I didn’t know that they could drive, though. Drive safe, piggy, oink, oink.”

They didn’t come today just to provoke a reaction or to intimidate me. The bastards were here to make sure that they had an alibi for whatever has just gone down at Maria’s house. It must be connected to our visit to Maria this morning, and the only other person that knew about our visit was Donovan’s protector, Clive Douglas.

I doubt, though, that Douglas would lower himself to throwing bricks, and with the three stooges here in the gym, they must have somebody else doing the dirty work. It’s all the same to me – it has to be Douglas and Donovan behind this and once this is done, I am going to bury them both.

With the blue light on, I arrive at Maria’s house in just over ten minutes and it is not hard to spot which car is Maria’s.

All the tires on the yellow Ford Focus have been slashed, the front windscreen is shattered, and the word “Whore” has been spray-painted in big red letters down both sides.

Of more concern is that, despite my telling Maria to lock the doors, her front door is wide open and I can’t see any sign of her through the windows at the front of the house. So, as I step inside, I call out to her.

“I’m in the living room, DC Smith. Come inside, everything is okay.”

I don't know if she has made a mistake with my name, or is smart and giving me a warning, but before I go in, I pick up the newspaper in the hallway and tightly roll it up.

Maria is sitting on the sofa, but she is looking right past me like a rabbit caught in the headlights, so when he steps out from behind the door with the baseball bat it is not a total surprise.

"I'm so sorry, DC McMillan, I had no choice. I tried to warn you."

"Shut your mouth, bitch, and you, move away from the door and stand there and listen."

He is a hard-looking bastard, with close-cropped hair, a weather-beaten face and a distinctly Eastern European accent, and the absence of any kind of mask suggests that he is not bothered about being identified.

I move as he asks, but I have no intention of fully cooperating with a thug. "I take it that you know I'm a police officer and in two minutes there will be two squad cars outside?"

This guy is a not just a run-of-the-mill rent-a-thug; my threat doesn't bother him in the least. In fact, he smiles and moves closer to me, pointing the bat at my face.

"There's nobody else coming, Sean, it's just you, me, and the bitch, and unless they give British cops steel spines, then yours will snap just as easily as anyone else's.

"Now in case you don't know why I am here, it's to deliver a warning to her and to you. It's quite simple, the bitch keeps her mouth shut and doesn't speak to the cops again, or that pretty son of hers won't see another birthday. And to you, Sean, you drop the case you are working on, or the last thing this Paki whore will see is me gouging her eyes out with a spoon."

As he finishes speaking, he turns his head very slightly towards Maria to emphasize his point, but it is enough for me to make my move. I grab the baseball bat with my left hand and pull it downwards; then I smash the blunt end of the newspaper into the side of his head and he falls backwards and smacks his head against the wall.

Unfortunately, unlike my skinhead friends, this guy is made of stronger stuff. He still has hold of the bat and is quickly back up on his feet.

The first blow from the bat crashes into my right arm and the second gets me in my ribs. He follows these up with a huge punch that catches me a glancing blow on the back of my head, and I know that if I go down on the floor I won't stand a chance.

Confident that he has knocked the wind out of my sails, he drops the baseball bat onto the floor and grabs me by my shoulders, but before he can land his planned head butt, I smash my knee into his testicles as hard as I can, and he doubles over in pain. At the same time, Maria slams the bat into the back of his skull and his face slams against the coffee table as he goes down.

If I think he is done, though, I could not be more wrong. As I reach forward to pull him back, he spins around and puts his whole weight behind a punch that nearly breaks my nose.

When I come to, Maria is standing over me and holding a towel to my nose to stem the bleeding with one hand, whilst still firmly clutching the baseball bat in the other hand.

"Where did he go, Maria? Are you okay?"

"I'm fine. Thanks to you, he's gone, but don't worry about him for now. Just keep still for a minute until the bleeding stops. You were knocked out for a few seconds, so you might be a bit dizzy or have a concussion."

Despite what has just happened, her voice is calm and reassuring, and when she takes my hand and helps me to the sofa, the memory of our night together comes flooding back. I desperately want to hold her and keep her safe, but before I do anything foolish, she gets up and goes to the kitchen to make me a cup of tea, and I stand up to inspect the damage in the mirror.

My eye sockets are already starting to bruise up nicely. No doubt I will have two lovely black eyes in the morning, and the whole of my right arm and my side feels like a truck has hit me at sixty miles an hour.

"Don't worry, I am sure your good looks haven't been permanently damaged, Sean. Is it okay if I call you Sean?"

Maria has come back into the room and placed two cups of tea on the coffee table. As she sits down, she leans forward with a tea towel and wipes away a smear of blood from one of the corners, then makes a comment about being glad that it is his blood and not mine.

I sit down next to her and add two sugars to my tea, and then I take a drink and instantly feel a rush as the sugar hits my blood stream. "I think you have earned the right to call me whatever you want. You were quite handy with that baseball bat for a petite woman, Maria, thank you."

This comment gets me a smile, and I get the same feeling I got when I first saw Maria in the pub on 15th October, 1994.

"You didn't do too badly yourself, Sean. That thing you did with the newspaper reminds me of a guy from my past. Funnily enough he was also called Sean and he looked a lot like you."

This is the first time that she has made any kind of reference to my dream-self, and even though I know there is no hint of suspicion in the comment, I make light of it anyway.

"Maybe you met my dad. I look a lot like him."

Her face changes completely and it looks like I have upset her or brought back memories she would rather forget.

"I hope not, Sean. You seem like a decent guy. The Sean I knew was a bastard. He ran out on me when I needed him the most."

Just in case I wasn't feeling guilty enough before now, that comment has taken my guilt to the next level, but I can't let it show and I feign sympathy.

"I'm sorry, Maria. I didn't mean to upset you. What happened?"

"It's okay, it's just not often that I talk about him. I really didn't know him that well. I only saw him twice.

"We were in the King George together on the night of Anthony Glennister's murder, but he ran away before the police arrived. I thought he was very good looking and very charming, but he wasn't the man that I thought he was."

"There was no mention of anyone called Sean in the witness statements, Maria. Have you seen him since then?"

I know she hasn't, of course, but I want to know more about what she thinks of him, of me.

"No, I never saw or heard anything from him again. He told me that he was from Romford and I actually hired a private detective to try to find him, but they gave up looking after two months. It was like he had never existed."

This revelation about the private detective is a shock, and I am amazed that she would spend time and money just to get back at me for running out on her at the pub.

"Why were you looking for him, Maria? I can understand your being angry with him running out on you in the pub, but otherwise you barely knew him."

"I wasn't bothered about his running out on me in the pub. He was a coward for doing that, but I got over it.

Despite what I thought about him, I still felt that he had a right to know I was pregnant with his son. I don't care now, though. We have managed just fine without him."

If I thought the punch in my face was hard, this punch in my guts was even harder, and for a few seconds I am lost for words. I may be a detective, but at times I can't believe that I don't pick up on the obvious. I was so distracted by meeting Maria again this morning, that I had not picked up on Ben's age, or any possible link to myself.

As I sit here staring at the picture of Ben on the wall, the resemblance to me is striking and his skin tone makes it obvious that his parentage is mixed, so to say that I am in shock would be an understatement. Finding out I have a son just seven or eight years younger than myself is not what I was expecting.

"That must have been tough, Maria. He is a fine looking young man. What is he studying at university?"

"He is a fine young man, and a very smart one. He is in his final year of a degree in journalism."

I don't know why but hearing this makes me feel a whole lot better about everything. I am responsible for this whole situation, but despite all of the shit Maria has gone through, she has still managed to cope and Ben seems to be doing well.

I am still furious, though, about what happened earlier, and I now want to travel again tonight, but not to gather any more information for the investigation. This trip would be for personal reasons.

"Maria, I need to go, but I am going to ask Detective Constable Swain to stay here with you tonight, and I will arrange for a squad car to be outside and call for a carpenter to come and board up your window until we can get the glass replaced. Why don't you make us some more tea while I make the calls?"

While she is in the kitchen, I call Catherine and ask her to arrange the squad car and a carpenter to come, and then I call DCI Morgan to update him. By the time I hang up, the squad car has already arrived and a few minutes later Catherine arrives and walks into the living room.

“Bloody hell, Sean, does the other guy look as bad? You look like you have gone ten rounds with Mike Tyson.”

I take Catherine through the whole chain of events since leaving work today – Donovan and his cronies turning up at my gym, the call from Maria, my Eastern European friend and the fight before he escaped.

“It sounds like you were lucky. It could have been a lot worse if Maria hadn’t intervened when she did.”

“Yep, I honestly think he would have killed us both if she hadn’t been so handy with the bat.

“Cath, I need you to stay here tonight. There is something I need to do. The uniform boys outside will be replaced at eight tomorrow morning, and her son is on his way home and should be here by nine-thirty. I need you to do something else for me as well – arrange for a squad car to go to Carol Baker’s house. I don’t think Douglas or Donovan have made the connection yet, but I don’t want to risk leaving her unprotected.”

Catherine nods and she knows now not to ask too many questions. “I won’t ask what you need to do, but just be careful, Sean. These people are dangerous, and you are not bulletproof.”

On my way out, I say goodbye to Maria and reassure her that she is safe, and then I drive home with a clear plan in my head of what is going to happen next.

Because of his high profile, I find what I need quickly after just a few clicks on the internet. I save the picture to my hard drive and print it out in color.

I am so exhausted from my session in the gym and from the fight that I don't need any other kind of stimulant tonight, and as I lie down on my bed in my gym kit clutching Clive Douglas's picture in my hand, I know that sleep will come easily as I chant my way back to 1994.

## The Past – Saturday, 8th October, 1994

By the time I get to Clive's house in Luton it is nearly 4 pm on Saturday, 8th October, 1994. Whilst I am spot-on with the date, my location and timing are a bit out. I have landed in Feltham two hours earlier than intended.

Because I don't have enough money for a forty-mile cab ride, I am forced to catch the train and then walk the rest of the way from the station, so it is a huge relief when I see his car parked in the driveway of his house.

Unfortunately, the driveway and the road in front are also full of other cars and judging by the sounds coming from the house and his garden, it looks like he has visitors.

As before, I make my way to the alley behind his house, but this time to avoid the nosy neighbors I climb the fence and secrete myself in a hidden spot among the pine trees, with a clear view of the house and garden.

There is a BBQ in full swing and Clive is standing just outside his back door with a beer in hand talking to a woman who looks about the same age, so she could be his wife.

The rest of the guests look like they could be neighbors, or other friends and family, apart from the three guys next to the BBQ.

Terry is flipping the burgers and every now and then Paul or Mark make a comment about him not doing it right, but they are not so concerned that they want to take over, and they go straight back to drinking and leering at a group of teenage girls after each comment.

I had deliberately chosen a Saturday to increase the chances of Clive being at home, but I was obviously not expecting him to be having a BBQ in October, and I was certainly not expecting to see the three stooges here.

It is just my luck that the weather is amazing today. But it makes no real difference – I will just need to make a few changes to my plan. Having so many people in the house might even work in my favor.

I certainly have no intention of giving up, or waiting until everybody has left, and if I have to do things a little more publicly than originally anticipated, then so be it. So, after watching for a few more minutes, I drop down out of the tree and make my way to the front of the house again.

As I suspected, the front door is unlocked, and with confidence that the music from the back garden will mask any entry, I go inside to the kitchen and put the kettle on. Then I move away back towards the front of the house until I am sure that it has boiled.

Satisfied that I have waited long enough, I lock the front door from the inside and head back into the kitchen and out the back door to the patio area.

Donovan and the Fletcher boys are still by the BBQ but are more interested in the girls and don't give me a second look. Clive has moved further down the garden to chat with his guests.

I need to get his attention to lure him into the house, but I don't want to make it so obvious that I get anyone else's attention, so I help myself to a beer and slowly make my way down the garden, mingling with the other guests as if I belong.

As I get close to Douglas, I recognize his neighbor, Frank, so I assume that the woman he is talking to must be Frank's wife Janice.

I wonder what they would think if they knew that instead of handing me over to his colleagues for being a peeping tom, good old upstanding copper Clive had tortured me and bashed my skull in with a hammer, before tossing me into a flooded quarry to die.

I would like to think that they might think twice about reporting anything to him in the future, but in reality, people like Frank and Janice have an undying faith in the police and would probably see no wrong in Clive meting out his own form of justice if it meant getting a criminal off the street. No doubt when I do finally bring him down, they will happily sign a petition to have him released. By the same reasoning, they probably think that Donovan and his boys are just boisterous lads.

They are discussing a recent spate of vandalism in the area, and Clive is telling Janice and Frank how the immigrants and the coloreds are to blame.

"Ten years ago, you barely saw a black face around here, now look at it – they are bloody everywhere. Unfortunately, they don't have the same moral standards as us, and they bloody breed like cockroaches."

Both Frank and Janice are hanging on his every word and it is only when Clive takes a break from his rant that he notices me standing behind Janice.

As I turn and walk back to the house, I hear Clive asking them a question, "Who is that fella with the black eyes? I don't recognize him. Do you know who that is, Frank?"

I reach the kitchen again without any incident and I know that it won't be long before DS Douglas comes to investigate. Just to make sure, I stand at the window and stare down the garden towards him.

It is obviously bugging him that he doesn't know who I am, and he keeps looking towards me. Not wishing to be rude, he continues his conversation, until finally his curiosity gets the better of him and I see him heading back to the house, so I move away from the window and wait behind the door.

He comes into the kitchen but doesn't see me behind the door. He starts to walk to the front of the house until I slam the back door and lock it. I know that I only have a few minutes at most to do what I came for before someone tries to get into the kitchen, but I want to enjoy every minute of it.

Clive is a big guy, though, and he is used to getting respect, so I know I won't be able to intimidate him. As he turns around to face me, the look on his face tells me that I need to choose my words carefully.

"You had better have a bloody good explanation for coming here and for locking me in my own kitchen. Who the hell are you?"

"An old friend sent me. He asked me to deliver a present to you."

I am already reaching into my pocket as I speak, and in response, Clive reaches over and takes a carving knife out of one of the kitchen drawers.

"Go careful there, fella. Unless you have got a gun in your pocket, this knife will be in your heart before you ever get a blow on me."

It's not a gun in my pocket, but it is a Taser, and if my memory serves me well, we didn't really start using them widely until at least 2008, so Clive should have no idea what it is.

"Calm yourself down, Detective Sergeant Douglas, it's not a gun. I told you, an old friend asked me to bring you a present."

By his stance, I can tell he wants to take me down right here and now, but at the same time, he is curious and he can't take his eyes off the Taser in my right hand.

"What old friend? What are you on about, and what is that in your hand?"

"Just an old friend – do you want this or not?"

I raise my right arm so the Taser is pointing towards him, and as he reaches out to take it, I pull the trigger and the two wired barbs fly forward and easily pierce the flimsy cotton of his shirt and lodge in his chest.

In eight years of policing, I have only had to use my Taser on two occasions. Despite what you see on TV, or in the movies, a blast from one of these babies will take a man down instantly on nine out of ten occasions.

Douglas is no different and with a delivery of fifty thousand volts, he is completely powerless on the floor, and his body violently convulses as I keep my hand on the trigger for another few seconds to make sure he is no threat to me.

When I stop, he is on his side and still shaking, so I roll him onto his back and pull out the barbs, then I lean over him and slap his face a few times.

"Wake up, Clive, I need you to be awake for this next little surprise. You do like tea, don't you, Clive? Yes of course you do. I remember you making a nice hot cup for me."

He is barely aware of what is going on around him, but I can't wait around any longer. The woman who I think could be his wife has come looking for him and is trying the back door.

"Clive, are you in there? The door won't open. Paul dear, can you and the boys help me? I think the back door might be stuck and I can't see Clive anywhere."

The door handle is rattling like mad and as I stand over Clive with the kettle of boiling water, the face of Paul Donovan appears at the window and we stare right at each other.

"Smash the bloody door down, boys – there's a geezer in there standing over Clive with a fucking kettle."

My intention had been to make Douglas feel the same kind of pain that he had put me through, but in the end, my conscience won't allow me to burn his face or his balls. I reason that this would bring me down to his level. But he does need to feel some pain. Before his boys can get inside, I empty the contents of the kettle across his hands, and he screams out in agony as the steam and the smell of scalded flesh hits my nostrils.

With the kettle empty, I drop it and start to run for the front of the house just as the back-door crashes open, and Mark Fletcher runs in, closely followed by Donovan and Douglas's wife.

Mark is right behind me as I reach the front door. As I try to unlock it, he gets me in a headlock and tries to pull me down to the floor.

Before Donovan can catch up, I lift my right leg and thrust my running shoe downwards as hard as I can on Fletcher's shin, which is enough to make him cry out and release his grip on me to grab his injured leg, then I am out of the door a second later.

Standing just a few feet away from the front door are neighbor Frank and Terry Fletcher, but when they see Mark writhing around on the floor, Frank suddenly doesn't seem so brave and he moves to the side to let me pass.

Terry looks scared also, but when Donovan appears at the door and tells him to grab me, he doesn't have any other choice than to make a lunge for me. He doesn't even see it coming when my knee slams into his nuts and sends him sprawling onto the lawn.

From there I don't look back and keep on running until I am at least half a mile away. There is no way that Donovan will come looking for me on his own, and I doubt very much that Clive will be calling the police anyway.

More than likely, he will think that this was one of his crooked connections, or somebody he has stitched up sending him a message. Either way, he will not risk getting the police involved, or having too many questions asked.

Tonight has been a good night, and while it has added nothing to the case, it has made me feel a whole lot better about the attack on Maria's house. I just hope that my coming here tonight has not resulted in any significant changes to the future as a result of either Douglas or Donovan subsequently recognizing me on the night of the murder of Anthony Glennister.

Douglas got a good look at me in the kitchen, but Donovan only saw me very briefly at the kitchen window, and even if they do recognize me as the kettle guy when they catch me on 15th October , 1994, what more can they do to me?

Donovan already remembered that I was the guy at the scene of his hit-and-run in '93, and Douglas thought that I was there to blackmail them both, so now they will also have me for scalding Clive's hands.

The result will be the same. Ironically, by the time Clive is ready to pour the boiling water down the back of my neck, it will have been me that inspired him.

So, with that thought in my head, and eager to get home, I check that the Taser has enough remaining charge. Then I jam the prongs against the side of my neck and squeeze the trigger.

## Present Day – Tuesday, 13th February, 2018

When I wake up it is still dark. My first inclination is to call Catherine to check that everything is okay, but it is not even five in the morning yet, and if there had been any problems Cath would have tried to call me.

Not even Douglas would try anything else with a cop inside the house and a squad car outside, so I roll back over and sleep until my alarm goes off at six-thirty.

I want to catch up with Catherine and to check up on Maria before we head into work today, so after calling her, I am on the road and pulling up outside number 247 at just before seven-thirty.

By the time Catherine lets me in, Maria is already waiting in the living room with a cup of tea and a plate of hot buttered toast.

"Sorry, I don't have anything else in the house right now, Sean, neither of us are big eaters in the morning. But I made you some toast."

With everything that went on last night, I had forgotten about Ben, but when she mentions that neither of them are big eaters, I am reminded again that I have a university-aged son, and the butterflies in my stomach come back.

"Thanks, Maria, toast will be great. I don't normally have breakfast most days, but that looks good, thank you."

As I sit and eat my toast, we make some awkward small talk between the three of us, until Maria eventually excuses herself to go to the bathroom, and I get down to business with Cath.

"Did you manage to speak to her again last night about giving a new statement?"

The smile on Catherine's face answers my question and I can't help but let out a little 'fuck yeh' in my head as she confirms it.

"In the end, I didn't need to persuade her. Not after that thug attacked you and threatened to hurt Ben. When you left she was only too happy to cooperate. If we can get her into the station today without Douglas getting wind of it, we can then drag Terry back in, like you were planning to, and put the frighteners on him in return for his cooperation. We are so close, Sean."

She is right and I would love to put the champagne on ice now, but Douglas will be on us like a rat up a drainpipe if he gets even the slightest hint that we are moving to pull Donovan in.

If that does happen he will use everything at his disposal to stop us, and if his corruption runs as deep as I think it does, it will not bother him in the slightest if Catherine or I become collateral damage.

"Thanks, Cath. I called Morgan just before I got here, and he has given us a hall pass for today's briefing, but before we take Maria in, I just want to go in and check that Douglas is not hanging around with any nasty surprises for us."

"Actually, Sean, as soon as Maria agreed to cooperate, I called an old mate and pulled in a favor. He has agreed that we can take Maria into Leeson Street Station for the interview. I knew you would be worried about someone in our nick blabbing to Douglas and hopefully if he does come looking for us, the interview will be done by the time he tracks us down."

This is music to my ears and I could almost kiss her, but before I do, Maria comes back into the room and sits back down.

"Maria, Detective Constable Swain was just telling me that you are now willing to give a new statement about what happened on the night of 15$^{th}$ October, 1994 – is that correct?"

She looks scared and is hesitant to answer at first, so I am worried that she may have had a change of heart overnight, but then she nods and answers, “If I don’t speak up now, nobody else will and I know that after last night, they will never leave me and Ben alone.

“It was bad enough before, but I knew that I just had to stay quiet to stay safe. Now that they know I have been talking to the police, it is only a matter of time before they get to me, or to Ben. I just want it to be over now so that we can move on, but I need your assurance that they won’t be able to get to us.”

It is another one of those moments where I wish that I could believe my own assurances, but with Clive Douglas involved, I have my doubts. We can protect Maria, Ben, and Carol Baker from the Donovan gang, but Detective Superintendent Clive Douglas has shown already that he has a much wider network of goons and informers to rely on.

Without Maria, though, there is no progress, so I give my assurance as convincingly as possible. “Give us that statement, Maria, and within twenty-four hours, I promise you that Paul Donovan and the Fletchers will be off the street and you will have all the protection at our disposal until they are convicted.”

Maria acknowledges my assurance and I tell her to go and get changed. I also tell her that Ben should stay away from university today.

“It’s just a precaution, but I think we would all be much happier knowing that he is here with a police car outside. We have also arranged for another officer to remain with him while you are with us giving the statement.”

While she goes upstairs to shower and change, Catherine stays in the house and I go outside to let the guys in the squad car know what is happening, and to brief the guys on the shift change who are due to arrive in a few minutes.

When I go back inside the living room ten minutes later, Maria has already changed and is sitting down next to Catherine, but they are not alone.

Even after more than twenty years, the burn scars on his hands are still clearly visible and he smiles when he sees me come in.

"You really should close the door behind you, DC McMillan, particularly after such a nasty incident last night. You never know who might be lurking around. You look surprised to see me again. I seem to have a habit of surprising you, don't I?"

Once again, I am lost for words, and I don't know if he is here to kill us, to warn us off, or to simply sniff around again to find out what we are up to, but I have no intention of giving him anything.

"Sorry, yes, I am surprised to see you, sir. It's really nothing for you to be concerned over, though, just an aggravated burglary. It's all under control and we will be taking Ms. Pinto into the station soon to give her statement."

The bastard smiles again and then points to my face.

"Judging by the state of your face, he must have been a very aggravated burglar, or did you trip over your skipping rope in the gym?"

The asshole is letting me know that he is on to me. Cath obviously knows what is going on, but Maria has no idea.

"He was trying to defend me, that thug was threatening me and my son."

Douglas puts his hand on Maria's hand and squeezes it. "Don't you worry about him, Maria. You must be a very special case to have two detectives and a police car watching over you. It's highly unusual to be given this kind of protection over a simple burglary, isn't that right, DC McMillan? Maybe, though, it's not just because of a burglary – what do you think, DC Swain?"

I go to answer for her, but he quickly shuts me up. "I was asking for DC Swain's opinion, not yours. DC Swain, do you normally provide this level of protection for a burglary victim?"

"It's not normal procedure, sir, but in this case and given that Ms. Pinto is connected to an ongoing investigation, we were worried that this break-in might have been connected. We had approval from DCI Morgan for the squad car outside and as for myself and DC McMillan, we were happy to stay overnight with the victim."

Douglas is on his feet and putting his coat on and I can't help staring at his hands again.

"Well, if DCI Morgan said it was okay, then it must be okay. As long as everybody is okay, that's the important thing. Don't let me keep you any longer from catching this burglar, he sounds like a vicious bastard. Oh, and DC McMillan, that suit looks very well pressed for someone that spent the night on the sofa – just saying. Have a good day."

As soon as he is gone, I tell Maria to get ready to leave.

"One of our colleagues will be here soon and will stay in the house with Ben. Go and let Ben know we are leaving and that you will be back in a few hours."

She heads upstairs to speak to Ben and I turn to Catherine.

"It's like he has a bloody tracker on me. Somebody in the station is feeding him information, Cath, and God help them if I find out who it is."

Catherine agrees, but also offers an alternative theory. "Either that, or he is just a bloody good copper. You don't get to where he is without being able to find things out."

"Maybe, Cath, but we still need to be careful who we confide in, including the rest of our own team. Go and get Maria – we need to get a move on before he comes looking for us and figures out that we are not at Blackwell Station."

Twenty minutes later, we pull into the carpark of Leeson Street Station, but straightaway I know that something is wrong. There is a welcoming committee waiting to meet us.

"What the hell is going on, Cath? What's with the delegation? Who is that sergeant?"

Cath tells me to wait in the car.

"Just hold on there, Sean. That's Rob Brydon. He was my training sergeant during my probationary period. Let me go and find out what's going on."

They chat for nearly five minutes and it is obvious from the body language that we are not welcome here, and when Cath gets back in the car, I am eager to know what is happening.

"What's the problem, Cath? I thought we were good to go."

"I'm sorry, Sean. Last night Brydon told me that everything was okay, but it seems somebody has got wind of what we were up to and we have been ordered back to Blackwell."

I am absolutely furious at this news, and now I am convinced more than ever that someone on our own team is working against us.

"What do you mean we have been ordered back to Blackwell? Douglas doesn't have that kind of authority over us. I'm not going anywhere until I have spoken with Morgan."

Cath pushes down my phone and stops me from making the call.

"Sean, it wasn't Douglas that gave the instruction, it was DCI Morgan, and if we want to see him before the morning briefing to find out what is going on, we had better get a move on."

Seriously, this case is on a knife edge and the next twenty-four hours are make-or-break for it. I can't believe that even my own boss seems to be deliberately obstructing me.

We make the drive back to Blackwell in complete silence. Once we are in the reception area, I tell Cath to take Maria to one of the interview rooms.

"Cath, you stay with her and don't let her out of your sight. I'm going to try to grab a few minutes with Morgan to get to the bottom of this. Call me immediately if you see Douglas sniffing around."

When I get to Morgan's office, it is just a few minutes before nine and he is gathering his files for the morning briefing.

"Sean, good morning, sorry about dragging you back here, but I had my reasons, of course."

I have been rehearsing what I was going to say to him on the way here, but my well-rehearsed speech is gone and I release my pent-up frustration.

"I would really love to know those reasons, sir. A neutral station was arranged for the safety of the witness and for the safety of this investigation – pulling us back here is putting us all at risk. Somebody is deliberately sabotaging this investigation and also most likely feeding information to Detective Superintendent Douglas – sir."

Kevin Morgan is well known for never losing his composure and despite this outburst from a junior officer, today is no exception. He closes the door and sits down behind his desk, then gestures for me to do the same.

"Do you feel better for that, DC McMillan? I brought you back here because of exactly the same reasons. I happen to agree with you. I think someone is feeding information to DS Douglas. I can maybe understand the initial intervention with Donovan, but it makes absolutely no sense that he is still hanging around.

"When you called me this morning to excuse yourself from the morning briefing, Douglas was here again in my office, asking if I would mind if he attended today's briefing. A few minutes later, he took a call and couldn't get out of here quickly enough. I take it from that look on your face that you had a visitor?"

"Yes, sir, DS Douglas showed up at Maria Pinto's house this morning. He was asking questions about why the squad car was outside and why we were making such a fuss over a burglary."

Morgan picks up his files and gets up to leave.

"If I were you," he advises me, "I would get moving on that interview. I have requested a trace on the call to DS Douglas's phone this morning, but until I have that, don't trust anyone, Sean. I suspect that our friend is already on his way back here, and there will be only so long that I can hold him for."

On my way back down to the interview suites, my mind is in turmoil. Despite my earlier concerns about Morgan, it is obvious that he is working in the best interests of the case and still has our backs. It must be one of the uniformed guys or another member of the team that is ratting us out to Douglas.

Whoever it is, I don't have time to worry about them now. We probably have thirty minutes at the most before Douglas is here with his nose in the trough again.

Catherine is waiting outside the room and is keen for an update, but I tell her we need to get started.

"It's all good, Cath. We need to get moving, though, before Douglas realizes where we are. Is she ready?"

Cath nods and we take our seats in the interview room, where Maria is nervously toying with a cup of coffee.

"Is everything okay, DC McMillan? Why did we have to leave the other police station?"

"Everything is okay, Maria, just a misunderstanding, that's all. Before we start the interview, I need to ask you if you would like anyone else to be present. It can be a friend or your lawyer if you have one, or if you don't have a lawyer, we can call the duty solicitor for you. Would you like somebody to be present, Maria?"

She hesitates for a few seconds as she thinks over the question, then she shocks me by requesting the duty solicitor.

I had not been expecting this. To get one of the duty solicitors this early in the morning is going to set us back at least an hour.

"Maria, are you sure about this? It is of course your right to have a solicitor present, but this is a routine interview and you are not being accused of anything."

"Yes, I think I should. Catherine told me that I should have someone to represent me, just in case anything changes."

This second shock is bigger than the first one.

"Okay, give me a few minutes to arrange it for you, Maria. DC Swain, please join me outside." And I excuse us from the room.

Before I can speak, Catherine starts first.

"Before you go off on one, Sean, I was going to tell you before we went inside, but you didn't give me the chance to speak. Things are moving so fast now that we can't afford to mess up. If we go in there and take a new statement from Maria without her having a solicitor present, any good brief will rip us to shreds in court.

"Donovan's brief will be shouting about police intimidation from the highest mountains and will pull in favors from his pals in the gutter press. You were so angry in the car on the way over here that it fell to me to be the rational one."

Once again, she is absolutely right, but it doesn't make me any happier.

"Shit, shit, shit, okay I know you're right, Cath, see if you can get someone here as quickly as possible. That bastard Douglas could already be on his way by now."

For the next hour, I am like a cat on a hot tin roof and every time that the door at the end of the corridor opens, I expect it to be Douglas coming to haunt me again.

Eventually, though, the duty solicitor arrives at ten past ten, and thankfully it is one of our regulars, Jean Monroe.

Jean is in her mid-fifties, and I have always respected the way in which she handles her cases. She is one of the rare breed of solicitors that actually knows when to advise her clients to cooperate when clearly the evidence is stacked against them, rather than continuing to allow them to dig a hole for themselves.

After a few pleasantries, Cath gives her a quick brief on the case, then leaves her inside the interview room for ten minutes to confer with Maria before the start of the interview.

"Something's not right, Cath."

"What do you mean, Sean?"

"It's nearly ten-thirty and no sign of Douglas yet. There is no way he doesn't know where we are by now."

Cath smiles and puts her hand on my shoulder, saying, "Ignore him, Sean. Anyone would think you are missing him.

Come on, let's go in and get started. I think they have had long enough."

Today, I am going to lead the interview of Maria, but before Catherine starts the tape I ask her if she has had enough time to confer with her solicitor, and if she is comfortable with us proceeding.

"Yes, I have, and yes, I am, thank you."

Catherine starts the tape and I proceed with the formalities.

"This interview is being recorded and for the benefit of the tape, the time now is 10.37 am and the date is Tuesday, 13th February, 2018. Present in the room are Detective Constable Sean McMillan, Detective Constable Catherine Swain, Ms. Maria Pinto, and Duty Solicitor Ms. Jean Monroe.

"Maria, before we start, I would like to tell you that you are not under investigation yourself, and you are free to leave at any time. The purpose of this interview is to ask you some questions about a statement you made on 15th October, 1994, in connection to a fatal stabbing that took place in the King George Public House in Feltham. Do you remember making that statement, Maria?"

Surprisingly, instead of looking scared, she looks defiant, like she wants to offload a quarter century of guilt.

"Yes, I remember it; I remember it like it was yesterday. It's not something I could ever forget."

With this attitude, the interview won't take long and we will soon be in a position to pull Terry Fletcher in for questioning.

"Thank you, Maria, now please think carefully about my next question. When you gave your original statement, was it completely accurate? You stated that Anthony Glennister was stabbed by an as yet unidentified black male – is that what happened, Maria?"

If there is any doubt in her mind about cooperating with us, this is the time for her to pull out. But after a brief discussion with Jean Monroe, she turns back to me with the same determination on her face.

"My original statement was incorrect – that is not what happened, I would like to give a new statement and to set things straight."

Before she can say anything else, Jean Monroe interrupts her and addresses us, "For the benefit of the tape, my client has advised me of her willingness to give a new statement, but I would like it to be noted at this time that her original statement was given under duress. I would further like it to be noted that she has also been the victim of continued harassment and intimidation from the night in question up to and including the present."

I nod and for the benefit of the tape, I confirm that the comments are noted and then I proceed with the interview.

From then on, it moves at a rapid pace. Maria describes the murder of Anthony Glennister and the subsequent threats exactly as I remember them, but she also provides a whole lot more detail on Paul Donovan's biannual reminders.

Her description of his home visits and veiled threats match exactly the statement given by Carol Baker, and my confidence in nailing him is right up there again.

By 11.20, I have everything I need and I end the interview, but I ask Maria and Jean Monroe to wait in the room for a few more minutes.

Outside the room, I share the next steps with Catherine.

"I need to brief Morgan again and get his permission to bring Terry Fletcher in. I really think we can end this today. I want you to take Maria home, though, and then get straight back here for the interview. If I need to, I will send uniform to drag him here by his balls.

"I'm going to ask Jean to wait around as well. With any luck, by the time that Donovan, Douglas, or bloody Desmond Carter get wind of this, he will already have coughed."

Catherine heads away with Maria, and I speak briefly to Jean, who agrees to wait around for a couple of hours but reminds me that her bill will be coming to the station. She then heads off to the canteen for an early lunch.

Before going to find DCI Morgan, I head upstairs to collect the two case files from my office. On my way in, I am surprised to bump into him on his way out.

"Sean, I was just looking for you. I thought you might already have been finished with Maria Pinto."

"Actually, sir, we have just finished. I was hoping to update you – and to get your permission to pull Terry Fletcher in."

I hadn't noticed at first, but he is looking flustered and doesn't seem interested in finding out about Maria's interview. "Sean, there has been an attack on Carol Baker's house. She is alive, but only just."

"What do you mean an attack? What happened, sir? We had a car outside her house."

On the way to his office, we continue talking and he shares everything he knows.

"At around five this morning, some bastard poured petrol through her letter box. Thankfully, the fire was spotted by one of the neighbors, and they were able to get Carol out before it was able to fully take hold. She took in a lot of smoke, though, and has some pretty bad burns on her arms and legs, so they are holding her in Queen Anne's hospital for observation, with two of our officers on the door."

"I don't understand, sir. Where was our squad car? Why the hell didn't they see what was happening?"

The answer to my question is obvious, but it is still a blow when he confirms it.

"They didn't see anything, Sean, because they weren't there. According to them they were ordered to stand down at 4 am, about an hour before we think the fire was started."

"Ordered by whom, sir?"

"Well, according to PC Bates, he was the one that took the call and it is noted in his log that DS Sarah Gray called him at 4.02 am this morning with specific instructions to stand down and return to base."

This makes no sense to me.

"So, DS Gray is working with Douglas?"

"Sean, I have told you before about curbing the emotion and engaging the brain. I haven't spoken to Sarah Gray yet, but do you really think she is that stupid? DS Gray knows as well as any of us that the call would have been noted in the vehicle log. I have already run another trace on the number, and I will not be surprised at all if this number is the same one that has been used to call DS Douglas."

I need to find this guy, and to update Morgan about Maria's new statement, but first I need to warn Catherine and Maria.

"Excuse me, sir, I need to call DC Swain and let her know what has happened – she is taking Maria Pinto home."

Morgan nods and tells me to go ahead. I pull Catherine's number up in my contacts and call her, but it just rings out and I start to panic.

"Shit, no answer!"

Morgan tells me to calm down and try again, and after it rings twice she answers, "Sean, what's up? We just arrived."

Relieved to hear her voice, I take a deep breath before speaking, "Cath, is the squad car there?"

"Yes, of course it is, it's right outside, what's going on, Sean?"

"I can't explain now, just go in and check that Ben is okay, and then get back here as soon as you can – and bring Maria with you."

I am obviously not making any sense to her and it is no surprise when she questions me, "Bring her back? What for? What am I supposed to tell her?"

"Tell her whatever you need to, Cath, just check on Ben and then get back here. I don't have time to explain right now."

Reluctantly she agrees and I hang up and turn back to Morgan.

"If it's okay with you, sir, I want to keep Maria Pinto here today in protective custody. We can keep her in one of the holding cells for now."

Morgan agrees that it is a wise move, and then he asks me about Maria's interview.

"I take it that before I pissed on your chips with the bad news about Carol Baker, you were on your way with some exciting news for me?"

"Yes, sir, Maria Pinto has completely changed her statement, and has now firmly implicated Paul Donovan for the murder of Anthony Glennister, and for a continued campaign of harassment and intimidation against her and the other witnesses. It's exactly what I suspected all along, but the big surprise is that it appears Mark and Terry Fletcher actually tried to intervene on the night to stop Donovan."

I knew this already, because I saw it myself, but I emphasize the point again for Morgan's benefit.

"Sir, Terry Fletcher has always been the weak link of the trio, but with this new information, I am convinced that I can turn him against Paul Donovan. I don't think he would rat out his brother for anything, but it makes no sense for him to take the rap for a murder that he tried to stop."

Morgan is clearly running the scenarios through his head, and he asks me to pass him a copy of Maria's new statement. He spends the next ten minutes reading through it in silence.

I am conscious that the day is slipping away from me, and there is only so long that I will be able to keep Maria here, but I don't want to interrupt him.

When he does finally look up from the statement, it could go either way. But when he nods approval, I know it is good news.

"Good work, Sean, if we can get her on the witness stand, we have a better-than-average chance of a conviction. Better than average is not good enough, though. If you can get one of his buddies to say the same, then I would say our chances will have increased to much better than average. Go ahead and pull Terry in."

This is like music to my ears and after thanking him, I head downstairs to speak to the custody sergeant, who agrees to send a car out to find Terry.

"Thanks, Mike – this is the address of the builders yard where he works, and this is his home address. Call me, please, as soon as you have him back here."

Catherine is already waiting outside the interview suites when I go back down, and she looks frustrated and extremely pissed off.

"Well, what's going on? Do we need to question her again? I can't keep her shut up in there forever, Sean."

"Not forever, Cath, but for today at least. We need to put her into one of the holding cells for her own protection."

I explain to her about the attack on Carol Baker's house, my discussion with DCI Morgan, and his agreement for me to pull in Terry.

"There is a rat in the office, Cath. These bastards know our every move. We can't risk losing Maria, and they have already shown us they are prepared to kill to keep our witnesses from talking."

She looks stunned and is momentarily lost for words.

"Jesus Christ, Sean, what the hell kind of hornet's nest have we stirred up?"

"I don't know, Cath, but it looks like a bloody big one. Uniform are out tracking Terry down for me, but for now I need you to speak to Maria and get her into a holding cell.

"Ben will be safe enough at home, but we need to keep her here as long as we can. Tell her whatever you need to – just get her in there, and then arrange to get her something to eat and drink."

I leave Catherine to deal with Maria, and then I head to the canteen to grab a sandwich and a coke, as it's now nearly 1 pm and the piece of toast at Maria's house this morning seems like a lifetime ago.

Jean Monroe is at one of the tables, working on her laptop, and I ask her if one of the chairs is free. "Do you mind if I join you, Jean?"

Jean is a studious looking woman with wire-rimmed glasses and greying blonde hair, but despite knowing her professionally for nearly two years, I have no idea if she is married or has family, and she is not the kind of woman that is likely to tell me anyway.

Her manner is always professional and polite, but as far as anything else goes, her private life is just that, private.

"Please, you're most welcome to sit down, DC McMillan, as long as you are not here to coerce me into leading a witness or anything else along those lines?"

This is the first time I have ever heard her say anything even remotely humorous.

"Nope, just here for my sandwich," I say with a laugh. "I didn't want to appear rude by sitting at another table." And I open my sandwich.

She looks up again from her laptop and smiles.

"That's okay then, and talking of being rude, how much longer do you think you will be needing me? My clock is ticking, and I will also be charging you for the incinerated lasagna you serve up in this place."

Wow, now sarcasm, if she was twenty years younger, she would be my kind of woman. She is right about the lasagna, though. The chef we have is not exactly Michelin-star standard. In fact, rumor has it that he is an ex-con out for revenge on the police by way of god-awful canteen food.

"Yep, sorry about that, I should have warned you. I always tend to go for something prepacked myself. Hopefully, you won't have to wait much longer."

I finish my sandwich and leave her to her work, heading back down to speak to the custody sergeant again.

"Any progress in finding my client, Mike?"

"With any luck, they should be dragging him through the door in a few minutes. He was at the builders yard and obviously wasn't too pleased at being asked to come in. There was a bit of a scuffle with his mates, and one of the boys was forced to discharge a couple of squirts of CS gas to clear a path to the car."

Hopefully, it was Donovan that got the brunt of it, and hopefully the fat fuck will still be feeling the effects when I pull him in, but can I really be that lucky?

"That's great news, Mike, thanks, I owe you one."

Catherine is nowhere to be seen near the interview suites, so I assume she must be in the office and I call and ask her to collect Jean from the canteen.

"The boys in blue are on the way in with Terry. Put Jean into interview suite two and then come and meet me in reception."

When I get back to reception, I am just in time to see Terry being dragged through the door and up to the counter. Judging from how red his eyes are, it looks like he got the gas and is not best pleased.

"Get your hands off me, you pair of twats. Get these bloody cuffs off me. You've got no right dragging me here like this or squirting gas in my eyes. I'm gonna have you for assault. I want my solicitor here right now."

The normal procedure is to process any prisoner through the front desk before interview, but technically Terry is not under arrest, and as soon as he sees me, he calms down slightly.

"I might have bloody known that you were behind this. You're wasting your time, mate, same as last time. I ain't saying shit about anything."

I nod to Mike and he tells the two constables to take Terry into interview suite one. I follow behind with Catherine, who has now joined me.

"Sit down, Terry."

"Piss off, copper, my bloody eyes are burning."

I push a bottle of water and a box of tissues across the table and tell him to sit down again.

"Listen to me, Terry, the sooner you sit down, the sooner you can get out of here."

He pours some cold water onto a bunch of tissues and swabs both of his eyes.

"I want my brief here, Desmond Carter. You know his bloody number. Do yourself a favor and call him. Until then I ain't saying naff all."

I know I am treading a fine line legally, but I am running out of options, so I just go for it.

"No problem, Terry. If you want Desmond Carter, we can call him, but I happen to know that you and Mark tried to stop Paul Donovan from knifing Glennister. We have a witness that will swear to it. You and Mark are both going to go down with Donovan for murder if you don't start wising up."

He is flustered enough now to drop the tissues and forget about his eyes.

"You're lying, McMillan. There ain't no bloody witness, piss off, I told you I wasn't going to speak to you. Get my bloody brief."

"Desmond Carter is only interested in saving Paul Donovan's ass, Terry. Come on, wake the hell up! You're just Paul's whipping boy. Cooperate and tell us the truth and I will personally make sure that you never do a single day of jail time. Carry on lying and I will make sure that they lock you away for life in the biggest hellhole in Britain."

The realization that I might be right is starting to occur to him. He has the same look as he had when Paul slapped him in the King George.

"I want my brief. You can't keep me here like this."

Turning to Cath, he appeals to her, "Tell him to stop."

Cath shrugs her shoulders and I carry on pushing him.

"Paul and Mark have played you for a fool your whole life, Terry. They don't give a shit about you. If they were sitting where you are now, they would have sold you down the river already. Think about it, do you really want to spend the rest of your life in prison? It won't be a nice cozy cell for the three of you. I will make sure that you get classified as a vulnerable prisoner and get sent somewhere on your own.

"The only problem with that, though, is the other prisoners tend to think of the vulnerable prisoners as easy prey. You might like that, Terry – a nice big lad to look after you. I'm sure it won't hurt so much after the first few times."

"Fuck off, no, you can't do that. You shouldn't be saying that."

He is nearly in tears, and I know that I have pushed him far enough, and can now pull back to being the good cop.

"Terry, we're the police, we can do whatever we want, but we know that you tried to help Anthony Glennister, and we know that your brother also tried to help him. We don't want to put either of you in prison for something that you didn't do. But if you don't help us, that's exactly what's going to happen. My boss has already given me his approval to have you arrested and transferred to prison. Once you are inside, we can't help you. Let us help you, Terry."

The tears are welling up in the corners of his eyes. He can't speak or doesn't know what to say.

"There is a duty solicitor in the room next door, Terry. She is a good woman, and she will make sure that you are legally protected.

"Let me bring her in to represent you and you have my word that if you tell us the truth about what happened on that night, I will arrange for full immunity from prosecution, for you and for Mark."

He doesn't answer, but he nods and wipes his eyes, and I leave the room to bring Jean Monroe in.

After bringing her up to speed on the case, we go outside to leave her alone with Terry for a few minutes, and Cath leaves me in no doubt as to her feelings.

"You were skating on bloody thin ice in there, Sean. If anyone ever found out what we have just done, we will be off the force in no time. For God's sake, you basically told him that you were going to arrange for him to be sodomized for the rest of his life."

If it weren't so serious, I could have found that funny, but I know how far off the legal path I have gone, and if he hadn't agreed to cooperate, we could have been up to our necks in shit by now.

"I didn't exactly say that, Cath. My intention was more to do with painting a picture in his head. It seemed to work, though, now let's get back in there and make it official before Desmond Carter and the rest of the cavalry turn up."

Once we are back inside the interview suite, both Terry Fletcher and Jean Monroe confirm that they are ready to begin and Catherine starts the tape and leads off with the formalities.

"This interview is being recorded, and for the benefit of the tape, the time now is 2.11 pm and the date is Tuesday, 13th February, 2018. Present in the room are Detective Constable Sean McMillan, Detective Constable Catherine Swain, Mr. Terence Fletcher and Duty Solicitor Ms. Jean Monroe.

"Terry, before we start the interview, I would like to tell you that you are currently not under arrest and you are not under investigation yourself. However, depending on the answers you give to our questions, this may change. Do you understand?"

He looks terrified, but he nods and mumbles a confirmation.

"Thank you, Terry, the purpose of this interview is to ask you some questions about a witness statement you made on 15th October, 1994, a subsequent interview you gave following your arrest on 18th October, 1994, and most recently the interview on 29th January, 2018. The witness statement and the interviews were in connection to a fatal stabbing that took place in the King George Public House in Feltham on Saturday, 15th October, 1994. Do you remember the incident and the statements that you made, Terry?"

"Yes, of course I remember, but I didn't kill him and neither did my brother – we tried to help him."

Wow, I am over the moon that he is going to cooperate, as I had expected to have to coax it out of him carefully. Instead, it sounds like he can't wait to spill his guts. We need to do this properly, though, and Cath does her best to keep him on track.

"Okay, thank you. Please, though, try to restrict yourself to just answering the question. Can you please tell me why you were in the King George Pub on that evening?"

"The pool tournament, you already know that. We were up against the Three Crowns."

"Who is 'we'? Who else were you with, Terry?"

He hesitates to answer and looks to Jean for support.

"Mr. Fletcher, you don't need to answer any questions that you are uncomfortable with, but I would advise against this course of action. It is in your own best interests to cooperate and answer the questions."

"My brother Mark, and Paul was there as well. He was the team captain. It should have been Mark, though – he is a much better player than Paul."

"Do you mean Paul Donovan?"

"Yes, Paul Donovan, he is my boss as well. He owns the builders yard where I work."

I am about to take over from Cath and ask a question, but we are disturbed by a knock on the door and Mike Bolton, the Custody Sergeant, comes in and hands me a post-it note, then leaves.

Catherine makes a comment for the tape to record his arrival, handover of the note, and his departure, and then I pass her the note and continue on while she reads it.

Desmond Carter is in reception kicking up a stink and demanding to see the Chief Constable. Not sure how long I can delay him.

Realizing time is running out, I take a risk and decide to push hard. "Terry, what happened after the tournament? Your statement talks about a fight between a black guy and Anthony Glennister. That's not true is it? What really happened? There wasn't any black guy, was there, Terry? It was Paul Donovan that started the fight and killed Paul, wasn't it?"

Jean leans towards Terry and tells him not to answer, and then addresses me, "DC McMillan, based on the interview on 29$^{th}$ January, I will overlook the fact that you have moved right along to the murder today without adequately setting the scene. However, I must ask you to refrain from trying to put words into the mouth of my client. I suggest you stick to asking non-leading questions."

Suitably chastised by Jean, I nod and ask again, "Terry, please, tell us about the fight."

"Me and Mark had nothing to do with it. It was all his fault. He's a bloody head case. He always has been."

"Who are you referring to, Terry, who is the head case?"

He looks at me like I'm the stupid one.

"I already said, didn't I? It was Paul Donovan."

My heart is racing. Given that Terry is a long-time friend and employee of Donovan's, his testimony is far more valuable then Maria's, but Carter could burst in at any minute and break up the party.

"What exactly happened? Please try to remember how the fight started and how Anthony Glennister died. I need you to be 100 percent sure of what you tell me, Terry."

The tears are beginning to well in the corners of his eyes again and Jean puts her arm around his shoulders and tells him to take a deep breath and think about his answer.

"You said that you can make sure that me and Mark don't get into trouble, is that true?"

"Yes, it is, Terry. If you fully cooperate today and tell us the truth about what happened, my superior officer has already agreed that no charges will be brought against you, or your brother in relation to this case."

This seems to satisfy him, and Jean nods her approval for him to continue.

"Okay then, by the end of the last game Paul was off his skull, and specky, sorry I mean Anthony Glennister, was creaming him. I thought Paul was just trying to put him off his shot, but when he put the black down, Paul went fucking berserk and smashed him over the head with his pool cue.

"We tried to stop him but he went bloody mental and put us both down on the floor. By the time I got up again, he had knifed the poor bastard."

"There was no need for it. He wasn't fighting back. After the smack on his head he had no idea what day it was. Paul was like a …"

Before he can finish the sentence, we are disturbed by a commotion in the corridor outside, and no prizes for guessing who it is. Morgan is obviously doing his best to placate him, but Desmond Carter is not a happy man, and is demanding to be let into the interview room, and whilst Terry is a bit slow, he immediately recognizes the voice.

"Is that Desmond Carter out there? What's going on, should we stop and let him in? He is my brief."

Jean Monroe throws me a disapproving look, but before she can say anything, I carry on.

"Terry, we are nearly finished. You just told us that it was Paul Donovan who stabbed Anthony Glennister, is that true? Did Paul Donovan start a fight with Anthony Glennister and kill him?"

Outside the room, the voices are getting louder and somebody tries to open the door, but it is quickly pulled shut again. It is enough to distract Terry, though, and I bang my right hand down on the table to get his attention again.

"Terry, did Paul Donovan start a fight with Anthony Glennister and kill him?"

"What? Sorry, I think I should wait to speak to Mr. Carter."

"Terry, remember what I told you earlier about Desmond Carter and about prison. Answer the question – did Paul Donovan start a fight with Anthony Glennister and kill him?"

This is a step too far over the line for Jean and she objects to my line of questioning.

"DC McMillan, any conversation you have had with my client before the start of this interview is completely inadmissible, and if I find out that you have been scaring my client with prison stories, I will be filing a formal complaint."

I am so close. I just need him to answer this one question, but I am running out of time.

"Terry, look at me and concentrate – did Paul Donovan start a fight with Anthony Glennister, and did he kill him?"

Jean stops him again.

"DC McMillan, please suspend the interview to allow me to speak with my client in private."

"The interview can be suspended as soon as your client answers the question: did Paul Donovan start a fight with Anthony Glennister, and did he kill him? Answer the question Terry, did he kill him?"

"DC McMillan, DC Swain, I insist that you stop the tape immediately and suspend this interview."

Catherine looks towards me for guidance, but I am determined to carry on.

"Not until he answers the question, Ms. Monroe. Terry, we know that Paul Donovan killed Anthony Glennister, don't go down for him. Answer my question, did Paul Donovan stab and kill Anthony Glennister?"

"Yes, he killed him. He smashed his head in with a pool cue, and then he stabbed him. I tried to help hi …"

At that moment, the door opens and DCI Morgan comes in with Desmond Carter, who is almost hyperventilating with anger, but Morgan stops him from talking and gives his own instruction.

"DC McMillan, DC Swain, this interview is terminated, please stop the tape."

We have everything we need anyway, so I am not too concerned about any kind of dressing down from Morgan, or the rant that I know is coming from Carter, and I indicate for Catherine to end the interview and stop the tape.

As soon as she does, Carter launches into us.

"This is an absolute outrage! I will be making an official complaint to the Chief Constable for unlawful arrest, unlawful use of force, harassment and anything else I can think of. You are both a disgrace to the force and I shall be strongly pushing for your suspension and dismissal."

Morgan moves in to calm him down, but he is far from finished and insists on speaking.

"Whatever you think you have here, think again, ladies and gentlemen."

As soon as he says this, I can't keep quiet and I stand up to defend us.

"Mr. Carter, what we have is a recorded interview with Terence Fletcher where he confirms that Paul Donovan assaulted Anthony Glennister with a pool cue and then stabbed him to death. That's what we have, so I suggest you now put your energies into a defense for Paul Donovan – he is going to need it."

If I was expecting for this to faze him, it doesn't. In fact, it seems to have the opposite effect. He smiles, then tells me to sit back down.

"I really think that you should, DC McMillan, I am about to give you a lesson in law, and I don't think you are going to enjoy it."

The smug bastard really needs to have the smirk wiped off his face, but I have no idea what kind of shit the slippery bastard has got up his sleeve. I know, though, that it's not going to be good.

"Did you know that Terence Fletcher is officially classified as having learning disabilities? No, I don't suppose you do. If you had known, you probably wouldn't have dragged him in here in such an unprofessional manner. In the old days, we didn't call it learning disabilities, or special needs, did we?

"Back then, people like Terry would have been called a spastic, or a mong, or a flid, but thank God for the PC Brigade.

"Because of them, people like Terry, people with learning disabilities that is, well, they have rights now. Do you want to know what one of those rights is, DC McMillan? You probably don't, but I'm going to tell you anyway. They have the right to be accompanied and represented by an appropriate adult when they are being interviewed, and for clarity, that appropriate adult must not work for the police, and they must have experience working with people with learning disabilities.

"Now correct me if I am wrong, but I don't believe that Ms. Monroe has any such experience, and whilst she is not a direct employee of the police, she is employed on a retained contract as an on-call duty solicitor.

"I, on the other hand, have no such connection with the police, and I have been representing Mr. Fletcher for more than thirty years, so I am perfectly aware of his particular needs and the way in which I can best support him. Do you see where I am going with this, DC McMillan?"

I can barely contain my anger. My case is falling apart again, and this crooked fuck is loving every minute of it. But thankfully and before I say something that might make things worse, Morgan answers on my behalf.

"I think we should all take time out, Mr. Carter. Your point has been made and we won't be detaining Mr. Fletcher any longer. I suggest that you address any complaint to me in the first instance, and I will investigate and take action if any of my officers have breached procedure."

Carter has been looking at me the whole time, but he now turns towards Morgan to respond.

"Not just breach of procedure, DCI Morgan, I am talking about deliberate and willful breaking of the law and breaching of Mr. Fletcher's human rights."

Morgan is keen to get him out and he puts his arm on his back and says gently, "Okay, thank you Mr. Carter. As I said before, your point has been made. I suggest that we finish now."

"Okay that's fine," Carter responds. "I think my point has been made with you, but I would like to get confirmation from these two before I go."

He wants a response from both of us, but he is looking directly at me again.

"Was my point made, detectives? You do understand what this means?"

Cath nods and confirms verbally, then reluctantly I nod, but he is still not finished with us.

"Okay, well that's progress. I am so glad I could help to fill in one of the gaps in your legal knowledge. Just in case you are still confused, though, let me put it in simple terms, and I apologize in advance for using colorful terminology.

"You don't have shit! Whatever comedy of an interview you have just put my client through is completely null and void, and I say again, you don't have shit!

"Come on, Terry, we need to leave. Paul and Mark are outside waiting for you. DCI Morgan, you can expect to hear from me before the end of this week."

As they leave, I am utterly shell-shocked. If this was not already the low point of my career to date, Jean Monroe adds to my misery as she also leaves.

"DCI Morgan, you can also expect to receive a letter from me by the end of the week."

Outside in the corridor, I hear Carter laughing as Terry explains how I told him he was going to get bummed by other prisoners for the rest of his life.

"It's not bloody funny, Des, I'm not even queer."

Morgan goes out to check that they have left, and then he comes back in and sits down opposite us.

"Well that was an almighty bloody cock-up, wasn't it? You will both be lucky to be working as traffic wardens by the time he has finished with you. I suggest that you both take a few minutes to clear your heads and consider what can be done to limit the damage, then meet me in my office at three o'clock. In the meantime, I suggest that you arrange for Ms. Pinto to be taken home, and get our officers called back to the station."

The expression on my face says it all, but Morgan interrupts me before I can protest.

"Is there something you want to say, DC McMillan?"

"Yes, sir, there is an extremely high probability that Maria Pinto will be threatened or attacked again. We can't withdraw her protection. Carol Baker is in hospital and I doubt that she will cooperate with us now, and Terry Fletcher's new statement is worthless. Maria Pinto is all we have. We have seen what these people are capable of, sir."

"Are you worried about the case collapsing or the safety of Maria Pinto, DC McMillan?"

"I'm worried about both, sir."

Morgan gestures for us to sit down, then he stares at us both for a few seconds before speaking again.

"By rights I should have you both suspended. I don't know fully what went down today, and at this point, I am not particularly interested, but I do know that you stepped over the line in your interview with Terry Fletcher. It is beyond belief that you could make such a basic mistake, but I do have some sympathy for the pressure you are under to close this case. As it is, I have absolutely no doubt that Desmond Carter will take this as far as he can, and it is going to be hard enough to defend your actions in front of the Chief Constable without also having to explain why we are using uniformed manpower to babysit our witnesses."

"With respect, sir, Maria Pinto was threatened in her own home and Carol Baker is in hospital – surely that is explanation enough?"

"Maybe to you and me it is, but we can't keep protection in place indefinitely, and the bean counters at HQ are all over me at the moment to cut back on overtime payments.

"Pull out the current protection for Maria Pinto, and I will ask Chief Inspector Moore from uniform to instruct his patrols to pass by her house every few hours. We can keep the presence at the hospital for Carol Baker for another few days, but that is as much as we can do for now. If we get any more information to indicate an imminent threat, then we will put the full protection back on."

This is better than nothing at all, but I know deep down that the threat is quite real and quite imminent already. For now, though, I need to keep quiet and work on damage limitation.

"Thank you, sir. Before we come and meet you, I just want to say that I take full responsibility for everything. DC Swain was acting entirely under my instructions and was not made fully aware of my intentions."

"Good, your point is duly noted and is fully in concurrence with my own opinion. It goes without saying that as the team lead I would expect you to take full responsibility for your own actions, and for the actions of your team.

"Ignore what I said earlier, DC Swain. You can escort Ms. Pinto home. DC McMillan you have until three-thirty to come up with your plan."

After Morgan leaves the room, Cath leans towards me and touches my hand.

"Thanks for trying to save me, Sean. It's appreciated, but possibly a bit too late. I could have stopped you at any time, but I didn't, so I guess that makes me equally as guilty anyway. So, what do we do now?"

I honestly don't know at this point, but it can't be over yet.

"For now, we do what we have been told, Cath. Take Maria home and break the news to her that we are pulling the protection while I get ready to see Morgan. I still want to pull Donovan in, but I can't even think about that until I get Morgan's blessing."

Cath looks shocked that I still want to carry on, and she lets me know how she feels in no uncertain terms.

"Are you completely crazy, Sean? Can't you see that it's over? We only have Maria Pinto – everything else is gone and after today's performance there is no way that Morgan is going to let us anywhere near Donovan, and DS Douglas certainly won't. You can be sure that he will know already what happened today."

From her reaction, it looks like I am pretty much on my own now, but that's fine, this is make-or-break time now and I have nothing much to lose. I can either carry on and break the case, or I can give up and wait for my suspension; it's an easy choice.

"I told you a few days ago that you can either support me or walk away and there would be no hard feelings. The offer stands, Catherine. With or without you, I am going to see this through to the end."

She doesn't answer me but stands up to leave.

"I need some time to think, Sean, I will call you when I get back."

Back in the office, it feels like everyone else is staring at me, but I know that I am just being paranoid and as of now none of them would have heard the news of my screw-up.

They will find out soon enough, though. Shitty news has a habit of traveling much faster than good news, and if they don't get the news from someone within the team, someone will pick it up from Desmond Carter or from one of the duty solicitors.

Office gossip is the farthest thing from my mind, though. For now, I need to salvage whatever I can to convince Morgan to let me continue. But what do I have left?

Terry's testimony is completely worthless, and even if we did try to submit it, the Crown Prosecution Service would dismiss it out of hand as soon as Carter made his submittal, and it is also highly likely at this point that Carol Baker might change her mind about cooperating with us.

This leaves me with Maria's witness statement and her willingness to give evidence in court. I don't know if this will be enough, but surely with this and the photographs from the hit-and-run scene, we can at least charge and hold Donovan pending further enquiries. This would then give me more time to try again with the other witnesses, and to give Carol time to recover enough for me to speak to her again.

Based on what has just happened with Terry, it now makes perfect sense why we didn't see DS Douglas again today. He would have known what was going on within five minutes of Terry being pulled out of work, and no doubt, he would have had a nice little discussion with Des Carter.

Knowing about Terry's learning disabilities status, there was obviously no need for him to intervene. In fact, it would have suited him better to allow us to continue with the interview, to discredit us, or to get us suspended.

He is probably having a good laugh at my expense right now, or congratulating himself over this victory, and I sorely regret now that I didn't pour the boiling water all over his bloody balls; believe me, next time I won't make the same mistake.

I push these thoughts to one side, as time is getting on and Morgan will be waiting to see me. I pick up the files and head up to meet him.

In the lift, my mind wanders back to Catherine's reaction when I said that I wanted to continue. I had expected her to be upset or annoyed, but I really thought that she would continue to support me. She has never struck me as the kind of person that would give up easily, and certainly not when she knows without a shadow of doubt that Donovan is guilty.

It's possible of course, that I might have just underestimated her commitment, but then I play over her last words again in my head, and one part in particular starts to nag away at me.

Before Catherine left the interview room, apart from calling me crazy, she had said "everything else is gone."

I hadn't thought much of it at the time, assuming that she was talking about Terry Fletcher and Carol Baker, so don't ask me why I did it – maybe it was a gut feeling, or some kind of premonition.

As I step out onto Morgan's floor, I stop for a second and open the Ravi Pinto file. Carol Baker's statement is on top, and everything else is there, apart from the envelope with the Polaroids.

Somehow, I knew that they wouldn't be in the file, but I can't accept that Catherine has taken them. It doesn't make any sense. They must have dropped out somewhere in my office, or maybe the interview room.

I can see through his window that Morgan has just finished his meeting with Sarah Gray, but he can't see me just yet, so I get back in the lift and press the button to close the doors.

My mind is racing on the way down to my office. Catherine is my partner and couldn't be working against me, not for a bastard like Douglas. I must have dropped the envelope somewhere. I simply must have; there has to be a logical explanation.

In my office, I tear my cabinets and drawers apart, and then I skim through all the other files on my and Cath's desks, just in case I have accidentally put them in another file, but there is nothing.

I know deep down that I am not going to find them, but I head down towards the interview suites to check anyway. Unsurprisingly, the interview suite is completely empty and Mike Bolton confirms that nothing has been found or handed into reception.

I thank him and ask him to call me if anything does show up. Then my phone rings and Morgan tells me to get a move on.

As I take a seat in his office, he is finishing a call, and I am mulling over whether to mention my suspicions about Catherine.

I am still struggling with the thought myself, though, and if I am wrong, any hope of Cath continuing to work with me will be gone. I still desperately need her support and I have no proof whatsoever that she is working with Douglas or had anything to do with the pictures going missing, so I decide against saying anything for now.

"Okay, Sean, what have you got?"

What I have is precious little, but I don't want to tell him what he already knows.

"Sir, all we really have now is the new statement from Maria Pinto. With Carol Baker hospitalized, it's going to be a while before she is fit enough to speak to us again, and there is a distinct possibility that she may retract that statement and withdraw her cooperation. I still believe, though, that with Maria Pinto's statement and testimony, we have enough grounds to bring Donovan in and charge him."

He frowns and shakes his head before responding, "Implicating Donovan in the death of her father was your leverage for bringing Maria Pinto on side. Do you think that if Carol Baker does pull out that the pictures alone will be enough to make her stand up in court?"

I had been dreading him bringing this up, and if he hadn't mentioned it, I hadn't intended mentioning the pictures myself.

"Actually, sir, we don't have the photographs either."

The look on his face makes me feel like a naughty child being told by their parents how disappointed they are in them.

"Christ, this just gets better and better! Is there anything else that you want to get off your chest, DC McMillan, or is that it with the surprises for today?"

"That's it, sir."

"Good, so why don't you tell me what has happened to the photographs and what you intend to do about it?"

I feel like throwing up, and if I wasn't sitting directly opposite Morgan, I probably would, but I hold it down and try to keep positive.

"They were in the file when I had it this morning, and I am sure they were still in there when we were interviewing Terry Fletcher. The only other places I had the file today were in my office, in reception waiting for Terry to arrive and in the canteen when I was having lunch. It is not in my office, the interview rooms are clear, and nothing has been handed in, but it must be in the station somewhere, sir.

"This shouldn't change anything as far as Maria Pinto is concerned, with or without Carol Baker or the photographs. Maria has already seen them and knows that it was Paul Donovan that left her father dying on the side of the road. She is a decent woman and I think she will stand by her statement."

Morgan is in a predicament himself. Any failure or fuck-up by his team is a direct reflection on his leadership and I can see he is weighing up the pros and cons in his mind before he answers me.

"Possibly you're right, Sean, the hit-and-run would have been the icing on the cake, but that ship has sailed and Maria Pinto really is our last hope. Unfortunately, long experience has taught me that nothing in life is ever certain, and I strongly suggest that you speak to Ms. Pinto again to make sure of her support before you completely kill your career and mine by dragging Donovan in again without any evidence."

It's another huge relief to hear this, and as I thank him I am already on my feet to leave.

"Thank you, sir, I'm going to head right over there."

"Hang on, Sean, not tonight. Give her some time to think it over, she will still be there in the morning. If she is still willing to cooperate, then you have my permission to pull Donovan in and arrest him on suspicion of murder."

"Understood, sir, thank you for your support."

"Don't get too carried away with your thanks, Sean. Given the circumstances of this case, my support comes with a caveat."

I am probably not going to like what he says next, but I don't have any other option, so I nod, and, in my head, I tell him to bring it on.

"If you pull Donovan in, the decision whether to charge him or not will be entirely yours. If things go tits up from there on, I will shut down the case immediately, and I will be expecting you to do the decent thing. I have no intention of letting my own career go down the pan for the sake of defending your mess. Do we have an understanding, DC McMillan?"

Given that I am not an officer in the Imperial Japanese Army, and I am not one of Hitler's generals, I think I can safely assume that he wants me to resign, rather than commit suicide for my screw-up, but resignation amounts to about the same, and as I have already said, I don't have any other option.

"Yes, sir, I understand, thanks again for your support."

As soon as Morgan turns towards his computer, it is a clear indicator that the meeting is coming to an end, but as I get up again to leave, he tells me to wait.

"While you were committing career suicide today, I was following up on the number trace, and as we thought, it is the same number used to call off the squad car outside Carol Baker's house and to call DS Douglas before he left my office this morning."

He scribbles the number down on his notepad, then tears out the sheet and hands it to me.

"It's a pay-and-go number, so not really much help, but take it anyway – you might get another one of those lucky breaks that handed you the Polaroids in the first place. My last piece of advice for today, Sean, is go home and get some rest. It's past four now anyway. Let's talk again in the morning before the briefing."

When I leave his office, the rest of the floor is completely silent, so clearly the rumor of my screw-up has done the rounds and they must have all been waiting patiently to see me getting frog-marched out of the office by Morgan. I hope that I haven't disappointed them too much.

I don't particularly want to go home yet, but neither can I face going back down to the sniggers or jibes from the rest of the team, so I drop down to the carpark and call Cath from my car as I drive home.

She will of course be looking for a full update, but her comments and the missing Polaroids are still on my mind, so I keep it short.

"Hi, Sean, I was just about to call you, I'm on my way back now. What happened with Morgan?"

"Hi, Cath, tell me first about Maria. You seemed to be gone a long time – how was she when you left?"

There is a brief pause before she answers. I probably would not have noticed before, but now I am paranoid about everything.

"As you can imagine, she was extremely unhappy when she found out that we were pulling back the protection. I had to stay with her for a while to try to reassure her that we will be right back if anything else happens. I have told her that she can ring either of us at any time of day or night until this is finished."

"Okay, thanks. Listen, Cath, we have both been ordered home for the rest of the day. I am on my way home now and I suggest that you do the same."

"Okay. What happened with Morgan, though? Are we moving ahead or not, Sean?"

I am hating myself for thinking that Cath might be the mole, but I can't take the chance and I lie to her.

"We didn't talk for that long. He was more interested in finding a way to limit the damage from any complaint, then he told me to go home and wait for his call tomorrow."

Again, there is a short pause, but this time it's because she knows that I am selling her a line of bullshit.

"Okay thanks, have a good night, Sean. Call me if anything changes."

"Thanks, Cath, have a good night."

I feel absolutely exhausted, but it's still early and I know that even if it was later, I still wouldn't be able to sleep, so before getting home I stop at an out-of-town Tesco hypermarket to pick up something to drink.

I still have under half a liter of Jameson at home, but with the day I have had, I need something better to calm me down. After scanning the shelves for a few minutes, I select an ornately decorated bottle of Japanese Hibiki Whisky.

At one hundred quid a bottle and 47 percent proof, it is a strong and expensive drop, but I also know that it's going to be as smooth as Michael Bublé singing a Sinatra song, which is just what I need right now.

I need comfort food as well, so I pick up a Mac & Cheese ready meal from the chiller section and then head to the checkout with my shopping that screams out sad bachelor.

I am so distracted that I don't notice Douglas behind me in the queue until the cashier scans my whisky bottle and he speaks, "I reckon we must be paying DCs too much these days. In my day we had to settle for a bottle of Bells or the Famous Grouse."

For just a second an image flashes through my mind of smashing the bottle over his head, but he is not worth it. Instead I turn and flash him a sickly smile.

"If I didn't know better, Detective Superintendent, I might be starting to think that you fancy me. You do know that there is a law against stalking, don't you?"

This wipes the smile off his face, but not for long of course.

"That's another thing that has changed since I was a DC – we had respect for our senior officers. I would suggest to you to learn to hold your tongue, but it doesn't matter. If the rumors are true, you might be looking for a new job soon anyway."

He then pushes his way past me to leave. As he does, he turns back towards the cashier and says, "Make sure you check his ID, love, he might look over 18, but you can't be sure with these kids with learning disabilities. They always look older than they actually are."

This asshole is everywhere I turn, and is beating me hands down, but to make it worse it looks like there is absolutely nothing I can do about it.

I would almost like to travel again tonight, just to go back and cripple the fucker, but that wouldn't help. So, on my drive home, I turn my music up loud to take my mind off this shit for a few minutes.

As soon as I get into my apartment, I switch on the oven and throw in the Mac and Cheese, and then I spend the next twenty minutes soaking in a steaming hot shower trying to make sense of things.

I hope that Morgan was not just making a show of his support with the intention of closing me down tomorrow. I don't think he would, but until tomorrow I won't know for sure. The thing with Cath has really got me worried, but I still can't believe it. I have been so wrapped up in this case that any kind of wavering or doubt from anyone else has had me seeing deliberate roadblocks that for the most part haven't been there.

It is not beyond the realms of possibility that I have simply dropped the pictures somewhere in my office, and I decide to look again tomorrow with a good night's sleep under my belt.

The shower has me feeling relatively normal again, but as I open the door, the smell and the smoke hits me, so I slam the bathroom door shut again, and soak a towel in the bath to cover my mouth.

I can't understand with all the smoke why my smoke detectors haven't activated, but seconds later I hear the building fire alarm kick in, and with a towel around my waist and one across my mouth, I make my way from the bathroom to my bedroom to put on my shorts, a t-shirt and my running shoes.

As I dress, I can hear somebody ringing my doorbell, which surprises me. With what happened to Carol Baker, my expectation had been to find my front door ablaze, but when I get back to my living room, I can see that the smoke is actually coming from my kitchen, and I realize straightaway what I have done.

My doorbell is still ringing, but before I answer, I force my way into the kitchen and turn off the oven. Then I open my windows to let the smoke out.

By now, the ringing has also been joined by frantic knocking and the voice of the building caretaker, Arnold, "Mr. McMillan, are you in there? Mr. McMillan, the fire brigade is on the way."

I feel like a right bloody idiot when I open the door to let him in, and I see the other neighbors all crowding around him for a look.

"Sorry about this, Arnold, I made a mistake and turned the grill on instead of the oven – all under control now, though, no need for the fire brigade"

He looks unconvinced by my explanation and tries to have a look, but I block the doorway with my arm.

"I said it's all under control, Arnold. Now if you don't mind, I've got a Mac and Cheese to throw away."

"Okay, but I will have to report this to the building manager – the fire brigade charge us now for false alarms, you know."

Right now, I really couldn't give a flying fuck about any charge or fine from the fire brigade, and with a parting, "whatever," I shut the door in his face and go back into the kitchen.

Most of the smoke has already gone, and the baking tray in the oven is covered in a mini Mount Vesuvius of smoldering cheese, macaroni, and plastic. With the heavy smell of smoke still in the air, I settle down in front of the TV with a Pot Noodle and a large glass of Hibiki.

As always, there is nothing worth watching on the regular channels, so I flick onto Netflix and after a few minutes, select the newest series of Line of Duty. This probably seems like a strange choice given the current circumstances, but I think deep down I am hoping to see something that might restore my faith in the force.

I had first watched Line of Duty when it came out in 2012, and it was partly the reason that I had been inspired to join a real-life cold-case squad.

My ability to dream-travel seemed, in my mind, to make me the ideal candidate for the job, but I would never have believed how close to reality the police corruption plotline was until now.

In eight years of policing, I had always refused to believe that there were any secret networks within the force, or any kind of widespread corruption. But over the last few days, I have seen it for myself.

During my travels back to 1994, I witnessed Detective Superintendent Clive Douglas's corruption, and was a victim to his crimes, and over the course of the next twenty-four years he would have had more than enough opportunity to build his own network of police officers of all ranks, solicitors, politicians and maybe even judges.

Watching Line of Duty does give me a ray of hope, though. One of the main characters is Detective Sergeant Steve Arnott, and throughout each of the episodes, he is always up against it; yet he always manages to come good in the end.

It is only fiction, of course, and I might be on my third large glass of Hibiki, but if a bushy-browed detective like Steve Arnott can beat the corruption and nail the bad guys, so can I.

I know what I need to do now. I need to go travelling tonight, but I don't need to go that far back in time – around 4 am yesterday morning should be fine.

My first stop needs to be Carol Baker's house before 5 am to get her out before the fire, or to stop the fire happening in the first place, then after that a quick trip to my office to lock away the Polaroids before they can go missing.

After that, the day can continue as before until after Maria's interview. This time I will let Jean Monroe leave, and I will take my chances and let Desmond Carter represent Terry. He should still be shitting it from the earlier pep talk, so I am confident that with enough pressure I can still get him to spill his guts.

Yep, this should be enough to put things back on track again, and if it takes a few more days before I can bring Donovan in, then fine, the result will be worth the wait.

Happy with my plan, I pause the episode I am watching, log onto my laptop and do a Google search for Carol Baker. I quickly find some good pictures from her Facebook page that I can use as my dream trigger.

While my printer warms up, I pour myself another whisky, and then I go back to watching episode 2 from series 4.

This series involves the investigation of a crooked DCI, portrayed by the lovely Ms. Thandie Newton, who is suspected of mishandling evidence, and the irony of this is not lost on me.

By the time it finishes the time is just after 9 pm, and I decide to have a final drink and watch one more episode before I stop for the day and start my travels.

# Present Day – Wednesday, 14th February, 2018

My phone is on silent, but the glass top of my coffee table amplifies the vibrations as the WhatsApp message comes through. I wake up confused, wondering where I am.

I don't remember finishing my last drink, but the glass is empty and the TV has timed out and switched itself off, which means that I must have crashed out on my sofa at least two hours ago. When I check the time on my phone, it is much longer than that. It is just after 2.30 in the morning.

I am kicking myself for being such a screw-up, but I still have enough time to travel tonight, and I splash some cold water on my face in the kitchen and pick up Carol Baker's picture from the printer.

I dress in sweat pants, gym shoes, and a loose-fitting gray hoodie, then I head into the bedroom, and lie back on my bed to start my chant. But then I remember the message and I sit back up and reach for my phone.

They are on the way to get Maria Pinto and her son now.

I read the message twice more, and then I stand up and pull out the piece of paper from inside my jacket pocket to check the number that Morgan had given me earlier today. It matches exactly the number from the message. Like everything else in this case, that makes no sense at all.

Why would somebody that I think is working against me now send me a message to warn me about something that is going to happen to Maria and Ben?

I start to type a reply to the message but change my mind and call the number instead. It rings twice and then the person on the other end cuts off the call.

Okay, so they don't want to speak to me, but they obviously want to warn me about something, so I type my reply to the message.

Who is this? What do you mean? Who is on the way to get Maria?

For a few seconds there is nothing, but then my phone vibrates in my hand and a new message comes through.

Too many questions, just get there now if you don't want them to get hurt.

The bile is rising in my stomach at the thought of either of them getting hurt. As soon as I am in my car, I call Maria. Instead of a ring tone, I get the message that the phone may be switched off or out of signal range.

In frustration, I throw my phone down onto the passenger side seat and accelerate up the carpark ramp and out onto the street. But I barely get fifty yards before the blue lights come on behind me, and I am forced to pull over.

For thirty seconds I stare out my rear-view mirror to see if the occupants of the police car get out. When they don't, I get out myself, and then the doors of the patrol car open.

"Stay right where you are, sir, let us come to you."

I reach into my pockets to get my warrant card out, but then I realize I have left it in my jacket pocket and I don't have my wallet or any other ID on me either.

"Guys, my name is Detective Constable Sean McMillan. I am on my way to an urgent call. Can we do this later?"

Both of the cops are big guys, and unusually they are both sergeants. As they box me in next to my car, I realize that I have been set-up.

The older-looking one of the two calls into his radio for some backup whilst his colleague looks me up and down without speaking. Then the questions start.

"Have you been drinking tonight, sir?"

"Listen, guys, one of my witnesses and her son are in serious danger and I need to get to them right now. I need to get going."

As I finish speaking, I turn to open my car door, but the second cop kicks it shut and grabs hold of my arm.

"All in good time, sir. How about you answer my colleague's question? You look a bit unsteady on your feet there – have you been drinking tonight?"

"Listen, you pair of bloody morons, I am a DC based in Blackwell Station with the Cold Case Squad, and if you don't let me go immediately, I will personally hold you responsible if any harm comes to my witness."

In response, the older guy grabs my other arm and pushes me back against the car.

"I really couldn't give a shit who you are, son – answer the question, or this is going to go from bad to worse pretty damn fast."

"Look, my phone – it's on the passenger seat – get it and check my messages. I know what this looks like but check the messages and you will see that I am not lying."

Still holding me, one of them looks through the window. He releases my arm and moves around the car to retrieve my phone. When he comes back a few seconds later, he is shaking his head.

"I think you might have been having a bad dream, sir.

The last message you received was from your mother this morning, asking you if you would be visiting anytime soon. I don't see anything else on here about any kind of emergency."

I was a bit groggy when I woke up, but I know that I wasn't hallucinating. These bastards are obviously part of Douglas's crooked network and sarge here had more than enough time to delete the messages. I am well and truly screwed now, and the only consolation, if there is any, is that the message was probably a hoax to lure me out of the apartment. Maria and Ben are probably perfectly safe.

Douglas knew I was drinking tonight, and he knew that I would be drinking heavily. All he had to do was get his informer to send me a couple of messages and then have a couple of his crooked cops waiting for me outside.

No point holding back any more. They know I have been drinking and the only place I am going tonight is to a police station, so I vent my frustration to test the reaction.

"How much does he pay you? It must be a decent amount for you to break the law."

They both know exactly what I am getting at, but years of practice allow them to keep stony-faced.

"Sir, we have reason to believe that you have been drinking tonight. Do you consent to providing a specimen of your breath?"

"No, I don't consent. Did Clive Douglas put you up to this? Is this part of your normal duties or does this attract a bit extra in your brown envelope at the end of the month?"

The older cop is smiling, and he tells the other guy to get the breathalyzer from the patrol car.

"Sir, I am going to ask you one final time and if you still refuse to cooperate I will have no other option than to arrest you.

So, for the last time, do you consent to providing a specimen of your breath?"

As the other cop returns with the breathalyzer, a police transit van appears at the top of the street and drives down towards us, and I have already made my mind up not to make it easy for them.

"Fuck you, you crooked pair of bastards. Pass a message on to your master – tell him that I am coming for him, and for Donovan and his pals."

This is probably what they want anyway. Between them, they wrench my arms behind my back and body-slam me to the ground. As they slap the cuffs on me, the older guy leans in and whispers in my ear so that he can't be overheard by the cops from the van, who are approaching us.

"Don't you worry about the boss getting your message – you are going to be seeing him soon enough and you can give him the message yourself."

As he starts to pull me to my feet, he slams his knee into my guts before pulling me fully upright and arresting me.

"I am arresting you on suspicion of driving whilst under the influence of alcohol. You do not have to say anything, but it may harm your defense if you do not mention when questioned something which you later rely on in court. Anything you do say may be given in evidence. Do you understand?"

The only thing I understand right now is that Douglas has screwed me over once again, and I doubt very much whether Morgan or anyone else is going to find out about my arrest anytime soon.

"As I said before, fuck you!"

He doesn't even bat an eyelid at my comment. Instead he hands me over to a young constable with the instruction, "He's a drink-driving case, and claims to be a DC from Blackwell nick, but he hasn't produced any ID. Take him in to Leeson Street and we will follow behind and book him in."

I don't struggle with the new arrivals as they put me into the back of the van. There is no point, and I doubt whether they have any connection to Douglas or the rest of his crooks anyway.

Leeson Street station is not far away. After driving for fifteen minutes, we pull up in the yard at the back of the station, and I am escorted in to the reception desk by the two crooked sergeants.

Sergeant Rob Brydon is manning the desk and recognizes me immediately.

"It's Sean McMillan, isn't it? You were here yesterday morning with Cath Swain. Guys, what's going on? Sean is a detective constable based in Blackwell Station."

The look of annoyance at my being recognized is clear on their faces, but they obviously have their orders and they don't waver.

"DC or not, he's been lashing back the whisky tonight and thought he would go for a little drive, so we need to keep him here until he sobers up."

Rob looks a little confused, but he is a by-the-book copper and accepts the explanation.

"Okay, did he give a roadside breath sample? If not, we can try for one now and call for the duty doc to come and take a blood sample."

This is not part of the plan, though, and the older guy tells Brydon that none of that will be necessary.

"Actually, we were hoping to allow him to sleep it off for a few hours as a professional courtesy – no need to ruin his career over a stupid mistake.

What do you say, Rob? We can throw him in one of your cells for a few hours, and then we can take him off your hands again before the end of your shift. No paper trail, nothing to worry about."

It looks like I have struck lucky that Rob Brydon is on duty. He is not happy at all with this request.

"I don't know who you think you are dealing with, but that's not how things work around here. This prisoner will be processed and treated exactly like any other, and within the letter of the law, and if you don't like that you are welcome to take him to another station."

I should have known he would not be far away, but the man is like a ghost when he sneaks around, so he catches us all off guard when he steps through the door and interrupts the debate.

"It's Sergeant Brydon, isn't it?"

Brydon must recognize him, because he addresses him accordingly, "Yes, sir, it is – do you have some interest in this arrest?"

"Not so much the arrest, Sergeant Brydon, but DC McMillan is assisting me with a highly sensitive case, and it would be greatly appreciated if we could allow this small indiscretion to slip under the radar."

Brydon is clearly uncomfortable with the situation, but at the same time, a highly influential senior officer is standing in front of him asking him to break the rules, and reluctantly he agrees.

"Okay, you can put him in cell number two, but he needs to be out before the shift changeover at eight."

Douglas thanks Brydon as one of his lapdogs removes my cuffs, and then Douglas excuses his boys and leads me to the cell himself with one of the station constables.

Once the door is open, he pushes me inside and follows me in.

"Constable, shut the door and give me some privacy please with the prisoner. Sean, have a seat on the bench."

The constable of course complies without question and as soon as the door is closed, Douglas sits down at the other end of the bench and turns to face me.

"Well, well, well, what are we going to do with you, Sean? I tried to give you some good advice, but you just don't know when to take it, do you? Have you seen yourself in the mirror lately? You look like shit – two black eyes, hungover, and pulled over for drink-driving. I imagine that DCI Morgan is already torn between loyalty to one of his officers and protecting the reputation of his squad after your adventures yesterday. If we add to that your obvious struggles with alcoholism, he really won't have much of a choice but to get rid of you."

He pauses before continuing in the same reasonable tone, "It doesn't need to be that way, though. I can make all of this disappear, and as a bonus I can throw a few nice cases your way that will guarantee you make sergeant within a year. That is what you want, isn't it, Sean? That's why you have been pushing so hard?"

This asshole really has got a nerve. He personifies everything that is wrong with policing, but he has shown once again tonight that he can fuck me over as and when he likes. And there is nothing I can do about it.

The real issue for me, though, is that I don't know whom I can trust any more. Catherine is still a major question mark and I still have my doubts about DCI Morgan, DS Gray, and the rest of the team for that matter.

This is part of Douglas's game, of course – divide and conquer, and then swoop in and pick them up when they are most vulnerable, just like I am now.

With the current state of my case and the threat of a drink-driving charge hanging over me, I couldn't be more vulnerable. There is no way I am going to make it easy for him, though. And he is way too smart to accept that I would roll over so easily.

"What about if I tell you to go fuck yourself?"

"Oh, that's easy, Sean. I go back outside and arrange for you to be breathalyzed. I think we both know how that's going to turn out, don't we? You've got eight years in. Do you really want to throw it all away for the sake of solving a long-forgotten murder? There is a bigger picture here and you need to open your eyes to see it."

"I took an oath when I joined the force – so did you, Douglas, only you seem to have forgotten yours. It's not just the murder. You know about the hit-and-run as well from the previous year, don't you?"

This makes him pause for a second before replying, "Oh that's right, Ms. Pinto's father. I really must commend you on making that connection and for digging up those pictures. Perhaps when we have more time, you can enlighten me as to where they came from. It's all a bit irrelevant, though, now that the pictures have gone, and I suspect that Carol Baker might not be as cooperative as she was previously. That really was a nasty business at her house. It would be a shame if the same thing were to happen to Maria Pinto or that son of hers. What was his name, Sean?"

He knew that he would hit a nerve with the comment about Maria and Ben, and he has his right hand around my throat pushing me back against the wall before I can even get to my feet properly.

"You need to bloody wise up and get with the program before I lose my patience and throw you to the lions, Sean. It's an easy choice – back right away from Paul Donovan and keep your career, or watch it go down in flames. You're a bottom-of-the-barrel DC that nobody gives a shit about. I could bury you in an instant if I wanted to. Is that what you want? Because if you do I am only too happy to be the one that pours the petrol over your career and lights the fire. By the time I am finished with you, you will be lucky to get a job stacking shelves in Tesco. It's your choice, Sean."

He releases his grip on me and sits back down on the bench to wait for my answer.

"It's not really much of a choice, is it? Do my job or turn a blind eye, either way I get screwed."

Douglas smiles at the thought that I am going to come onside.

"Try not to think of it as getting screwed, Sean, think of it as losing a battle to win the war. Once you see the benefits of working with me, you will realize that you have made the right choice. We're on the same side, Sean. We still put the bad guys away, we just use slightly more flexible methods to get the job done. So, do we have an understanding, DC McMillan, or do I need to arrange for the breathalyzer?"

"Just get me out of here. I need a shower and some sleep before work."

"That's not really an answer, Sean. Do we have an understanding?"

I could vomit at his arrogance; but for now, and as far as he is concerned, we have an understanding.

"Yes, we do, now get me the hell out of here."

The smile on his face would make the Cheshire cat jealous, but then he gets his usual smug look again.

"That's great, that's really great, Sean, you are going to go far, but for now I think you could do with a few more hours to cool off and reflect on the implications of what could happen if you change your mind. Don't worry, you will be released in time for work in the morning. In the meantime, why don't you have a lie down and sleep off the booze? I'll be in touch sometime later today to check on you."

I know that there is no point arguing with him, but as he gets up to leave, I ask about Maria and Ben.

"I want an assurance that you will back off from Maria Pinto and her son, and Carol Baker as well. You need to make sure that nothing else happens to them."

His parting words leave me in no doubt that he is the master of manipulation.

"That's not down to me, Sean, it's your actions from here on that will determine what happens to them. That's always been the case, Sean, it was never down to me. You just couldn't see it – I hope you do now?"

As the door slams behind him, it is not yet four in the morning and I suspect that I will be here until at least seven-thirty, so I lie back on the bench to try to make sense of things.

I must have been exhausted, though, because the next thing I know somebody is shaking my arm.

"Sean, wake up, we need to get you home and cleaned up."

Catherine is standing over me looking concerned, and I am in two minds to come right out and accuse her of working with Douglas, but I need to be a bit more subtle if I want to have any hope of carrying on.

"How did you know I was here?"

"Rob Brydon called me half an hour ago. Come on, it's nearly seven-fifteen. You can explain what happened in the car."

As we pass reception on our way out, Brydon is still on duty and I return his nod and thank him as he looks up from his paperwork. If it comes to it, I am sure that he would be someone that I could rely on to back me up, but I am a long way from that point right now.

On the way to her car, we don't say a word. It is Cath that finally breaks the silence after we have been driving for a few minutes.

"Okay, so maybe it's a bit much to ask for a word of thanks for coming to get you, but I think I at least deserve an explanation as to why you spent the night in the cells.

"Rob Brydon wouldn't tell me anything, other than the fact that you were brought in drunk at around 3 am. So, what happened? You went home after yesterday's interview and decided that getting wasted was the best way to deal with things? This is not like you, Sean."

I am in no mood for explaining myself to her and if my suspicions are right, she knows everything anyway.

"You're right, Cath, it's not like me, but then there seem to be a lot of people not acting like themselves lately."

"What the hell is that supposed to mean, Sean? Is there something you want to get off your chest? I have supported you right from the beginning of this mess and through every single one of your lies. Don't you dare try to pin any of this on me."

Her reaction is genuine and sincere, and I am once more caught between my belief in her and my suspicions.

"Sorry, Cath, that wasn't aimed at you. It just feels like we are being sabotaged at every turn, and my banging head doesn't help right now.

Drop me home and then I will meet you in the office to explain everything before the morning briefing. Do you know if Morgan knows anything about this?"

"No, I don't think so. Rob said that he had only called me. That's something else you need to explain as well. Rob is not the kind of guy that bends the rules, even for a fellow officer."

I ignore her last comment, and thankfully by now we are pulling into my street and she spots my car at the side of the road.

"Bloody hell, Sean, don't tell me you got pulled for drink-driving? Don't answer that, I don't want to know, just get yourself cleaned up."

She drops me next to my car, and as she drives away I notice that my roof light is on, so one of my doors must not have been closed properly. The keys are also still in the ignition and as I reach in to take them out and to close the door, I am hit in the face immediately by the smell of the dead rat that has been left on the driver's seat.

There is also a note underneath the rat reminding me of my obligations.

Play ball, Sean, or the next body you find in your car won't be a rat.

For a few seconds I consider leaving it there, but the thought of it festering away on my seat all day makes me change my mind and I pick it up with the note and throw them both into the gutter. Then I head up to my apartment.

The smell of smoke is still there, but it is much less noticeable than last night. Hopefully, in a few days it will be gone completely. By the time I have shaved and showered I am ready to face the world again.

The time is just before 8.15 am and just in case Douglas wants to play silly buggers again, I have booked an Uber for eight-thirty. While I wait, I quickly make some toast and a cup of tea, in case I don't get time for anything later today.

By the time I get to the office it is nearly nine o'clock, exactly as I had intended. Cath has already taken a seat in the briefing room, so I am able to avoid having to give her any kind of update for a while longer.

This doesn't go unnoticed, though, and as I sit down, she lets me know it.

"You might be able to avoid me for now, Sean, but you're number two on today's agenda, so I hope you gave some careful thought to your update while you were sleeping things off last night?"

Her attitude is no great surprise, and it's also no surprise to see Clive Douglas sitting next to DCI Morgan yet again.

"I see our friend Clive is in attendance again, Cath. He must have bought himself a season ticket, what do you think?"

Before she can answer, Morgan clears his throat and starts with the introduction of a new detective constable to the team. Then he kicks off the briefing by asking DS Gray to take us through progress on her missing person's case.

Thankfully, by the time Sarah is done and questions have been asked, I have had nearly another twenty minutes to work out what I am going to say.

When she is finished, Morgan hesitates before looking down at his clipboard, and I get the feeling that he is as nervous about my update as I am. I doubt if he knows about my escapades last night but, given that our last conversation discussed the possibility of my resignation, he is probably worried and understandably so, and Douglas hovering over him like a vulture will not be helping things either.

"DC McMillan, you're up next. Please let us know about progress on the Glennister case."

As I stand up, I can feel every pair of eyes in the place boring into me, but the only person I can see is Douglas who is absolutely salivating in anticipation of my update.

"Actually, sir, we have had a couple of set-backs that have weakened our position."

This statement seems to change the whole vibe in the room and whilst Douglas keeps the same expression, Morgan is looking both puzzled and worried.

"DC McMillan, if you are referring to your interview with Terence Fletcher and the attack on Carol Baker, I agree, these are both set-backs, but I asked you to take some time to consider your next steps carefully. What about your witness to the murder of Anthony Glennister?"

I wish I had been able to speak to Morgan before the briefing to share my real intentions, because now he must feel like I am letting him down massively.

"Sir, I need some more time today to decide if there is any point in carrying on with this investigation."

Douglas slumps back in his chair trying to hold back his obvious satisfaction at a job well done, but Morgan looks like he is about to explode, and the whispering and sniggers in the room are not helping the situation.

"DC McMillan, I suggest we have a chat after the briefing. For now you had better excuse yourself before I say something that I might regret."

As low points go, I am obviously on a roll, and this is up there with the humiliation following Terry Fletcher's interview yesterday and the time that I pissed my pants in school as a nine-year-old. The only thing that could make it worse now is getting a congratulatory text message, which is exactly what I get as I leave the briefing room.

The message makes it obvious who it is from, but if I am in any doubt, the arrogant bastard has not even tried to hide his number, or to use a pay-as-you-go.

Good lad, Sean, keep playing along and finish the case in a couple of days, then we can meet for a drink this weekend to discuss ways to work together for our mutual benefit.

I deliberately don't go back to my office because I don't want to pass Cath in the corridor after the briefing. Instead I waste fifteen minutes over a cup of tea in the canteen, before heading straight to Morgan's floor and waiting around for him to get back from the briefing.

When he does appear at just after ten, he has a face like thunder and he makes sure that the rest of the office knows how pissed off he is when he sees me standing waiting for him.

"I hope to God that you have got a bloody good explanation, DC McMillan?"

Surprisingly though, as he shuts the door and sits down behind his desk, he is once more calm and controlled.

"I take it, Sean, that what I heard this morning was just for the benefit of DS Douglas?"

I should have known that he was just play-acting for the benefit of the crowd, and I am mightily relieved.

"Yes, sir, it was. My apologies that I wasn't able to bring you in on my plan beforehand. Unfortunately, I was a little tied up last night and this morning."

For the next ten minutes, I explain in detail to him the chain of events since leaving his office yesterday and Catherine picking me up this morning, and the look on his face tells me that he is struggling to believe it.

"This doesn't make any sense, Sean. DS Douglas is an old-school copper and bending the rules is how things used to be done, but this goes way beyond rule bending. What you are talking about is corruption and illegal activity on a massive scale. There is no way that we are going to be able to make this kind of allegation stick without firm evidence, and right now the only thing we appear to have is your word against his, or am I wrong?"

Unfortunately, he is absolutely right. So, for now, my plan is the same as before – finish with Donovan and come back for Douglas at a later date.

"You're not wrong, sir. Douglas is not my priority right now, though. It's still Paul Donovan. You offered me your support yesterday to pull Paul Donovan in again if Maria Pinto was still willing to stand by her new statement. Well, with your permission, I would like to speak to her again today."

"Are you intending to come clean and tell her that the pictures, and possibly Carol Baker's witness testimony for her father's death, have gone?"

This is a question I had been asking myself over and over again, but I have decided that I will.

"Yes, sir, if she is prepared to risk her life, and her son's life, to help us, then she deserves the truth. If she decides to pull out after I tell her, then it's over and I won't push it any further, and you will have my resignation as promised."

My response seems to meet with his approval and he nods and says, "That's good, Sean. What's your plan today? If you need it, I can throw some more officers your way to protect your witnesses, or to cover any of the other donkey work you need."

"Thanks, sir, but for now I need things to appear normal. Douglas is expecting me to wind the case down over the next couple of days, so I don't want him to think that I have gone the other way again. If things go as I hope they will today, they are going to get interesting very quickly, so I may need to call on your support at short notice."

Morgan hands me a card with his mobile number on it, then he wishes me luck.

"Don't take any unnecessary risks, Sean. That pair of black eyes you have should be enough of a warning about what they are capable of."

So far so good – just Cath to convince now, but I am still fifty-fifty about her loyalty to me. In the lift on the way down to our floor, I work on my game plan.

She is waiting at her desk when I get to our office, and before she can speak, I tell her to get her bag and coat.

"Come on, let's go for breakfast. I don't want to explain myself in here, too many nosey fuckers listening in."

She follows me without question, but the mood as she drives us to the café is a clear indicator that it is not going to be easy, and her refusal of the offered breakfast confirms it.

"Just a coffee for me, Sean, if you are going to bullshit me again, I would rather do it on an empty stomach – less to mop up if I vomit. I'm sure you understand. So, is that it then? Are we giving up?"

Her question sounds genuine enough, but I can't help thinking that she is looking for confirmation to pass on to Douglas and because of this I would rather send her the other way to see what gets back to him, or not. Either way I will have confirmed if she is the rat or not.

"Absolutely not, Cath. What I said in the briefing was just to get Douglas off our case. Yesterday was a set-back. We lost Terry in spectacular fashion and the attack on Carol Baker is all down to me, but it only makes me more determined to carry on and nail that bastard, Donovan."

She looks like she is thinking about what to say next, and I chance my arm and tell her about the Polaroids.

"I lost the Polaroids from the Pinto file as well, so the case against Donovan for the hit-and-run is dead in the water."

This doesn't seem to be a surprise to her, and my fifty-fifty doubts as to her loyalty are now rapidly moving up to seventy-thirty.

"Okay, so what happened last night, Sean? Why was Rob Brydon calling me this morning to pick you up?"

If I tell a complete lie and she is working for Douglas, she will know right away that I am playing her, but I can't tell her the complete truth either, or she will know that I think she is working for him.

"You were right this morning, Cath. I was annoyed at screwing up and instead of picking myself up and working out a plan to salvage the situation, I got wasted on expensive whisky and decided to go for an early morning drive. It was just my luck that the boys in blue were taking a break outside my building and they pulled me over. Fortunately, they took me into Leeson Street, and your mate Rob was on duty and recognized me. The rest you know."

"Okay, so where do we go from here, Sean? The Pinto case is over, and we have been warned to stay away from Donovan. Do you still think Maria is going to stand by her statement?"

I take a bite from a bacon sandwich, then a sip from my tea before I answer her, "Yes I do. Morgan has given me his blessing to speak to her again, and if she agrees to continue on, we can pull Donovan in and charge him."

I may be wrong, but I could almost swear that her chin dropped a little when I told her this, and as she excuses herself to use the bathroom my doubts hit eighty percent.

As I finish my sandwich, I can almost imagine her in the bathroom on the phone to Douglas relaying our conversation, and by the time she returns to the table, I have already paid the bill and am ready to leave.

"Okay, come on. Let's go, Cath."

"Back to the station?"

"No, Maria Pinto's place – do you remember the way or do you want me to drive?"

Something is clearly bothering her. She hesitates to leave, so I pick up her keys from the table and I walk out to her car with her just behind me as I open the driver's side door.

"Sean, are you really sure about this? If this goes pear-shaped, then we might as well both hand in our papers now."

I ignore her and start the engine, then I wind down the passenger side window.

"You can walk away now, Cath, and there will be no hard feelings. But with or without you, I am going ahead with pulling Donovan in. Make your choice, Cath."

She climbs in without saying anything else and I set the GPS for Collister Drive in Feltham. I turn the music on to distract us both from the obvious tension in the air, but the whole time she is fiddling with something in her handbag and I have a good idea what it might be.

When we arrive at Maria's house, the first thing I notice is that her car has been towed onto her driveway and is now covered in a tarpaulin to mask the damage and the graffiti until she can get it fixed.

There is a light on at the front of the house, so I assume that Maria is in, but it is Ben who answers the door.

"Oh hi, you've just missed Mum. She wanted to get out for a few hours to clear her head. She went into London shopping."

This is the last thing that I want to hear and, unfortunately, I take out my frustration on Ben.

"Why the hell didn't you try to stop her? You know what happened on Monday night. We can't protect her if she is wandering around God knows where."

This winds him up and he gives it back to me with added interest.

"Sorry, it's not bloody me that got her into this mess – you're the ones that talked her into making a statement against the animals that attacked our house, and where was your protection then? Look at the state of you, you can't even protect yourself. Mum is a grown woman, and if she wants to go shopping, then she is not going to listen to me or anyone else."

I call the mobile number that she gave me, but after a few rings it goes straight to her voicemail, so I leave her a message.

"Maria, this is Detective Constable McMillan, please give me a call back when you get this message. There is nothing to worry about, but it is better if you stay at home for a few more days until we are sure that the threat has gone. Okay, just call me back please."

Ben is already closing the door on us, but I hold out my hand to stop it.

"What about you, Ben – no uni today?"

"No, no classes today, so working on a paper at home."

Knowing he at least is at home makes me feel a bit better and before we leave I hand him one of my cards and ask him nicely, "If your mum comes home, please ask her to call me, or let me know."

He nods and then shuts the door and Cath asks me what next.

"I think back to the station for now," I answer her, "and wait for Maria to show up."

I drive again, and on the way back, I try to lighten the mood as best I can.

"I guess as far as partners go, I can't exactly be described as ideal, Cath, and I'm sorry for dragging you into my mess. If it's any consolation, this isn't quite how I envisaged my first case lead going either."

She seems almost relieved that I have broken the ice, but she has no intention of letting me off the hook this easy.

"Is that meant to be an apology, Sean? Because you're going to have to work a damn sight harder than that if it is. This case is on the verge of collapse, but despite everybody else seeing it, you still can't see it yourself, plus you seem hell bent on dragging me down with you. When are you going to wake up and admit that it's over?"

"I gave you the chance to walk away, Cath."

This comment really gets her annoyed, but the more annoyed she is, the less attention she is paying to the road ahead, which is exactly what I want.

"Seriously, Sean, you gave me the chance to walk away? How the hell would that have looked to the rest of the squad if I had simply abandoned you in the middle of a case? You didn't give me any choice at all. All I have ever wanted is for you to be honest with me, but the further we got into this, the more you've kept me on the outside. It's bullshit, Sean, and you know it."

As always, she is right and if our positions were reversed I would probably have walked away from her a long time ago, but I need to keep her pissed off with me.

"I wasn't sure that I could trust you, or if you were up to the job. It was never anything personal, Cath."

"You couldn't trust me, are you bloody serious? I'm the only person you can trust. You have got a bloody nerve accusing me … hang on, where are we going, Sean? This is not the way back to the station. Oh, you can't be serious, Sean, come on, this is crazy."

She has answered her own question about where we are going, and as we pull up outside Donovan's Builders Yard, she is still trying to convince me not to go inside.

"Sean, if you do this, you might as well call Douglas yourself to let him know you are here. What do you actually think you are going to achieve by coming here?"

I really wish I knew the answer to that question. Realistically, by the end of today, I will have either charged Donovan or I will be handing in my resignation, and I think the only reason we are here is that I don't want to risk not having the opportunity to wind him up again.

If Maria changes her mind and withdraws her new statement, then my chance will have gone, so that is why we are here now.

"You worry too much, Catherine, I just need to get a few bricks to finish a patio I am building."

"Sean, you live on the third floor of an apartment block."

"Oh, that's right, I must have been thinking of something else. Ah well, while we are here, we might as well go in for a look around."

I am out of the car and walking through the gate before she can respond and Terry Fletcher spots me immediately and disappears into a crusty looking porta-cabin that must be the office.

As I get to the steps of the cabin, Paul Donovan steps out of the office with Terry tucked in behind him.

"Is there something that we can do for you, officers? Maybe a nice bit of timber or some new pipework?"

Catherine grabs my arm and tells Donovan that we are leaving

"Sorry, wrong address," she says, "just a mix-up."

If Cath thought that this was going to diffuse the situation and satisfy Donovan, she could not have been more wrong. It sends things in completely the opposite direction.

"No, I don't think you did make a mistake. Mr. Bacon here seems like he wants to say something. Well, say what you want to say, copper, then get the fuck out of my yard before I call the police and report you as trespassers."

As he was speaking, I have been climbing the stairs and am now just one below Donovan, and Cath tries to pull me back down again.

"I think your girlfriend is worried about you, Sean, it's probably fair enough, though. You weren't exactly Mr. Muscles in the gym and judging by those bruises you had probably better leave the fighting to her."

This is enough for me, and without thinking I push Donovan hard in the chest and he falls backwards into Terry Fletcher, who in turn falls against the door, and Cath moves in between me and Donovan.

"Sean, that's enough, don't let him wind you up!"

Emboldened by Cath's words, Terry joins in and urges Donovan to do something.

"Go on, Paul, smash his bloody teeth in – he went for you, so it will be self-defense."

Cath still has hold of my arm to stop me doing anything else, but she looks over her shoulder to tell them both to back off and then she turns back to me again.

"Is this how it ends, Sean? Come on, you are better than this. Think about what you are doing – please, Sean."

It's at times like this that I really wish I wasn't a copper, because by now both of these clowns would be picking their teeth off the floor, but I'm not finished yet.

"Hey, Donovan, make sure you let Clive know that we were here. Be sure to send him my love."

Terry looks confused, which is no great surprise, but Donovan is smiling.

"Oh, don't you worry, Clive knows what you are going to do before you do, mate. You should know that by now."

Cath is obviously fully aware of the Douglas connection, but this is getting way to personal for her, and she urges me to leave again.

"That's enough, Sean. Whatever is going on here, I don't want any part of it, so either come with me now or you're on your own."

Donovan is loving this and is happy to keep the jibes coming to amuse Terry.

"Go on, Sean, take your girlfriend home before she starts to cry. Go and get the Kleenex, Terry, the waterworks are about to start."

Terry takes this as an instruction and turns to go into the office before Donovan stops him.

"It was a joke, ya bleedin mong. Stand there in case PC Plod takes a swing at me again."

I hadn't noticed Mark Fletcher coming up behind me until he speaks, "Don't worry, Paul, I saw it all as well. I already called Des to let him know that this pair of twats were here harassing you."

I push Cath's arm away and I move closer to Donovan again.

"Don't worry, Paul, were leaving now, but there was something that I wanted to ask you."

Still with a look of invincibility about him, he shrugs his shoulders and says, "Yeh, whatever, get on with it then."

"Do you remember the week before the murder of Anthony Glennister? You were at a BBQ. Do you remember that?"

This has him worried now and his face changes completely.

"What the hell are you on about, what the hell has that got to do with anything?"

"There was a guy in the kitchen with a kettle full of boiling water."

Now really flustered, he yells at me, "Go on piss off and take the bitch with you!"

As Cath pulls me away, I throw out my last comments, "Do you remember him, Paul? I bet you remember what he did to Clive's hands. Terry certainly remembers the knee in his nuts, don't you Terry?"

I swear even from ten yards away I can see Terry wince at the memory of my knee slamming into his family jewels, and as I turn to walk out of the yard, I piss myself laughing, much to Cath's astonishment.

"You've lost it, Sean – seriously, what the hell was all that about?"

"Just a bit of psychological warfare, Cath. I think I won that battle. Do you want to drive or shall I?"

Catherine takes her keys off me, but she refuses to start the car until she gets some answers.

"This is utter bullshit, Sean. Harassing Donovan is one thing but throwing around unfounded insinuations about a senior officer is something else entirely.

"Don't be at all surprised if DS Douglas is waiting for us when we get back to the station. How in God's name are you intending to get us out of this? And what the hell was that about a BBQ and Clive's hands? He burnt his hands rescuing someone from a fire years ago."

Before I can answer her my phone rings and without even looking at the screen I know who it is.

"Just get me back to the station, Cath. It's probably best that you don't take any further involvement in this."

The phone continues to ring in my hand and she asks me if I am going to answer it.

"It might be important, Sean. It could be Maria or Ben – you should take it."

"No, it's nobody important, Cath, not important to me anyway. Are you going to drive me back to the station, or should I call a cab?"

Reluctantly she starts the engine and heads back towards Blackwell, where I have absolutely no doubt either Morgan or

Douglas will be waiting for us. My phone rings twice more but I cut it off both times. Thirty seconds later, I get a text message.

You are finished, Sean, I am going to make it my personal mission to bury you. I was wrong about you having potential, you're a lietime loser.

As soon as we pull into the station parking, I am out of the door and expecting a confrontation before Cath has even stopped the car properly, but there is no welcoming committee and inside the station, everything appears to be normal.

I don't bother to wait for Catherine. Instead I go straight to my office and call Maria's cell phone again, but as before it appears to be switched off or out of range. I call her landline to find out if Ben has heard from her.

He answers after four rings, but he hasn't heard from her since she left the house this morning and I am now starting to get worried again. I thank him and remind him about calling me, and then I torment myself mentally with the worst possible scenarios.

It's getting on for one o'clock now and Ben said that we had just missed her when we saw him this morning, so she must have gone out at around eleven. He said that she was going out for a few hours, so she could be back home by two at the earliest, but if she really has gone into London, then she could be much longer.

This is driving me mad. But, short of scouring London for her, there is bugger all I can do but wait for her to get in touch, which I am sure she will when she gets the message.

I continue to torment myself until Cath knocks on my door and brings me back to reality.

"I think we should try to speak to Morgan before he gets a call from DS Douglas. Whatever you think, Sean, I do care what happens to you."

I lie to her and tell her that I have already checked with his assistant. "He is out at a meeting with the Assistant Chief Constable. She said that she will let me know when he is back in."

"Okay, I'm just going to use the bathroom. Can I get you a tea or coffee on my way back?"

I'm really not in the mood for anything right now, but to shut her up I accept the offer of tea. As she turns away, I take the Glennister file from the bottom of one of my drawers.

I don't know why I am bothering, though, I know the file inside out by now, but it makes me feel better to hold Maria's statement in my hands, and I start to read through it. Then I spot the piece of notepaper that Morgan had given me with the phone number.

Under any other circumstances, I would never have contemplated what I am about to do, but when you have lost everything there is nothing else to lose. I walk to Catherines desk and call the number.

At first, there is nothing. Then I am sure I can hear a faint buzzing sound. As it rings off, I call again, and I open her handbag. This time there is no mistaking the sound of a cell phone vibrating, and after a quick rummage around, I pull out a cheap blue Nokia and watch as it buzzes away on the desk.

So that's it then, no doubt any more that Cath is the rat. This is about as certain as it gets without her admitting it, so before she gets back I flick through the address book to see what I can find, then I put the phone back down on the desk and wait for her to get back.

When she reappears with the drinks in her hand she actually has a smile on her face and is obviously expecting us to kiss and make up. Then she spots the phone on the table, and I half expect her to either drop the drinks or throw them over me.

In the end, she does neither. Instead she calmly puts them down and pulls up a chair opposite me.

"So, what now, Sean? My big secret is out? It's not what you think, though."

"So, what is it, Cath? How long have you been in Douglas's pocket?"

This makes her laugh slightly and shake her head.

"It's really not that simple, and I wish I wasn't in his pocket. It's because of you, though, Sean, all your sneaking around and lying to me. You might think you've been played, but believe me, he has played me as well."

Either she is a damn good liar, or I have seriously missed something here, because I am more confused than ever.

"What the fuck do you mean, it's because of me? What – did I tell you to go away and get in bed with Captain Corruption? Because I don't remember saying that, Cath."

"Oh, for Gods's sake, open your eyes, Sean. Douglas can sniff out an opening a mile away. He contacted me after we pulled Donovan in for the second time. He makes it all sound so nice and plausible, making out that he was looking out for my career and worried that you might be corrupt. With all the lies and you suddenly turning up with long-lost pictures and previously unheard-of witnesses, what the hell was I meant to think? I honestly never thought it would go this far."

I could almost scream with frustration right now, but I need to find out as much as I can from her.

"So, you didn't think it would go as far as Maria getting threatened in her own home, and me getting attacked, or go as far as Carol Baker nearly dying in a fire. These people are maniacs, Cath, if anyone gets in their way, they are taken care of."

"Of course, I didn't, Sean. I would never have let that happen."

"But you bloody did, Cath, and you are still protecting him now. Come with me to Morgan's office and we can end this right now. We can pull Donovan in and we can get Douglas out of the picture at the same time."

"I can't do that, Sean, I'm sorry I just can't."

There must be more to it than this. He must have something on her, or she is just scared witless like everyone else.

"What has he got on you, Cath? Is it that bad that you are prepared to be his on-call bitch for the rest of your life? Because that's how this is going to end if you don't speak up."

If it was anyone else she would probably be in tears by now, but Cath is made of stronger stuff and she doesn't waver.

"I only ever wanted to be a cop, Sean. That's probably hard for you to believe, but I remember seeing a black female police officer in The Bill when I was younger and from then on that's all I ever I wanted to do. I know I have taken a wrong turn, but neither of us has to go down for this if we play smart."

"Play smart? You mean side with Douglas. No way, Cath – you might be able to live with yourself, but I couldn't. Turn yourself in, Cath, because if you don't, once I have finished with Donovan, I am coming for Douglas, for you, and the rest of his rotten bunch."

Cath pulls her handbag towards herself and gets up to leave. "You're a bloody fool, Sean, and you're on your own now."

I'm glad she is leaving, because my temper is rising, but I still have a few questions.

"When did you take the Polaroids from the file? Was it when I left the interview room to get Jean when we had Terry Fletcher? It's been bothering me how you did it with Terry in the room, but now it makes perfect sense."

She doesn't answer, and she turns to leave but I pull down on her handbag.

"What did you do with them, Cath? Did he get you to destroy them, or has he kept them as additional leverage against Donovan in case he steps out of line in the future? That's what I would have done – yep, I think he still has them."

"I suggest you let go of my bag, Sean, unless you want the whole station to be made aware of this conversation. Believe me, I have nothing to hide, and you have nothing to say."

"Okay, just one more thing before you go, would you let him kill me to protect your career, Cath?"

I think now that she might cry, and she looks ready to crumble, but she somehow manages to stay composed enough to answer me.

"For God's sake Sean, just drop it and walk away."

As soon as she is gone, I grab my jacket and head out of the station to hail a cab back to my apartment to collect my car.

During the course of the cab ride, I decline two more calls from DS Douglas and another from an unknown number, then I switch off my phone to make it harder for Douglas or anyone else to trace me. I switch it back on when I realize that Maria won't be able to contact me either.

My last-ditch plan is to find Maria in the hope that she will still be willing to stand by her new statement, but I have no idea where she might be in London. My only option is to head back to her home to wait until she shows up. But before I go there, I head upstairs to my own place to collect my Taser and my CS spray.

The residual smell of the smoke from my apartment alerts me to a problem as soon as I step out of the lift, and I know with 100 percent certainty that I had not forgotten to close my door when I left for work this morning.

It is wide open now. Without even going inside, I can hear voices and what sounds like my drawers being rifled through.

Whoever they are, they are obviously expecting to be able to work undisturbed. Cath or anyone else has not managed to tip them off yet.

Inside the apartment, Terry Fletcher is busy under my kitchen sink pulling everything out onto the floor, so I assume that the other voice I heard in my bedroom or the bathroom is Mark.

I don't wait to find out, though, and before he even realizes I am there, I kick Terry hard between the shoulder blades and his face slams against the pipework of my sink with a satisfying crunch.

My only regret is that I didn't kick the twat hard enough to knock him out, and as he falls backwards onto my floor with blood streaming from his mouth and forehead, he calls out to Mark for help.

Mark appears at the bedroom door at exactly the same time as I do, but the meat tenderizer that I grabbed from the kitchen catches him squarely on the right side of his head, and he drops to his knees.

Unfortunately, during the course of his search of my apartment, he has found one of my old extendable steel batons and as I move forward to strike him again, the baton smashes into my right ankle, and Mark is up on his feet as I drop to the floor.

Taking full advantage of the situation, Mark turns with the baton and rains down blow after blow on my back and my arms, but I manage to protect my head, until Mark gets distracted by Terry calling out to him again.

"Mark, where the fuck are you? My bloody nose is broken."

This is enough for Mark and with a last kick in my side, he turns and runs back towards the kitchen and calls out to Terry to get up. But he doesn't wait for him as he runs out the front door, and I slam it shut trapping Terry inside with me.

As Terry cowers in the kitchen, I can hear Mark desperately hammering on the door for a few seconds, but then it stops, and I turn back towards Terry.

"I told you before, Terry, they don't give a sht about you. You're the whipping boy, the gopher, the fall guy, the spastic."

Between insults, he is crying but I am beyond caring now. My only priority is keeping Maria, Ben, and Carol safe, and nailing Donovan.

"Fuck off, pig! I need a bloody ambulance. This is bloody assault. You're a copper. You can't do this."

"What were you looking for, Terry?"

He looks completely confused, and it is really no surprise that he has been classified as having learning disabilities.

"What, what do you mean? I don't know."

"You don't know, or you can't remember? You really are a moron, aren't you, Terry? Maybe they didn't tell you because they don't trust you. That's probably it. You can't blame them, though. Why would they trust a bellend like you?"

As he ponders my last comments, I reach into one of the kitchen drawers and take out my spare pair of handcuffs. I grab one his wrists.

"Wait, what the hell, no!" Terry protests loudly, "you need to get me to a doctor."

He continues protesting as I drag him into my sitting room and handcuff him to one of my radiators, and then I pull up a chair in front of him.

"I think it's a bit of a waste of time calling a doctor, Terry. By the time I have finished with you, an undertaker will be more appropriate."

He is absolutely shitting his pants, but thirty years playing the thug means he has difficulty in downplaying the bravado.

"You're bluffing. You're not going to do anything, you're a copper. You can't do shit to me."

Just to emphasize my intentions and to add some drama to the proceedings, I get up and spend the next few minutes gathering various items and placing them on my coffee table in full view of him.

It's quite shocking when you realize just how many dangerous items there are in the average household, and by the look on Terry's face, he is thinking exactly the same thing.

I have assembled a veritable torture kit, and along with the hammer, pliers, craft knife, kettle of sugared water, and a bottle of bleach, I also add my Taser and CS gas.

When I sit back down in front of him, he is still giving it the big man, but much less convincingly or as loudly as he was before.

"You do anything to me, and my brother and Paul will fucking kill you."

I don't answer. Instead I let him keep talking until he finally goes silent.

"It doesn't need to be like this, Terry, just tell me what I want to know, and I won't need to hurt you."

He is now shaking and is probably close to shitting himself, so I am hoping that I don't need to go too far to find out what I need.

"I already gave you a statement. I told you everything. I don't know anything else."

The idiot obviously doesn't realize that his statement is worthless, and I am worried that I am running out of time.

"Terry, I don't give a shit about what Paul did to Anthony Glennister right now. I need to know what Paul and Clive Douglas are planning now. Do you know if they have gone after Maria Pinto?"

For some reason this makes him smile. "Is she the Paki?"

My backhand slap catches him right on his ear. At first, he is stunned, but then the tears come again as the shock wears off.

"Watch your mouth, Terry, or I won't be so polite the second time. What are they planning to do?"

"I don't know, honestly. They don't tell me anything, please let me go."

As he continues to sob and plead for me to let him go, I stir the kettle to mix up the sugar nicely with the water, then I ask him a question.

"Have you ever heard the term 'sugared' Terry?"

"You have done a few short stretches inside, so of course you have"

"Just in case you have forgotten, let me remind you what it means. 'Sugared' is a term used to describe somebody who has had boiling water laced with sugar poured over their skin. If my memory serves me correctly, it's a form of prisoner-to-prisoner punishment that originated in the US"

"Apparently, when sugar is added to boiling water, it acts almost like an acid and melts the skin away. Would you like to be sugared, Terence?"

He is now utterly terrified. He is shaking so badly that I can hear the handcuffs rattling against the radiator.

"I don't know anything, please I don't know ..."

I cut off his sentence by stuffing a tea towel in his mouth, then wrapping it tightly with a big piece of gaffer tape to mask his screams. Then I upend the kettle over his left hand.

If I thought Clive Douglas's screams were bad, this is ten times worse until he realizes that I have been bluffing and the water is cold.

I let another minute go by until his breathing nearly comes back to normal, then I remove the gaffer tape and the towel from his mouth.

"How was that for you, Terry? Next time I wont be bluffing"

His tears are coming so fast that he can't even speak, and he looks like he is in danger of going into shock, but it makes no difference to me.

"What are they planning, Terry? Either tell me now or I am going to boil this kettle. I might even add a nice splash of bleach for good measure and its going to go over your head."

He still thinks I am bluffing until I walk towards the kitchen.

"No, wait, please, don't boil the water. I'll tell you."

After what I have just done, I never doubted that he would tell me. How could he not?

"That's good, Terry. Now tell me, what are Paul and Clive planning? Did they say anything about Maria?"

"They both went looking for her. Clive called Paul to meet him up near Kings Cross, then they told me and Mark to come and see whether you had any files here."

My stomach is in my throat now, but I desperately need to remain calm.

"Are you absolutely sure about this Terry? How long ago did Clive call Donovan?"

"I'm not sure, maybe about an hour ago, just before we came here."

"And Paul definitely said he was going to Kings Cross to meet Clive Douglas?"

"Yes, I think so. He said he was going Paki hunting, that's what he said. Don't hit me again."

I don't have any more time to waste, and because I think there is a possibility of him pissing on my carpet if I leave him here, I release the handcuffs.

"Get the fuck out of my sight, Terry, and if I find out that you have been lying to me, you had better bloody emigrate to Australia."

He can't get out of my apartment quickly enough, and on the way down to my car, I call Morgan who thankfully answers immediately.

"Sir, Donovan and Clive Douglas have gone after Maria Pinto. She is somewhere in London, but I can't get her on the phone. Donovan and Douglas are meeting up in Kings Cross Station."

Morgan listens, and then tells me to take a breath.

"Okay listen, I can get some officers into Kings Cross to see if we can intercept them, but it they have already fanned out, it will be like looking for a needle in a haystack. In the meantime, I will get a trace out on DS Douglas's phone."

He then asks if Catherine is with me and I quickly explain about her pay-and-go phone and the collusion with Douglas.

"Okay, that's not good news, but dealing with DC Swain will have to wait. Get yourself up to Kings Cross as soon as you can and I will meet you there."

In my car, I dial Maria again, but she still doesn't answer. Once more it goes to voicemail.

"Hi, this is Maria, leave a message after the beep."

"Maria, get yourself into a police station now. I can't explain – just do it. And then call me please."

Kings Cross Station is more than an hour's drive away, and with the time getting on for three-thirty in the afternoon, I set a course for the M4 to try to beat the worst of the evening rush hour.

My natural inclination is to call Cath, to appeal to her better nature, but if I do, there is a risk that she will tip them off that I am onto them. So instead I call Ben.

"Ben, it's DC McMillan again, did your mum get in touch?"

He is obviously getting annoyed at my constant calls, but his response gives me some good news.

"She called about an hour ago – she said she was going to meet a friend for dinner and would be home around nine."

I am annoyed that he hadn't bothered to call me, but I am so relieved that I let it go.

"Did she say where she was meeting this friend, Ben?"

There is a pause for a second, but then he answers, "U'm no, she didn't say, but there is an Italian place in Piccadilly that she likes – sorry, I can't remember the name."

"Ben, that's great, thank you."

I am about to hang up, but he asks if everything is okay with his mother.

"All these calls are getting me worried. Is she going to be okay? Can I go and get her?"

"Ben, everything is fine. There are some officers on the way to find her just as a precaution. Please stay where you are."

He accepts my explanation and as soon as I finish with him, I call Morgan again to update him on Maria's possible location.

"That's great news, Sean. I will get a couple of officers into Piccadilly. There can't be too many Italian places, so if she is there we will find her. How far are you from Kings Cross?"

The satnav is showing that I am just outside Hammersmith, so still another forty minutes at least, possibly longer if the traffic in Central London is bad.

"At my current rate, I should get there at around four-thirty, sir. I take it that there have been no sightings of Donovan and DS Douglas yet?"

"Nothing, Sean, and DS Douglas has turned off his phone."

This is a bad sign, and possibly an indicator that Cath has heard what we are doing and informed Douglas, but I should have expected it anyway.

"Okay, thanks, sir, I will call you if I hear anything else."

While I have been talking, the traffic has got noticeably heavier and my speed has dropped down to less than sixty miles per hour, so I flick on my strobe light and siren to clear myself a path, but I have only been driving for another few minutes when I get a call from Maria.

"DC McMillan, sorry, I just picked up your messages. I think my phone is playing up, the signal has been in and out all day. What's the panic?"

As soon as I hear her voice, a huge wave of relief washes over me, and I drop my speed and turn off the strobe and siren.

"Maria, thank God! I've been trying to get hold of you all day."

"Sorry, Sean, I didn't realize I was under house arrest. I just needed to get out for a few hours to clear my head."

It was said jokingly, but I can see her point, and being stuck in your own home with a police car outside probably does feel like house arrest.

"Of course, Maria, that's fine, I just feel that you would be safer at home for a few more days. Where are you now?"

"I'm having lunch with one of my friends near Piccadilly Circus. It's a place called San Carlo Ciccetti. Should I go home now?"

I would love to say yes, but with Donovan and Douglas on the lookout for her, it is better that she waits for the boys in blue.

"No, stay where you are, Maria. There should be a couple of police officers already in Piccadilly by now. I will send them your location. Hang on until they get to you, and then give me a call back please."

I pass on the new details to Morgan and a few minutes later my phone rings again and I recognize Maria's number.

"Wow, that was quick, Maria, are the officers with you?"

When she replies my chin drops to my knees, and it is all I can do to stop myself from pulling a handbrake turn and driving the wrong way down the motorway.

"Sean, something is wrong. I called Ben to check on him, but he didn't sound right. I think he was trying to tell me something, but then the line went dead and I can't get hold of him now."

"Okay, calm down, Maria, what exactly did he say?"

"It's not what he said, it's what he didn't say, Sean. He told me he was busy and couldn't talk, then he was about to say something and that was it, the phone just cut off. Please do something, Sean, send someone to check on him."

I tell her to stay where she is and then I tell her that I am going there myself.

"Maria, it's probably nothing, but I am going there now. Keep trying to call him and let me know if you manage to speak to him."

Morgan is my next call, and he promises to get a squad car to the house immediately.

"Sean, you get yourself back to Feltham as fast as you can. There will be a squad car there in seven or eight minutes. I'm nearly at Kings Cross, so I will continue the search here, just in case they are still around. Don't worry, son, they won't be stupid enough to hurt the lad."

Unfortunately, I don't share Kevin Morgan's optimism, and with my siren and strobe blazing, I am off the motorway at the next junction and tearing up the road in the opposite direction within a few minutes.

I am wondering now if Terry has played me after all. I really don't think he is intelligent enough, though, so perhaps he was played himself by Donovan. Whatever the explanation, if anything happens to Ben or Maria, I will track that bloody weasel down and personally make sure he gets a whole-body sugaring.

Another ten minutes pass and then Morgan calls me again.

"Stand down, Sean, Maria Pinto has been taken in to Hyde Park station and the squad car has reported that everything is normal at her home. It sounds like there was just a problem with the phone line. The Hyde Park boys are going to arrange a car to take Ms. Pinto home."

This comes as a huge relief, but I want to be sure myself.

"That's great news, sir. If it's okay with you, I might as well just carry on and wait for Maria to get back. I still need to speak to her anyway."

"Sure, go ahead, Sean. Give me a call when you get back to the station later."

I should be feeling much happier now. But, based on the events of the last few days, I am taking nothing for granted until I see it with my own eyes, so I keep my siren going until I reach the outskirts of Feltham.

Just as Morgan said, the squad car is parked on Maria's driveway, and finally I can start to relax a little knowing that there are police officers inside with Ben.

The front door is unlocked, so I step inside and head to the living room where I can hear Ben in discussion with someone whose voice I recognize.

"Oh finally, Detective Constable McMillan, I was starting to think that you might not be coming. Sit down, join the party."

Detective Superintendent Douglas is standing next to the TV. Donovan is on the sofa next to a terrified-looking Ben and the older of the two sergeants from my drink-driving arrest is standing behind them.

The other sergeant is behind me and pushes me further into the room. Then the realization hits me that no other squad cars or officers are coming to the rescue.

"You look a little lost for words, Sean. Come, come don't be shy, we are all friends here. You know Paul obviously, my two uniformed colleagues are Sergeant Huntley and Sergeant Bellmarsh, and then of course we have young Benjamin here. Sit down please, Sean, I won't ask again."

Sergeant Huntley pushes me down into an armchair and then takes up a position hovering behind me with his baton ready to slam down onto my skull if I make any kind of move.

"Do you really think you are going to get away with this, Douglas?" I ask. "You can't possibly think that you can get away with holding us hostage here. What do you think this is going to achieve? Whatever you do, I am never going to give up hunting you and the rest of your lackeys. You are everything that is wrong wi ..."

Douglas cuts me off with a wave of his hand and Huntley slaps me around the back of the head to shut me up.

"That really is a lovely little speech, Sean, but nobody is holding you hostage. Quite the opposite, you are free to leave at any time. I told you before, it's your actions, not mine, that will determine what does, or doesn't, happen to anyone. All you need to do is drop the case against Mr. Donovan and then we can all get back to some real police work and young Ben here can continue breathing."

I am desperately trying to figure a way out of this, but I know if I make any kind of move, my minder will be all over me and Donovan of course won't hesitate to hurt Ben. I need to keep them talking as long as I can, but currently the only people coming are the Hyde Park boys with Maria, and they are probably at least ninety minutes away.

"You don't think putting away a murdering bastard is police work?"

This obviously annoys Donovan, but Douglas silences him before he can say anything.

"Sticks and stones, Paul, let me do the talking. This discussion is for the grown-ups. Do you know your problem, DC McMillan? You're still not seeing the bigger picture, are you?

"Paul has been one of my best informants for over twenty-five years and without the information he has passed onto me, there would be at least another fourteen or fifteen murderers still out on the streets. When you add to that all the muggers, druggies, rapists, and other assorted scumbags, I would say that the couple of deaths that you think he is responsible for are fairly insignificant on the scale of things."

If he wasn't a police officer, Clive Douglas would make a great politician. He certainly knows the art of spin as well as any politician that I have ever heard speak.

"Is that how you justify this to yourself, Clive? You win some, you lose some. What about Carol Baker? Would her death have been justified to protect this fat fuck?"

Before he can launch himself at me, Sergeant Bellmarsh moves forward and pulls him back down to the sofa and Douglas reprimands him again.

"Paul, I told you, sticks and stones, ignore him. He's deliberately trying to bait you. Just cool it; there will be time enough later for breaking heads."

When he finishes, he turns to face back towards me. "Sorry about that, Sean, too much red meat in his diet. Now, where were we? Oh yes, that's right, I was telling you about the benefits of turning a blind eye occasionally. The problem with young officers these days is that they don't understand anything other than the rulebook. This is where you are at a disadvantage, Sean, but you don't need to be – just open your eyes and come to the light. Your partner did. She's a smart girl."

With everything happening, I had almost forgotten about Cath.

"She didn't come to the light. You manipulated her, just like you do everyone else."

He turns towards Sergeant Huntley and laughs, then turns back to me.

“Is that what she told you? Well, maybe I did manipulate her, but it didn’t take much work. She thought you were fabricating evidence and was only too happy to come running into my arms. It was her that first approached me, not the other way around, Sean. She couldn’t wait to sell you down the river. You look upset, Sean, have I touched a nerve? The truth hurts, doesn’t it?”

The truth does hurt, and there is no reason for him to lie, and with the way I have been behaving, I can understand why Cath might think I was fabricating evidence. She was probably right when she said that it was my fault that she went to Douglas.

It doesn’t excuse her actions, of course, but I refuse to believe that she would have gone to him if she had known what he was really like.

“However you spin it, Douglas, you used her, just like you are using these two clowns.”

This time the slap is on the left side of my head, and Sergeant Huntley warns me, “Next time it won’t be my hand, just watch your mouth.”

The slap to my head is highly amusing to Donovan and he can’t keep quiet about it.

“Use your baton on him, Mel, split his fucking skull open, or better still, let me do it.”

Once more, Douglas shuts him up and then he asks me again if I am going to drop the case. “

You know it’s the right choice, Sean, just drop the case and everyone gets to go home. Don’t let your pride stop you from making the right decision. What do you say?”

I know this is crunch time, and I am desperately trying to remove the emotion and personal connection from my thought processes – but, like it or not, Ben is my son.

Granted, until a few days ago, I had no idea that he even existed, and even now I can't fully believe it, but do I betray my principles over this relationship, or do I go with my head and do what is right?

In the end, my principles and my belief that even Douglas and Donovan would not murder a fellow police officer and an innocent young man in cold blood lead me to do the right thing.

"Fuck you, Douglas, I'm walking out of here right now and I'm taking Ben with me. Don't even think about trying to stop us."

Considering my refusal to cooperate, he still looks calm, and I get the impression that he expected this answer.

"I guess that's it then, Sean. I admire your principles and under different circumstances we might have been friends; but, unfortunately, I don't think we are going to be taking warm showers together anytime soon. Don't let us keep you any longer."

I don't know why I thought that he was going to let us go, call it naïve hope or the belief that there may be some good in him, but before I can get up, the baton is around my throat and pressing against my windpipe to restrain me in the seat.

"You're not going to like this, Sean, but it's down to you, think about that as you watch."

Bellmarsh has his baton around Ben's neck. At first, I think that he is going to strangle him, but then I spot the hunting knife in Donovan's hand and I struggle to break free from Huntley's grip.

"Don't do it, please, you don't need to do this."

Douglas shakes his head.

"You had the chance to change this, Sean, it's on your conscience now."

Then he turns to Donovan and nods. "Do it, Paul."

Without hesitation, Donovan rams the blade of the knife so hard into the side of Ben's throat that the point comes out the other side, and I am powerless to stop it or to help him.

With a wound like that there is no way anyone could survive and, with blood gushing from the two gaping holes in his neck, he dies in front of me in just a few seconds, and Donovan stands up and walks towards me.

"What about this bastard, Clive? Killing the kid was a necessity; killing this asshole will be a pleasure."

Douglas seems to have other plans for me, and he tells Donovan to back off.

"Go and stand next to Sergeant Bellmarsh. Mel, put your baton away. I don't think Sean is going to give us any more trouble."

As soon as he releases his grip, I let loose at them before I have even got my breath back.

"You are done, Douglas, what kind of a monster are you? You're a police officer, for God's sake, how the hell do you sleep at night? And you, Donovan, you're a bloody psychopath. I'm going to bury the whole lot of you. I'm gonna burn down your entire castle of corruption."

None of them react to my rant, and there is no reason why they should; it's four against one and, if he wanted to, Douglas could have me killed as easily as he had Ben.

"That's all very nice, DC McMillan, but we know that none of that is going to happen. Let me tell you what is going to happen now."

"I don't give a shit about anything you say, you bent bastard, the only thing that is going to happen now is that you are all going to jail. You have been getting away with this for way too long and that murdering fucker has been living on borrowed time."

I turn to face Donovan for extra emphasis of my last point. "Guess what, Paul? Your twenty-five years are up, and you're out of time."

Gunshots in a small room are deafening and the first two hit Donovan squarely in his chest, then the final shot takes off half of the right side of his face and showers Sergeant Bellmarsh with his blood and fragments of skin and bones.

When I turn to look at Douglas, he is still pointing his service-issue Smith & Wesson Model 36 revolver in Donovan's direction and he looks as calm as if he were shooting cans at a fairground.

"It always amazes me, how powerful this gun is, Sean.

I know that you youngsters prefer the glamour of a Glock or a Sig Sauer, but when it comes to power and reliability, you really can't beat a good old-fashioned revolver. Mind you, this is the first time that I have seen its effect on a human. Quite impressive, don't you think?"

I am utterly speechless, and I'm not the only one. Huntley and Bellmarsh both look like they are in shock and it is clear that this scenario was not part of the original plan.

Satisfied with his marksmanship skills, Douglas lowers his weapon, and then he takes a deep breath ahead of delivering his final words.

"I can see you're a bit confused, Sean. I suppose that's fair enough and I don't blame you.

So, let me finish by telling you what is going to happen now. In a few minutes, Sergeant Huntley is going to call this in and request for backup and an ambulance. When our colleagues get here, he is going to describe to them how they arrived to check on Benjamin and Maria, but when they got here, they found Mr. Donovan standing over the lifeless body of Benjamin with the bloodied knife still dripping in his hand. What then ensued was a standoff, until I arrived, closely followed by your good self, and after Paul ran at me with the knife, I had no other option but to shoot him."

The guy is absolutely mad, but he is convinced that they will be believed.

"You will never get away with it. Do you really think the rest of the force is as corrupt and as stupid as you?"

"Probably not, but who are they going to believe more – a highly decorated detective superintendent and two well-respected sergeants with more than thirty years combined service, or a snot-nosed DC barely out of training?

"Unfortunately, Paul was becoming a liability. With him gone there is no need for you to pursue your cases and there is no risk of him telling tales outside of school"

"I did us both a favor, Sean. You wanted him in prison; I did one better. You should be thanking me."

"And what about Ben, you bloody animal, was that a favor to me as well?"

"Not a favor, Sean, collateral damage, but don't forget who caused it."

As he finishes speaking, he slides his gun back into the holster inside his jacket and tells Huntley to make the call, then he turns back to me.

"I reckon you have a couple of minutes at most to decide on what you are going to say.

Those shots were loud enough to wake the dead, so some of our boys are probably already on the way."

I have no idea how to respond. Even if I did, I don't want to waste any more breath talking to him, and I need to get home, so I simply get up and walk towards the door, but he hasn't finished with me just yet.

"It's over, DC McMillan – the sooner you realize that, the better it will be for you."

I cannot ignore this, and I cannot let him think he has beaten me, so despite my better judgment, I turn back to him and respond, "This is far from over; this is just the beginning, Douglas."

As with everything else, my threat doesn't bother him in the least and as I turn back to leave he finishes with some final words of wisdom.

"Sean, one last thing before you go – obviously, we have had a difference of opinion when it comes to this case, but you were right about Donovan."

"Right about what?"

"You were right when you said he was 'out of time'. Good luck, Sean."

Its Douglas that is going to need the luck, not me - I have said it before; I have all the time in the world. As I step outside, I can already hear sirens approaching in the distance but I don't intend to wait around to explain myself.

I have caused Maria enough distress already and the murder of her son is not something I am going to put her through.

I need to dream travel again and my ticket is in a half-empty bottle of Absinthe in my apartment.

Outside the house, Sergeant Huntley and Sergeant Bellmarsh are hard at work setting up a cordon in readiness for the arrival of the response teams. They barely even acknowledge my presence though and they don't protest or try to stop me as I get into my car to drive away.

A small group of the neighbours are already pushing up against the barrier tape to see what has happened and as I start the engine, I can see Detective Superintendent Douglas in the doorway talking on his phone.

No doubt, he is putting the wheels in motion to cover his tracks or to further extinguish any remaining sparks of my credibility. Whatever he is discussing, I don't have time to think about it and I pull away just as the first Police car arrives.

The drive back to my apartment is a complete blur and I struggle to comprehend what has just happened. I knew of course that DS Douglas was crooked and that Paul Donovan was an animal, but I never thought in a million years that Douglas would allow Donovan to kill Ben and certainly not in the way that he did.

The murder of Anthony Glennister was the result of an unplanned drunken attack and the death of Ravi Pinto was the unforeseen aftermath from the reckless driving of a stolen vehicle. What I have just witnessed, though, is nothing less than pre-meditated murder.

Cold blooded pre-meditated murder of Ben Pinto by Paul Donovan on the orders of Clive Douglas – followed by the cold-blooded execution of Donovan by Douglas.

The murder of Ben is clearly a warning to myself, to Maria and to anyone else who might think about speaking up, but the execution of Donovan makes no sense other than to indicate that Douglas was more terrified then I thought - perhaps of what Paul Donovan might reveal if he thought he might be facing life in prison.

I refuse to believe that Douglas executed him solely to put an end to my investigations; this was much more, this was about the self-preservation of DS Clive Douglas and the rest of his corrupt network at all costs.

My current priority is saving Ben, but bringing down Douglas and the rest of his cronies is next on my list – now more than ever, I am determined to take them down whatever it takes.

It is nearly 6pm as I arrive home and the door to my apartment is still open – inside, my spare handcuffs are hanging from the radiator where I left them and there is a small bloodstain on the carpet from the injuries to Terry Fletchers head.

I can't help wondering if Ben might still be alive if I had gone ahead and carried out my threat to torture Terry. In the end, my conscience and my own moral standards had not allowed me to lower myself to the same level as the very people that took Ben's life. With the benefit of hindsight, I wonder if I would still have made the same decision. Fortunately, I don't need to consider my answer to this question to much, my unique ability means that I still have the opportunity to put things right.

In readiness to travel, I lock and deadbolt the main door to my apartment to keep out the visitors that I know will surely come looking for me, and then I sit down on my bed with the remainder of the bottle of Absinthe. The last time I drank absinthe it had burned my throat and nearly made me spew.

I am under no illusions that it will be any different this time around.

It makes no difference though, I don't have the luxury of time or a whole load of more pleasant alternatives to choose from. After a couple of deep breaths I swallow the remaining contents of the bottle in three long swigs.

The strength and sheer volume of the absinthe causes an immediate feeling of nausea in my stomach and I cough a small amount of acidic vomit into my mouth. More importantly, my head starts to spin and I can feel my level of control rapidly deteriorating. I don't have a picture of Catherine Swain – I don't need one, I have been working with Catherine pretty much every day for the last few months and I can picture every single detail of her face.

Location and target are not my worry, accuracy of the time and date is – this will be the first time I have travelled within the present day and I am only going to get one shot before I am hauled away to explain myself.

I lay down, close my eyes and concentrate on Catherine, my office and the events from earlier today.

14$^{th}$ February 2018, 14$^{th}$ February 2018, 14$^{th}$ February 20…..

# The Past - Wednesday, 14th February, 2018 – Around 1.15pm

"What the hell, Sean, I said let go of my bag, are you even listening to me? You have seriously lost it. What the hell is the matter with you? Let go of my bag right now or you are going to regret it."

As always when I dream travel, it takes me a few seconds to get my bearings and the shock of realising just how accurate I have been leaves me speechless for longer than I would have liked.

"I won't ask you again, Sean, take your hand off my bag right now."

I already know the response to my next question, but as I release my grip on her handbag, I ask it again anyway.

"Okay, just one more thing before you go, would you let him kill me to protect your career, Cath?"

Regardless of what Cath has done, I can't help feeling some sympathy for her situation as she once again fights to compose herself and answer me. Douglas has manipulated her as much as he has manipulated anyone else. I know that she would never have walked away from me if she had known what he had been planning for Ben.

I mentally add Cath to my list of future priorities as she pulls her handbag away and responds.

"For God's sake Sean, just drop it and walk away."

As soon as she is gone, I grab my jacket and head out of the station to hail a cab back to my apartment to collect my car. This time, I have no intention of going in and confronting Terry and Mark, there is nothing for them to find anyway.

I know already that intentionally or unintentionally, the Kings Cross lead from Terry will send me on a wild goose chase.

Maria is perfectly safe if she stays in London – Ben is the target and if my memory serves me correctly, Douglas and Donovan must have arrived at Maria's house at around four.

My last call to Ben was around 3.45pm when he had given me his mum's location in Piccadilly, and then I had called Morgan a few minutes later. Maria had subsequently called me to say that she was ok, before calling me back at around four to tell me that she was worried about Ben. This means that I should have more than enough time to get to Collister Drive in Feltham to get Ben out of the house well before Douglas and Donovan show up.

Regardless, I don't intend to take any chances with time or with anyone getting wind of my intentions, so after declining the calls from Douglas and the unknown number, I switch off my phone and remove the SIM card.

Shortly after, my taxi arrives at my apartment block, and a few minutes later, I am in my car heading towards an out of town Retail Park. Curry's electrical mega-store is right at the entrance to the park and after a short discussion with the salesman, I opt to buy the Sony SX2000 Digital Voice Recorder. It sets me back nearly two hundred quid, but it has a 16-gigabyte memory and an unbelievable boast of up to 636 hours of recording time.

I should only need an hour at the most, but more importantly the salesman assures me that the voice recording quality is the best available in the market and is far superior to the quality of my IPhone. This is particularly important given that the recorder will be in my pocket, so after asking him to set it up, I make the payment with my credit card and I head back out to my car and set the GPS to take me to Maria's house.

Other than Maria's car under the tarpaulin on her driveway, the rest of the street looks perfectly normal and with the time approaching two-thirty in the afternoon, I am confident of saving Ben from the clutches of Douglas and Donovan.

I am less sure however, of what I am going to do after that – I have seen and experienced first-hand what they are capable of, but if I don't face them down now, I will just be putting off the inevitable. My actions have directly contributed to putting Maria and Ben in harm's way, so whatever the risk to my own safety; I resolve to put that to one side and to confront them when they arrive.

From outside the house, I can hear the volume of the television and it takes a few minutes of banging the door and ringing the bell to get Ben's attention. When he does finally come to the door, he appears to be more annoyed then surprised to see me again.

"Seriously, you called about an hour ago. I already told you that mum has not called. You don't need to come round or call every couple of hours."

"Actually Ben, I came to tell you that I think I know where your mum might be. When I spoke to her last, she mentioned to me that she was planning to have lunch with a girlfriend in Piccadilly Circus."

This comment registers a spark of recognition in his face and he nods his agreement, "Oh yeh, you might be right, she has a favorite Italian Restaurant that she likes to visit when she is in London. Did you really come all the way here just to tell me that though, why didn't you just call me?"

I don't want to worry him unnecessarily, but I need him out of the house and ideally somewhere public - like an Italian Restaurant in Piccadilly Circus.

"Ben, I need you to go and meet your mum in London. I don't have time to explain and there is nothing for either of you to be overly worried about, but I do need to insist that you leave the house now. There is an Uber already on the way and it will take you directly to the restaurant."

Whichever way I had delivered that message, it would have worried him – thankfully my delivery is sufficient for him not to argue with me and after a couple of minutes, he is back at the front door with his jacket and shoes on. The Uber driver already has the destination, but I reconfirm it with him before I stress to Ben the importance of finding Maria and contacting me.

"The driver will drop you as close as possible to San Carlo Cicettii in Piccadilly Circus – please go straight there and please ask Maria to message or call me as soon as you are with her. Tell her not to worry, it's just a precaution, I can explain everything when she calls me."

As the cab pulls out of the driveway, I check the time again – it is just past 2.45pm, more than enough time to test the voice recorder and prepare for the arrival of Douglas and Donovan. My intention is to goad Douglas into the same kind of conversation that we had previously, in the hope that I might at least gain some firm evidence to take to Detective Chief Inspector Morgan. For fifteen minute's I test various locations for sound and recording quality, but eventually I opt for my original idea to simply keep the recorder in my pocket – it will be far easier to have it on me if I need to leave in a hurry. Next, I lock the backdoor to limit the access options and I leave the front door open a few inches then settle down in the living room to wait.

By 3.50pm, my heart is racing and it occurs to me that I need to find a way home before 6pm – the thought of catching up with myself in the present is a scenario that I cannot even begin to comprehend. It is an unlikely scenario though.

Once they realize that Ben is not here, I doubt that Douglas is going to waste time talking to me for longer than necessary. I will either be murdered and disappear in front of his eyes, or he will warn me off again and go back after Ben or Maria – either way, I will have the opportunity to get home well before my sleeping self is disturbed in the present.

Shortly after, I hear a car parking on the driveway and they are so arrogant that neither of them bother to enter the house discretely. Douglas calls out to Ben and introduces himself. "Hello, Ben. My name is Detective Chief Superintendent Douglas; I need to speak to you please."

When he doesn't get any response, I hear him tell Donovan to check the living room and a few seconds later, he swaggers in. When he sees me sitting on the sofa, he hesitates for a second before regaining his bravado.

"What the fuck are you doing here? Clive, get in here mate."

Unlike Donovan, Clive Douglas doesn't display any sign of surprise at seeing me and he doesn't even speak until he has got himself comfortable in the armchair opposite me.

"I take it from your presence here that we would be wasting our time searching the rest of the house for young Benjamin? It appears that I may have underestimated you, that's okay though; all good things come to those who wait. The question now is what we do with you. I know what Paul would like to do with you, but that would be such a waste of your obvious talents."

While Douglas has been talking, Donovan has been furiously texting someone, but at the mention of his name, he moves in behind me and looks towards Douglas.

"What are we going to do with him Clive, the kids not here, but if we do this asshole, the cases collapse and we get back to normal. There is no way those bitches will testify if we get rid of this piece of shit."

The voice recorder has been running for twenty minutes and I sincerely hope that the impressive battery life and memory was not an exaggeration, even if Douglas doesn't say too much to incriminate himself, it looks like Donovan is quite happy to do it for him. I don't have anywhere near enough yet to be conclusive though, I need to push them for more.

"Why don't you boys tell me what you are doing here? Clive, you said something about searching for Ben, why exactly are you looking for him – and why are you looking for him with the main suspect in a murder case? If I didn't know better, I might think that you were intending to hurt him".

Clive smiles and nods in the direction of Donovan, "are they on the way yet?"

"Five minutes away, Clive. What are we going to do with him, he knows too much already"?

Douglas continues to look me up and down for a few seconds, obviously considering his words carefully before responding. "And what would make you think that we were here to harm Ben, Sean? I was already in the area with Mr Donovan, so I took the opportunity to check on the welfare of Ms. Pinto and young Ben. That was a nasty incident a few days ago."

"Oh I don't know Clive, what about the gun in your jacket and the hunting knife in Paul's pocket. Do you normally carry a weapon during routine investigations?"

This makes Douglas smile again and he looks over the top of my head towards Donovan.

"You see Paul, he's a smart lad. You would do well to pay attention, you might learn something".

Donovan is flustered, "How the hell did he know about my knife"?

Before Douglas can answer, Sergeants Huntley and Bellmarsh come into the room and take up positions directly behind me and in the doorway - no prizes for guessing then whom Donovan had been texting earlier. Douglas then tells Paul to join him. "Paul get over here next to me and give me your knife".

He reluctantly removes the knife from his pocket and hands it over, "What do you want it for"?

"Don't you worry yourself about that Paul, just stand there and be quiet".

Douglas turns back to me and is about to speak, but then he stops himself at the last second before pointing the knife towards me. "We seem to have ourselves a bit of a dilemma, Sean. On the one hand, Paul here has been one of my best informants for more than a quarter of a century, but on the other hand, I know that you are not going to let this drop. Killing you would be the easy option, but the paperwork and investigations into the death of a cop - even of a lowly Detective Constable would bog me down for the rest of my career. I could of course let you take Paul in, but then I would be running the risk of him spilling his guts in exchange for a lighter sentence. I think we both know that I am not going to let that happen, so that just leaves me with one final option, I kill Paul! Think about it, Sean, the cases go away, the dirt on me disappears with him and you get to reconsider your options for a mutually beneficial partnership".

Donovan is obviously none too happy with the last option and is not shy about letting us know. "For God,s sake, Clive, don't put ideas in his head, even if it is just a joke".

Despite the reference to a joke, he knows very well that Douglas is not joking and so do I – after the execution earlier today, he made it very clear to me that Donovan had become a liability. One of us is going to die in the next few minutes, I am certain of it; it's just a question of who?

Douglas gets up from the chair and picks up a photograph of Maria and Ben from the windowsill – when he speaks again he is still facing away from me and looking down at the photograph.

"She is a fine looking woman, Sean, I really don't want to hurt her, or the boy, but you're not leaving me with many options. Help me out, Sean. Which option would you choose?"

It's a no win situation with no right answers, I cannot incriminate myself on my own recording by telling him to kill Donovan - but neither do I want him to kill me. Disappearing in front of someone twenty-five years in the past is one thing, disappearing in the present is something entirely different. In the end, I stand up and tell him that I have heard enough, "This is over, Douglas. I'm leaving right now and don't even think about trying to stop me".

Still facing away, he nods his head and places the photograph back down on the windowsill. "You're a stubborn young bastard, McMillan. Just remember that you brought this upon yourself."

I know instantly that this is the moment that one of us is going to die, but as Douglas spins around, I am surprised to see the knife still in his hand instead of the revolver. Donovan realizes far too late that he is the target and the blade slams into his stomach and buries itself to the hilt.

As he slumps to his knees, Douglas still has a firm grip on the knife and he twists it in Donovan's guts to inflict maximum damage. He is seconds away from death and whatever I once thought of Donovan's mental state, Douglas is far more dangerous and psychotic.

Douglas is now on his knees and looking directly in Donovans eyes as he addresses me and continues to twist the knife. "You knew this was the only option, Sean, you knew this was the only way I was going to let him spill his guts. You can go now, don't go far though. We need to talk again soon."

The man is an absolute maniac and I don't need telling twice, I came here to get Ben out of the way and to get some recorded evidence. By now, Ben should nearly be with his mum in London and I am hopeful that the recorder has captured enough to take to Morgan. Without waiting for Douglas to speak again, I push past Sergeant Huntley in the doorway and run out to my car.

My hands are shaking so badly that I struggle to get the keys into the ignition until I stop and take a deep breath to calm myself. I cannot even begin to imagine the logic that Douglas applies to his decision making process - either he is completely mad, or the man is a cold and calculating genius. I suspect that he may be the latter, but for now my priority is in getting home as soon as possible.

Until now, I hadn't given much thought to how I would do it, and at just before four-thirty in the afternoon in a leafy suburb of Feltham my options are decidedly limited.

The mind has an amazing way of thinking though and after driving for a few minutes; I spot an opportunity up ahead. I release my seatbelt and press down on the accelerator until it hits the floor. When I veer off the road and onto the pavement, my speedometer is just touching ninety miles an hour. The impact of the front of my car on the massive Oak Tree is sickening – and as I fly through the windscreen my face is torn to shreds and my skull is smashed to pieces as it collides with the trunk of the tree.

## Present Day – Wednesday, 14th February, 2018

The light in my eyes is so powerful that I am temporarily blinded and I consider for a moment that perhaps I am still dreaming. The voice is very real though and the barked order leaves me in no doubt as to what is happening.

"Stand up and keep your hands where I can see them. Do it now!"

Before I can react, I am man handled from the bed and pushed facedown to the floor by at least two assailants. A knee presses down hard into the small of my back and my arms are viciously jerked behind me. It is only when the cuffs snap shut on my wrists that I realize who it is and when the main lights go on I am surprised to see Catherine standing in front of me. Sergeant Huntley is standing to the left of her and they are accompanied by four heavily armed firearms officers. The senior officer tells the guy with his knee in my back to stand me up, then he turns to Catherine.

"Is this him DC Swain?"

"Yes it is. This is Detective Constable Sean McMillan."

I am about to speak, but Catherine moves towards me and speaks first.

"Detective Constable McMillan, I am arresting you on suspicion of murder. You do not have to say anything, but it may harm your defense if you do not mention when questioned something which you later rely on in court. Anything you do say may be given in evidence. Do you understand?"

"Cath, no. This is crazy. You can't believe this, it was Douglas. Please, Cath."

She looks embarrassed and is going to say something, but is distracted when Sergeant Bellmarsh enters the bedroom. He is wearing search gloves and in his left hand, he is holding a bloodstained hunting knife.

"This was in one of the kitchen drawers; the blood on it still looks fresh."

Despite my protests of innocence, I am dragged out of my apartment and into the lift. Catherine can barely make eye contact with me as we descend to the ground floor. The road outside is filled with Police vehicles and DCI Morgan and DS Douglas are standing next to the back of a Police transit van. I try to speak to Morgan but he stops me.

"Save it, Sean. Don't say something you might regret", then he speaks to my escort, "go on get him out of my sight."

The look of disappointment and disgust on his face says it all, but as the rear door slams shut, I refuse to accept that this is the end. Far from it – this is just the beginning.

# ABOUT THE AUTHOR

Ernesto H Lee, is originally from the UK, but has mixed Spanish and German heritage and now commutes regularly between his homes in London and Madrid. Previously he was working in Dubai and other areas of the Middle East for more than twenty years, but he has recently now retired and is a full time author.

Out of Time is the first in a planned series of books that focuses on the exploits of Detective Constable Sean McMillan – The Dream Traveller.

The second book from the series will be available before the end of 2018.

For questions or enquiries, he can be contacted via email at:

ernestohlee@gmail.com

Made in the USA
Middletown, DE
23 August 2019